THE DOOMSDAY BUG

The Fall of Humanity Has Begun

T. R. REMINGTON

iUniverse®

THE DOOMSDAY BUG
THE FALL OF HUMANITY HAS BEGUN

Author Credits: Frederick Bonds

iUniverse books may be ordered through booksellers or by contacting:

iUniverse
1663 Liberty Drive
Bloomington, IN 47403
www.iuniverse.com
1-800-Authors (1-800-288-4677)

ISBN: 978-1-5320-5599-7 (sc)
ISBN: 978-1-5320-5601-7 (hc)
ISBN: 978-1-5320-5600-0 (e)

Library of Congress Control Number: 2018910951

Print information available on the last page.

iUniverse rev. date: 01/10/2019

1

A Killing In Senegal

"Those of us who have survived the pandemic thus far no longer fear going to Hell. Hell has come to us."

Arnaud De Vos
Acting Secretary General
United Nations

Ansar pushed back the brush as he quietly moved along the small trail that led to the last reported site of the baboon party they had been observing. This group was much smaller than the main gang further up the river. Only about 24 baboons, mostly females with a few males. A third of the party were juveniles, making it one of the younger parties on the reserve.

Thank God for GPS, he thought, *we'd never find them without it in this thick underbrush.*

Salome, a doctoral student at the University in Dakar and Dr. Hagen's assistant, listened intently to the directional beacon in her headset. "They're within 1500 yards, ahead and to the left," she quietly said to Ansar.

Ansar Hagen was a senior scientist at the German Primate Center in Senegal. He was researching vocalization pattern variations of different baboon parties. Today's trip into the reserve wasn't about his research, however, it was to find out why this particular party they were tracking had separated from the larger group and had not moved out of the area with the other parties. *Damn unusual,* he thought. Poachers were always a threat but usually it involved one or two animals, not an entire party. *May be nothing at all,* he thought answering himself.

"Everyone gather round," he said in a subdued voice.

There were four others in the group he led. Salome was using the GPS tracker, then there was Kurt and Stephan (both well-experienced assistants) and Assane, a local guide who worked with the Project. Assane also acted as their bodyguard carrying a G-41 assault rifle as he was also a soldier in the Senegalese military assigned to the research center. All of them carried side arms as the area was heavy with poachers, big cats, and the baboons themselves could be quite dangerous if approached wrong.

"We want to approach this group very quietly and passively, I want to know why they are not moving with the rest of the group and I would prefer not to disturb them, so let's stay together for now and do this slowly. Keep alert. There may be poachers in the area."

"Kurt, have the video camera ready, keep it running from this point on."

"You've got it," replied Kurt as he hurriedly checked the settings on the camera.

Video recording was a vital part of Ansar's research but today it served two roles. One to document any unusual behavior or conditions that may have caused the group of baboons to stop moving with the others and two, to record any possible poaching activity.

Poaching apes, and in particular, baboons, was big business in Senegal and most other regions of Western Africa. Ever-increasing human population placed a heavy burden on local food sources and in this region, baboon meat was sold at a premium at the market. The Senegalese government had placed a ban on all sales of ape meat but that had done little to quell the rising demand for it. As a result, the ape population in Western Africa was falling at an alarming rate. The macaque population was so low now, nearly all species of them were put on the protected list. Ansar's baboons were also in danger of disappearing if the trend continued. Out here on the reserve, there were few government soldiers to enforce the ban and poachers moved about unchecked. Teams like his were the first line of defense in this war and it was not without casualties.

"Let's move out," he said, as the group began to push forward once again.

"Under a thousand yards straight ahead," said Salome.

The underbrush began to give way to larger Acacia trees as they came to a clearing. It was eerily quiet. Ansar and Assane both scanned the area with their binoculars. Ansar looking for baboons while Assane looked for threats. Both saw nothing.

"Salome, are you sure of the location beacon?"

"Yes, doctor, I am picking up three collar signals directly in front of us. No movement at all. We should be seeing two of them just in front of those two trees 100 yards ahead of us," Salome replied.

Ansar began to feel a knot tightening in his gut. Something did not feel right. His body was on high alert as the hairs on the back of his neck were standing straight up.

"Assane, you seeing anything?" he whispered.

"No doctor, there is no movement anywhere. Just a small group of bushbucks off to the right about 3500 yards. They are not on alert so I don't think there are any cats nearby. I didn't notice them before because of undergrowth but there are a few vultures circling about ahead."

Ansar fought the urge to go back. His intense curiosity of the situation was driving him as he moved forward. *Were the baboons dead?* he wondered. *What would have killed the entire group?*

"Doctor, look...to your right," said Kurt. "There's blood on the grass."

Ansar took a few steps toward the bloodied grass and then noticed what looked to be a carcass lying in the grass.

"Assane get over here," Ansar said sharply. "What do you make of this?"

Assane pushed aside the tall grass with the barrel of his rifle to expose what appeared to be the mutilated body of a female baboon.

"Cats?" queried Ansar.

"No, not cats, I am not sure. The skull has been crushed and it's missing an arm. It looks like it was beaten to death," said Assane still examining the body.

"Doctor, there are two more over here," said Stephan who had noticed an area where the grass was flattened and also blood-stained.

"Two bodies here too," said Kurt. "One has a tracking collar. It's our group alright."

Ansar hurried over to where Stephen and the others had found the other bodies. Assane followed right behind, eyes scanning the immediate vicinity for movement.

"Same as the other ones," said Ansar. The baboons had been severely beaten and mutilated.

As the group moved about cautiously, more dead baboons were found laying in the tall grass. Now the horrific truth was becoming apparent, the entire party of baboons had been slaughtered. But by what (or who)?

"Doctor, I have never seen this before," said Assane. "This is not cats or hyenas. Nothing kills like this out here. Not even poachers would do this."

"Salome, are all the collars accounted for?" asked Ansar. "Salome?"

Ansar turned to see Salome tearing up, just staring at two of the juveniles bodies. She was going into shock.

"Salome!" Ansar gently grabbed her and turned her away from the gruesome sight. "Salome, snap out of it. We need you to find the other collar beacons."

Salome, looked into Ansar's eyes. He smiled and she slowly came back to him. "Come on," he said.

Salome put her headset on, fumbled about with the receivers controls.

"Uh, sorry," she whispered. "No doctor, there is one more signal coming from that direction." She said as she pointed off toward a stand of trees off in the distance. "About 800 yards."

"Stay together everyone," Ansar said as he unclipped his holster. "I suggest everyone check their sidearm's before we go any further. Just in case."

"Doctor," said Assane, "you should take a look at this." Assane had been scanning the general direction with his binoculars that Salome had pointed to. "At the base of those trees."

Ansar lifted his binoculars and focused in on the tree base. There sitting in the grass was a male baboon with a tracking collar.

"It looks like one of them survived," he said still looking at the animal.

"There's another one just behind the same tree doctor," said Assane.

"What are they doing?" asked Kurt.

"Just sitting there it looks like," said Ansar. He increased the magnification and refocused. Now he could see the male baboon quite well. Ansar noticed that the baboon was sitting motionless except for the occasional sudden spasm. "It looks like its sick," said Ansar. "It's having seizures. This doesn't make any sense at all."

"Maybe we should get back to the truck and get some help on this one," said Assane, obviously unnerved about the situation.

"Yeah, I think that would be best. I don't know what is going on and I am not sure I want to find out without more help," said Ansar to the group. "Let's slowly make our way out of here."

The group began to make its way to the brush line they had come in through. Assane turned to look through his binoculars at the two animals they had seen at the base of those trees. "Doctor, the baboons are gone."

"What? No they looked too sick to move that quickly."

"There," said Assane pointing, "two animals coming through the grass toward us."

It was then that the group heard a scream coming from the baboons that they had never heard before. The vocalization sounded demonic. The groups movement had been spotted by the two remaining baboons who now, were moving toward them far faster than baboons were known to run and closing the distance rapidly.

"We'll never outrun them," yelled Ansar. "Draw your guns. We'll have to shoot them."

Kurt and Stephan drew their Glocks and took the safeties off. Salome, who had never fired a gun before, drew hers but did not know how to flip the safety. Ansar grabbed it from here and took it off safety. Handing it back he said, "Make sure you point it at the baboons before you pull the trigger." She nodded her head and turned toward the direction the animals were coming from.

Assane, stepped in front a few steps and took aim with his rifle. It had a longer kill range and he would try to take the animals down before they closed the distance much more.

He fired at the lead baboon but it was moving very fast, coming in and out of sight as it raced through the waist high grass. He spent the first magazine and quickly threw in another firing a few more rounds and finally, one found its mark. The lead baboon dropped immediately. Now Assane quickly began to fire upon the second animal but it had closed the distance rapidly.

At that time, Ansar saw the lead baboon Assane had shot get back up and resume running toward the group.

Assane had emptied the second clip and was fumbling for the third magazine when he looked up to see a baboon racing toward him. The speed the animal was moving took him by surprise and before he could fire the weapon the ape was upon him. The baboon's large canines sank into Assane's left shoulder and tore the arm off at the joint. Its next bite crushed Assane's skull, but still, it continued to beat and tear apart the now lifeless body.

Ansar and the others opened fire on the baboon that was attacking Assane without effect. The second baboon was now upon them. Ansar fired the contents of his pistol into the oncoming animal. Two rounds hit the target but it did not slow the animal. Ansar was dead with the first blow from the baboon.

Salome, seeing the brutal attacks panicked and ran into the brush, followed by Kurt and Stephan who had fired all of their rounds and were now defenseless. The baboons followed them into the brush.

Moments later the screaming stopped. The baboons sat motionless besides the bodies, except for the occasional small seizure.

The video camera Kurt had been carrying was laying on the ground a few feet from his body...still running.

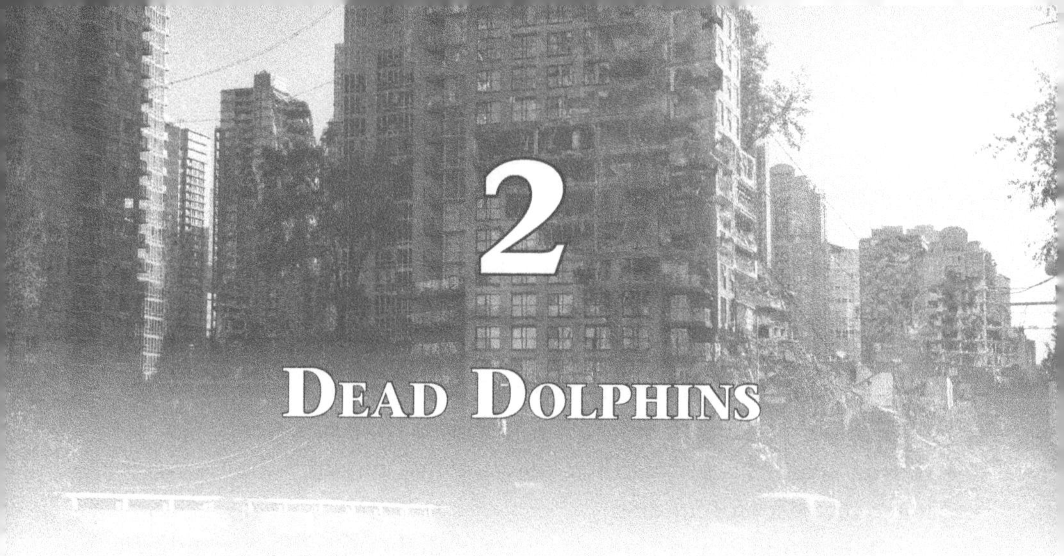

2

Dead Dolphins

Nature seeks balance. The dynamic between predator and prey cannot be corrupted without dire consequences. Humanity has upset the balance and now, nature is retaliating. What use are guns against microbes. How do you defeat an enemy that is inside you?

Feodor Belitnikov
Director, World Environmental Agency

It was summer 2013 that Dr. Jonas Allen began to suspect something had changed in the balance between us (humans) and them (diseases). Many researchers claimed that the planet was in the middle of the largest shift in microorganism resistance they had ever seen and the appearance of new variants of viruses and other microorganisms that had pandemic potential had health researchers everywhere scrambling for answers.

Jonas was the chief investigator for the CDC's division of preparedness and emerging infections (DPEI) out of Atlanta, Georgia. Now in his forties, Jonas had been with the Center for 16 years, having started in the E.I.S. He had risen through the ranks quickly and proved himself to be an outstanding investigator. His job was to evaluate reports of disease outbreaks and determine the type of response required by the CDC and other health agencies. It was kind of like detective work only the criminals were microorganisms, the crimes were disease outbreaks, and the victims, of course, were people.

Jonas was at his desk when Terry, a fellow investigator in Jonas' department and a good friend from college plopped himself down in the chair opposite him.

"Jonas, did you see this?" asked Terry as he tossed a report on the desk in front of him.

"What's this? Honestly, Terry, I can't take on anymore right now. I'm up to my neck in data reviews on this MERS-coV situation." Jonas said as he pushed his chair away from my desk symbolically divorcing myself from all of it.

"The ministry of health in French Guiana sent us an update on those diseased dolphins that washed up onshore a couple of weeks ago. They thought we might be able to help them on this," he said. "The director told me to throw it on your desk."

"Great! And why did he pick me out of all the other investigators here?"

"Well, he asked me if I knew of anyone in your department that liked dolphins and, of course, I immediately thought of Ellie," he said with a sheepish grin. "So I told him you love dolphins."

"Jesus, Terry, stop volunteering me for everything and I don't love dolphins, Ellie does."

"Hey, if Ellie found out that you knew about sick dolphins and didn't try to help, how long would your marriage last? I'm just trying to help my friend," he said now laughing out loud.

He was right, actually, Jonas had married Ellie because of her love for nature. She found beauty in everything and had become quite a superb nature photographer. They had gone to the Caymans for a working honeymoon (working for her as she never went anywhere without her cameras) and there, they had done one of those swim with the dolphins encounter. After that, she was hooked. He had even bought her a black coral dolphin necklace on their anniversary last year which she now wore everywhere.

"Okay, fine, how many dolphins were there?"

"Only four that they know of. It doesn't list any others being found," said Terry looking through the file.

"That hardly sounds like a major issue. What is the attraction to this case? Anyone die other than the dolphins? "

"No, it's not anything like that...yet," he said hesitantly.

"Well what is it then?" Jonas asked now curious.

"The dolphins died of fulminating Toxoplasma pneumonitis."

"That's not likely," said Jonas. "Are they sure?"

"Yeah, they did serotyping on the organism they isolated and its atypical Toxoplasma gondii, maybe type II according to their results."

"But that doesn't make any sense. Toxoplasma doesn't kill like that unless...was there any sign of immune-suppression in the dolphins? Any sign of another illness? Maybe a retrovirus infection. If the immune systems were compromised then this would make some sense," Jonas said still trying to analyze the information in his head.

"No, they didn't say they found anything else. The animals appeared to be beaten up a bit, probably from being washed ashore. Autopsies showed large amounts of Toxoplasma in the lungs as well as tissue cysts throughout the rest of the body. There was a higher density of cysts in the brain especially around the limbic region but that's not too out of line with a Toxoplasma infection."

"No, I agree but still the fact that the organism killed four healthy members of a pod doesn't seem right. Did they send any cultures?" asked Jonas as he glanced at the photographs.

"Yes, they're down in the lab right now. Walter said he'd get to it but he has those Crypto samples to run still from the Ashton outbreak. Should be available in a day or two."

"Good. I'll check with Walter later and see if they find anything interesting."

"Hey Terry, do you remember a similar incident back a few years ago...2006 or 2007 near Italy? Wasn't that Toxoplasmosis also."

"I can look it up to be sure, but yeah, I do remember a report on the deaths of some dolphins with the same cause of death. Why? You think something is going on?"

"Not sure. Probably not. Why don't you run a search for reports both on the CDC database and on the web for similar incidents? I'd like to take a look at anything you find."

"No problem, I'll let you know what pops up."

"Thanks Terry, hey are you and Brenda coming over Friday?"

"Absolutely, wouldn't miss it for anything," Terry said retreating into the hallway.

"Good, I'll let Ellie know," Jonas shouted.

Friday night get-togethers with their small circle of friends here had become an addiction with them. This week it was their turn to host the get-together. Of course, it would be a cook-out, probably barbeque as everything down south involved barbequing something and it was summer after all. Personally, he was a bit tired of it. *I would kill for some Chinese food,* he thought, but Terry and Sam Watson (another investigator in his department) had reviewed so much of the influenza information coming out of southeast Asia, they had come to the conclusion that some of the problems came from the way they prepared their food, so they decided not to eat Chinese food especially buffets. So that left him grilling pork and chicken, the same things found in Chinese food. Sam defended it by saying at least it's local and we can grill the crap out of it. Judging by the amount of beer he drank at these cook-outs it's not likely anything could survive the alcohol level in his gut anyway. Sam was up in Oregon on assignment so he would only have to make Terry happy which wasn't too difficult. Sam was a different story. He was downright belligerent.

Nevertheless, it was a way for all of them to vent a bit and undo some of the damage done by the stress of the job they did. It also helped them counteract some of the depression we experienced brought on by combing through thousands of pages of data on diseases and mortality rates, not to mention the photos. The running joke was that it wasn't the diseases that would kill them, it was the depression that could cause us all to shoot ourselves. He wasn't sure how many of the group took anti-depressants but based on the amount of alcohol they drank, he was sure there were a few. Of course he always insisted that they stay the night if they drank too much as we had a couple of extra rooms and sleeping bags. Also, Ellie did not drink at all and since they had been married, he didn't drink much anymore either. Ellie was a bit of a health nut and Jonas learned to appreciate her views more and more. Still, there were times when the job would get to him and he would try to numb myself. It seldom worked. He would act stupid, wake up with a major headache, and have to suffer through a day of Ellie's not so quiet disappointment.

Ellie's dolphins would have to wait, Jonas thought to himself.

The Saudi's were in an uproar over this MERS coV and there was some concern by them that it was a weaponized virus since only Saudi's had died from it. Actually, that was not true as at least four of the people who had contracted it were European but most likely acquired it in Saudi Arabia during their recent trips there. Of those four, two had died of the virus. The virus was deadly but it wasn't easily transmitted. For now, the urgency was a matter of politics and not virulence.

3

An Evening With Friends

"The violence and brutality of this disease is not due to the organism that infects its victim. That has always been inside us. The microbe merely amplifies it to suit its own means at the expense of its host."

Dr. William Huff
Center for Behavioral Studies
John Hopkins University

"Jonas, are you watching the grill? I smell smoke!" yelled Ellie from the upstairs bedroom window.

"Got it, babe. Everything is okay...just a little change in wind direction," replied Jonas as he quickly moved the ribs and chicken to a cooler part of the grill. Of course, he burnt the ribs a bit...not too bad. He did it every time so it was kind of a tradition. This time he got wrapped up in the Braves game on the TV and lost track of time. *Just once*, he thought. *Well at least Terry won't bitch about the meat being undercooked.*

"Hey neighbor, need a fire extinguisher?"

Jonas looked around to see where the voice was coming from. Then he noticed a hand reaching over the privacy fence with a couple of cold beers.

"We can drink these or put the fire out with them? What do you want to do?"

"Come on over Jim, bring the beer," said Jonas cracking a grin as his neighbor came through the gate.

"I'll say this about you, Jonas, you are consistent," laughed Jim. "I cannot remember a time you did not set the meal on fire at a backyard barbeque," he quipped.

"Fine, Jim, next time you cook and I'll make the jokes," Jonas replied opening a beer but taking time to swipe the cold bottle across his forehead. "Damn its hot today, what is it 92? 95?" he complained.

"Naw, its only 89 today. You've just been standing too close to the bonfire," he said laughing again. Jim held his hands up as if surrendering. "Hey, man I'm just jokin'. It's hot, for sure."

"Where's Molina? She run off with the pool boy?"

"Naw, anyway we fired him. Now she's just got me to look at," replied Jim chuckling. "She's dropping the kids off at her sisters. She'll be here in a few minutes."

Jim and Molina Cooper were about the best neighbors you could ask for. Jim worked for Lockheed Martin as a fuel systems engineer and Molina was an elementary school teacher right down the street at Morningside Elementary. They had two kids: Marcus, age 7 and Bryce, age 9. Jonas often joked with Ellie often about not having kids, just renting the Coopers kids until they got tired of them. That usually met with the same look of distain whenever he said it and apparently he said it way too often. Ellie definitely wanted kids but between the two careers, the timing was never right.

The doorbell rang and Jonas could hear the commotion coming from the front room.

Terry Andrews and his wife, Brenda had just arrived when Ben and Amanda Hoyle pulled up in front of the house.

"Hey, sounds like everyone is here," said Jonas pushing himself up from the lawn chair. "Ellie," he yelled. "Be sure to let me know when Ben pulls into the driveway so I can hide the beer," he yelled, winking at Jim.

"Hey, screw you. I brought my own," yelled Ben from inside the house. Ben stepped out onto the patio laughing, "Besides you buy lousy beer anyway," he said as he held up a case of Heineken.

"Oh now you are living high on the hog," barbed Jonas.

Terry emerged from the house, "Don't worry about him Jonas, I didn't bring anything. I'd be proud to drink your beer."

"Thanks Terry, some of us have to live in the real world," said Jonas smiling at Ben.

Dr. Ben Hoyle had come to work in Jonas' department after a brief career as a researcher/professor at the University of Southern California.

He found he did not like the politics of the academic world. Things didn't happen fast enough for him and after four years, he left to work at the C.D.C. as a clinical parasitologist. Eventually, he found his way into the D.P.E.I. He was married to Amanda, a psychologist who had grown up in Atlanta and whose parents were part of Atlanta's inner circle. Her father, Warren Silverstein owned several radio and television stations that were eventually bought out by Ted Turner's company.

"What can I say guys, that's what happens when your in-laws live in East Cobb. You start thinking Lexus instead of Dodge, sushi instead of hamburgers, you know...the life of privilege," joked Ben.

"Well you ain't gettin' any of that with that tiny little paycheck Uncle Sam gives you to look at germs all day so you better stick to drinking Bud Lite," Terry said lifting his beer as if to give a toast.

They all had a good laugh at Ben's expense as they settled into talking about the Brave's game, the weather, and who had the lowest golf handicap.

Ellen called out to Jonas to get the ribs and chicken into the kitchen. "Let's eat," she yelled out to the guys.

After dinner, the girls dismissed themselves to the front room each carrying a large wine glass filled with a chilled chardonnay, except Molina who stole one of Ben's beers.

"You know they're going to start talking shop," said Ben's wife, Amanda. "And I don't want to hear it. It's damn depressing to listen to it. I don't know why they want to talk about that stuff after seeing it all day."

"I hear you, Amanda," said Ellie. "Jonas gets home and the first thing out of his mouth is hey babe, you wouldn't believe the disease that hit Topeka yesterday or guess how many people died of worms today. Christ! Look at me, now I'm doing it. Seriously, someone change the subject. Anything, weddings, babies, NASCAR, something.....here's to anything but germs," said Ellie, raising her wine glass.

Jonas and his friends had moved to the summer room as the bugs were out in full force tonight.

"These damn mosquitoes are getting worse," said Terry, "I thought they sprayed this county."

"They do but the skeeters are developing a resistance to the pesticides they use," replied answered Jonas. "I read in the paper a few days ago that the latest one they use is almost worthless now."

"Why bother then?" asked Jim, "If it isn't working what's the use?"

"Well spraying, even with a pesticide that is not very effective still reduces the numbers which helps," replied Jonas. "Without it, we'd be overrun. Then we'd have all the problems associated with mosquito infestations like dengue fever, yellow fever, malaria..."

"Malaria?" said Jim surprised by the term. "We'd have malaria here?"

"Oh hell yeah," replied Terry. "We use to have malaria in the south until they started to eliminate some of the places the mosquitoes bred. Draining the swamps near cities, spraying programs, developing repellents all helped to eliminate the threat. They had malaria even up in Washington D.C. before the capital was built. That is how the Center for Disease Control got its start. It was originally called the Office of Malaria Control back in the forties."

Jim shook his head, "That's nuts. I did not know that," he said.

"Okay, so long as we're learning stuff here, I want to ask you guys something," Jim said leaning in toward them.

"We just saw that new zombie movie and it scared the hell out of Molina and me. Now I know it's done up for the movies but is that type of thing possible? I mean you guys see this stuff all day so you would know right?" he asked.

The other three had a good chuckle but then Terry responded seriously. "I don't think it's possible at all. After all some of the things zombies do are simply impossible according to natural law. Reanimating dead bodies, victims becoming zombies immediately after being bitten…all that just doesn't happen."

"So no zombie apocalypse?" said Jim.

"No way," Terry replied.

"Now wait a minute, let's think about this," said Jonas. "Jim brings up an interesting challenge. Sure maybe a zombie disease isn't possible but there are some diseases out there that resemble it. For instance, that Nodding disease that is spreading through the Sudan, it has some odd behavioral symptoms like the nodding seizures."

"Yeah but that's not anything like a zombie-type disease," said Terry, interrupting Jonas, maybe old-school zombies…the "Night of the Living Dead" type, but the new concept of zombies are aggressive, eat flesh, and they..."

"I know that Terry," said Jonas, "but I was simply using that as an example of how a disease can affect behavior. I wasn't saying it was like a zombie disease."

Ben got into the discussion, "Well let's all pick a disease that could be a zombie disease candidate."

"Jesus, Ben, we spend all day trying to stop the spread of disease and on our off time you want us to invent ways to make them worse?" chuckled Jonas.

"Wait a minute. That sounds kinda interesting now. I don't know much about what you guys see in the real world, but I'd like to hear some more about this," said Jim obviously extremely interested in the discussion.

Jonas looked at Jim, then at Terry.

"What?" said Terry looking back at Jonas.

"Hey, you started it," replied Jonas with a smirk on his face, "Make a zombie disease for the man."

"Okay," said Terry, staring back at Jonas. "One word: Rabies!"

"Christ, Terry, that's an obvious choice," said Ben.

"Can't you come up with something more interesting?"

"Wait a minute," said Jim, "Why not rabies? I know about that disease, it makes you go mad and you bite people and then they get the disease too." Jim, sat back and smiled, proud that he could contribute to the discussion. He designed fuel systems for aircraft, talking about diseases was as foreign as speaking French.

Ben responded, "Sorry Jim, it couldn't happen with rabies. First, rabies doesn't do that to humans. Infected humans basically get sick and die. They might go mad since it causes encephalitis, that's inflammation in the brain Jim," Ben said looking at Jim assuming he may not understand the term.

"I got it," replied Jim, "It infects the brain."

"Right," said Ben, "but in a different way than animals. Rabid animals get very defensive. Usually, people get bit because they come across a sick animal and approach it. The sick animal becomes aggravated and attacks out of fear. It bites you and you get rabies. Sure, infected humans can attack you but it's rare and I have never heard of a rabid human biting someone."

"So rabies is out?" asked Jim.

"Yeah but it was a reasonable choice," said Ben rolling his eyes as he looked at Terry, "unless of course..." as he turned his head and looked at Jonas.

"What?" asked Jonas.

"Well you're the one who does some work with the Department of Defense. Any attempts to weaponize rabies?" asked Terry.

"I couldn't tell you even if I knew and you know that, replied Jonas, "but I'm sure someone's tried. Besides, most weaponized diseases are meant to spread rapidly and kill just as quick. It would be hard to make rabies do that. Any of the hemorrhagic fevers would be ideal. Take Ebola. It can kill you in as little as 8 days from being infected, but therein lies the problem. It kills too quickly. The victims get too sick too fast and it limits how widespread the disease can travel plus you have to come in contact with infected body fluids so transmission is easily controlled."

"Could you imagine, though, if someone was able to tweek that virus enough to lengthen its incubation period or even worse, make it transmittable through respiratory droplets like influenza?" said Ben.

"Come on, Ben," said Terry. "You know as well as anyone, most of the bigger powers have vaults full of weaponized Ebola, Marburg, Smallpox, SARS, and loads of other nasty things. They would love to try out on some unsuspecting enemies. They're just scared shitless to do it. They know the outcome. Even if they have a vaccine or treatment for it. They would have to assume someone else would release their own virus cocktail on them. Hell, it'd be worse than nuclear war. At least with a nuke you have to enter a code and push a button. With viruses, you open the wrong vial and a large portion of the population dies within the month."

Jim had been sitting silent taking all of the discussion in. "You guys are serious aren't you?" he asked.

Yeah, but there isn't much of a threat with the really big stuff. It's just too difficult to work with so only the big guys have it...like us," said Jonas, trying to move the conversation in another direction. Weren't we talking about zombie diseases?" said Jonas, glaring his eyes at Ben.

Ben, on cue replied, "Yes, yes we were. Okay, here's my pick... Nanoviruses."

"What? That's not even a real virus," complained Terry.

"Oh, and you know that for sure," Ben fired back laughing. "Seriously, they are doing nanotechnology in the medical field that would have microscopic robots move through the body to deliver medications, repair damaged tissue, even get pictures of tumors. So, if they can program a nanovirus to do that, then what's stopping them from programming them to go to the brain of any target and start messing around with the victim's behavior? I know it's not real yet, but it's not out of the realm of possibility."

"Now that's creative," said Jonas clapping his hands. "I would never have come up with that...it's brilliant."

"Thank you, Herr Doctor," said Ben bowing his head.

"What about you, Jonas?" asked Jim. "What's your pick for a zombie-type disease?"

"I really can't think of one that would do that type of thing, Jim," replied Jonas. "I would probably look at a higher order organism like a fungus, maybe Cordyceps which we know causes behavior changes in ants. Or maybe a protozoan. Hell, even flukes and worms can alter host behavior, so I have to go in that direction. I think viruses and bacteria are too aggressive and too limited in their effects. Schizophrenia has been linked to infestations of worms and protozoan's so there is your insanity behavior but they just aren't that zombie-like. I am going to have to say... (Jonas hesitated)...I'm on board with Ben's nanovirus," Jonas laughed and smiled at Ben.

"Honestly, it actually makes sense...that's the scary part," Terry said as he lifted his beer in the air. "To nanoviruses wherever they are!" he toasted.

"To nanoviruses!" the others said together as they toasted the apparent winner of the night's zombie disease debate.

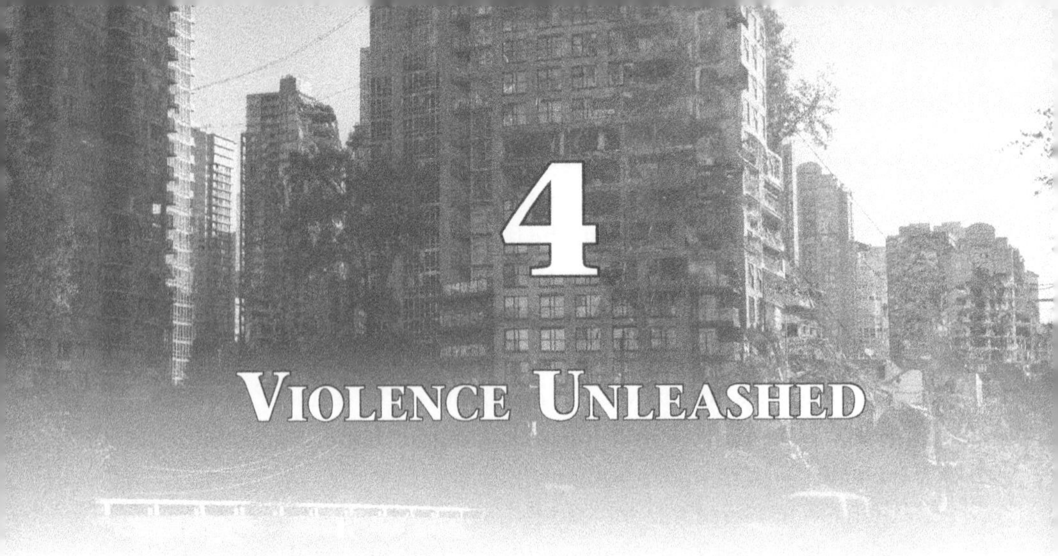

4

Violence Unleashed

"All around the globe, scenes of unimaginable horror are being witnessed. Human minds hijacked by this disease unleashing the darkest demons that dwell deep within the primal mind. Suicides, rapes, killings all on a scale never imagined. This is the end of man.

Bradley Adams
CNN News Correspondent, Mali

It was another long, hot day and the growing numbers of sick refugees waiting for treatment had taken its toll on Dr. Bashad and his staff. He had already seen almost fifty patients and it wasn't even noon yet. Bashad's colleague, Dr. LaRoche was at the south end of the encampment with a couple of staff members treating patients that could not make the trip to the main infirmary. Drs. Amir Bashad and Girard LaRoche had come to the M'bera refugee center via London as part of a team sent by Doctors Without Borders. The desperate plight of over 80,000 displaced refugees from the ongoing war in Mali had affected Amir deeply, having lost his brother and two sisters in Iraq from a suicide bombing. To Amir, the war against the jihadist movement in North Africa had become personal.

The M'bera refugee center, located in the southeastern corner of Mauritania, just over the border with Mali, was critically overpopulated. The U.N refugee agency, UNHCR that ran the camp had struggled to keep up with the demand for food, water, and sanitation. Healthy refugees entering the camp immediately fell sick with a wide range of diseases that continued to sweep through the camps inhabitants. Malnutrition and dehydration were a constant problem, but diseases like malaria and cholera were commonplace.

Dr. Bashad's last report to the UNHCR described the appearance of a flu-like illness that had swept through the encampment over the past few months. At first, the initial impression was that it was a mild type of influenza. The patients complained of headaches, fatigue, swollen lymph nodes, and a persistent cough. Most did not have notable fevers though some of the patients that had other illnesses such as AIDS did show high prolonged fevers and a steady worsening of the illness. He had reported that in the past ninety days, at least sixty four people had died from the illness either directly or as a secondary infection. It was difficult to tell as so many people were already ill with something else. Initial test results on blood, sputum, and stool samples revealed little surprises. Other than the common infective agents he was already familiar with treating, the reports showed a large number of Schistosomiasis cases as well as an alarmingly high number of atypical Toxoplasmosis cases. He knew that ScDr. Bashad's last report to the UNHCR described the appearance of a flu-like illness that had swept through the encampment over the past few months. At first, the initial impression was that it was a mild type of influenza. The patients complained of headaches, fatigue, swollen lymph nodes, and a persistent cough. Most did not have notable fevers though some of the patients that had other illnesses such as AIDS did show high prolonged fevers and a steady worsening of the illness. He had reported that in the past ninety days, at least sixty four people had died from the illness either directly or as a secondary infection. It was difficult to tell as so many people were already ill with something else. Initial test results on blood, sputum, and stool samples revealed little surprises.

Tensions ran high at the refugee camp. A combination of crowded conditions, theft, tribal in-fighting, and the occasional rebel attack pressed everyone here to their limit. Violence had escalated when French troops were on sight, but the U.N. peacekeeping force had re-established control and showed great tolerance to the animosity many refugees exhibited towards any foreign presence.

"Samara," called Dr. Bashad. "Come over here for a minute."

A young volunteer nurse, Samara, had been with Dr. Bashad for several months now and was more experienced than many of the visiting nurses that came and went with the various organizations that assisted at the camp.

"Yes, doctor," she replied walking quickly to where Dr. Bashad was.

"Samara, this young man is dehydrated. Let's give him a bottle of rehydration solution. Have him stay here for at least one hour, and have him drink another before he leaves. If there are any problems let me know. I'm going to take my break."

"Yes doctor. Will you be in your unit?" she asked as she helped the young man up to his feet.

"Yes. I'll have my radio on me so you can get a hold of me if there are any problems," he replied smiling and patting the young man on the back.

"You'll feel better shortly, just do what the nurse tells you to do."

The young man, about 16-17 years old, grasped the doctors hand and held it to his forehead,

"I will doctor. Thank you."

Amir left the infirmary and walked the short distance to his quarters, a pre-fabricated housing unit complete with a fan and a private toilet. Compared to what the refugees had to live in, the medical staff lived in luxury. There were a number of Belgian soldiers that had tents near his quarters as they were in charge of protecting the medical staff should any riots or attacks break out. Most everyone spoke French so he would often invite some of them over to play cards or just talk. Not right now though, he had a couple of hours before he had to return and it was the heat of the day. *Must be near one hundred*, he thought as he entered his quarters. He was exhausted. He took off his glasses and laid down on his cot. He quickly fell asleep.

Amir had dozed off for about an hour when a Belgian soldier entered his tent. It was Sergeant Dumont who was in charge of security for the medical staff.

"Doctor. Doctor wake up," said Dumont shaking his shoulder gently.

"What? What is it?" said Amir half-asleep and fumbling for his glasses.

"Doctor, Doctor LaRoche has been trying to contact you. He says it's important."

"LaRoche? Is he back?" asked Amir.

"No doctor, he is still in the south quarter," replied Dumont helping Amir up out of the cot. "He says it's urgent you contact him. He is on channel five."

"Thank you Sergeant." Amir picked up his radio and tuned it to channel five.

"Amir to Girard. Come in Girard." Amir spoke into the radio. "Dr. LaRoche are you there?"

"Dr. Bashad, this is Girard. Thank God you got back to me," replied LaRoche. "You must get over here. Something is going on with the sick.... many of the.....mini seizures.....cannot tell what the cause ......"

"Girard...Girard...can you hear me?" said Amir. "Girard can you hear me?"

"Yes, I am here....batteries low.....reception." the transmission from Dr. LaRoche was weak.

"Can you hear me now?" said Girard in a louder voice.

"Yes. It's better. What is going on?" asked Amir now extremely concerned as it was unusual to get calls from the out teams unless the situation was very serious.

"Doctor, many of the people here are acting strangely. Headaches, hallucinations, seizures.....then they become.....never seen anything like....." the transmission faded out momentarily. "....attacking each other. Don't know how many of them are dead.....violence is still spreading in all directions....." again the transmission faded.

"Dammit!" yelled Amir. "Girard are you there. I cannot hear you.

"Doctor I am here," It was Girard still transmitting, but the batteries in his handheld radio were running very low.

"Is this some kind of rebel attack? asked Amir.

"No, no rebels. Attacking each other," replied Girard. "Cannot describe what is happening." Girard was now highly excited and stumbling for words.

Amir could hear yelling and screaming in the background as he listened to Girard.

"Girard. Can you get out of there? Girard, get out of there now."

"....seems to be....psychotic reaction....extreme violent behavior....mass hysteria...."

Outside, Amir could hear a tumult off in the distance and suddenly the sound of gunfire.

"Girard. Who is shooting? Girard are you there?" he asked frantically.

"Troops opened fire on the crowd....too many...."

In the background, Amir heard screaming and gunfire and some kind of screams he had never heard before...animal-like. *What the hell was that?* he muttered to himself.

"Girard are you there? Girard what is happening? Do you hear me?"

There was no response. Girard had been killed along with his assistants.

Amir looked off to the south and saw thick plumes of black smoke. A fire had broken out. By now, the panicked refugees were fleeing in all directions. Most thought rebels were attacking the encampment, but as the violence spread rapidly it became apparent that the attack was from within the refugee population.

Like a chain of dominoes, the violent attacks began somewhere in the south quarter of the encampment and moved outward in all directions. As the brutal attacks continued, more and more bystanders began to become violent and in turn, attacked even more refugees. The insanity spread as hordes of psychotically driven refugees attacked their neighbors, even the animals. They left nothing alive in their wake. Hundreds of bodies lie strewn behind the expanding ring of killing. Bodies beaten and ripped apart, some obviously killed by gunfire from the peacekeepers who also fell victim to the sea of human violence.

Inside the infirmary where Dr. Bashad has been a little over an hour ago, the young teen he had treated for dehydration, began to hallucinate. Small facial twitches became obvious as the sound of yelling and panicking became louder. Then, as if someone had flipped a switch, he attacked the patient in the cot next to his, biting her neck and tearing out a large chunk of flesh. Two powerful blows to the head and she was dead. Two of the nurses grabbed him to pull him off his victim. He turned on them and emitted a bone-chilling scream. He attacked both with an I.V. stand killing them quickly. Now a panic spread throughout the infirmary and three more patients went into seizures only to then attack anyone near them. The attacks were brutal and swift.

Amir had heard the screaming and had run toward the infirmary dodging fleeing refugees. Along with him were Dumont and another soldier. Stopping a short distance from the hospital tent entry, the youth he had treated burst through the door flaps grabbing a young child near the entrance and began to beat him to death. He was covered with blood and screaming in that blood-curdling pitch. Amir was in shock at what he saw. Three more attackers appeared as they began to attack anyone near them. Then Dumont and the other soldier who also witnessed the brutal attacks opened fire on the four attackers dropping the youth and two others quickly. The fourth attacker rushed them brandishing an arm it had ripped off one of his victims. He took several rounds in the chest before he fell only a few feet from the doctor. Not quite dead, Amir noticed the attacker was still having mini-seizures, then they stopped.

"Doctor, come with us!" said Sgt. Dumont, as he grabbed Amir's arm and pulled him in the direction of the nearby Pandur personnel carrier. As they ran toward the waiting vehicle, the turret gunner opened fire on a group of six attackers who were rushing the vehicle. Amir was shoved into the vehicle by the sergeant who turned to cover his other soldier with them only to watch as he was over-run by the insane mob despite firing his weapon at point blank range into the crowd. The some of the attackers tore apart the body as the rest of the mob continued toward the vehicle. Dumont, now inside the vehicle, shut and locked the hatch while screaming at the driver to get them out of there. The turret gunner was still unloading his gun on the crowd which, by now had grown to over forty attackers. Amir sat in shock as he listened to the screaming and gunfire. Dumont looked out from one of the viewports as the carrier moved quickly through the crowd making no effort to go around people. "Doctor, come with us!" said Sgt. Dumont, as he grabbed Amir's arm and pulled him in the direction of the nearby Pandur personnel carrier. As they ran toward the waiting ve

"What the hell was that?" screamed Sgt. Dumont, looking at Amir. "What in God's name was that?" He began to shake, tears forming in his eyes as the trauma of the event set in. Wiping his eyes, he turned toward the driver.

"Emergency pickup point Blue. Don't stop until I tell you to," he ordered but by now the young soldier driving the vehicle was already heading for that point as fast as the Pandur could go. "And try not to get us killed," barked Dumont as he grabbed the headset off the hook on the radio. "Dumont alpha charlie seven seven to Flanders zebra tango seven at Nema do you read?"

"This is Flanders zebra tango 2 at Nema, go," replied the voice on the other end of the transmission.

"Emergency contact...M'bera refugee camp has been attacked and over-run. Hostiles are unidentified. Numerous casualties. Unable to return to camp due to hostilities. Proceeding to emergency pickup point Blue due west of camp. Three vehicles. I have no contact with other squads. Do not have a count at this time, but estimate twelve enroute. ETA to pickup is twenty-two minutes," said Dumont holding his head in his hands.

"Roger, Dumont alpha charlie seven seven. Pickup is in the air and inbound to you. Confirm ETA of 22 minutes."

"Confirmed, Dumont out." said the sergeant, who now exhaled deeply as he lay back against the seat. By now the turret gunner had come down into the vehicle and closed the hatch.

"We're in the clear, sergeant." he reported. "Two other Pandurs are following. No other refugees are with us."

"Here," said Dumont as he handed the headset to the gunner. "Contact the other two vehicles and tell them we are going to the emergency pickup point Blue. See if any of them know if the other four squads made it out."

"Yes sergeant," replied the gunner. "Sergeant...back there..."

"What is it?" replied Dumont.

"I panicked...I opened fire on the attackers...but then I started to shoot anyone near us."

"You and me both, son," said Dumont patting the gunner on the shoulder. "You didn't have a choice."

Sergeant Dumont turned to Amir who by now was shaking off the shock of the event.

"Doctor, I know what I saw. That was no rebel attack. I watched people near me start to have convulsions and then attack others. It was like..." he searched for words. "Like something out of a zombie movie."

Amir looked at the sergeant, searching for answers but he had none.

"I don't know what happened back there...not zombies...no such thing," he said shaking his head. "Not zombies," he whispered. "but something."

A short time later, at the CIA headquarters in Langley, a communications officer hurriedly walks down the hallway and enters the office of Alex Donaldson, director of science and technology, special projects division.

He hands the letter to the director. "We've intercepted a series of communications from U.N. peacekeeping force at M'bera refugee camp, sir."

"Thank you, son. That will be all," replied Donaldson waving his hand slightly to dismiss the officer.

Reading the communications, he closed his eyes and sighed. *Son of a bitch!* he whispered to himself. Putting the letter down, he picked up the phone and dialed a number.

"Vanguard Consulting," said the female voice at the other end of the call.

"Ulysses," he replied.

There was a long period of silence on the phone, then a male voice answers.

"Yes."

"The Trojan Horse is loose," stated Donaldson, his voice giving away the anxiety he was holding in.

"Are you sure?" replied the male voice.

"Yes."

"I'll call back with instructions," said the voice and then the line was disconnected.

5

A Change For The Worse

"We are the cause of our own demise. We have exploited the earth's resources without concern of any consequence. We ignored the signs. We thought ourselves outside natural law. God help us!"

Dr. Luciano DiAmato
Pontifical Academy of Science

Damn, this week is going by fast, thought Jonas as he pushed aside the files he had been working on. He had not slept much in the past forty-eight hours. The recent pressure brought on by the Saudi's regarding the MERS-CoV outbreak necessitated the extra hours. He had spent hours going over the recent serotyping results given to him by Walter and the reports sent by the Saudi ministry of health. It did not help the situation to find that 16 new cases were reported this week. There was some suspicion by the Saudi government that the SARS-like coronavirus was "manufactured" which was just a nicer way of saying someone made a virus to kill Arabs specifically. Jonas had already dismissed that possibility before he even saw the reports. The virus simply did not have the characteristics of a weaponized virus. It was too slow and too inefficient. Not to say it wasn't a serious health risk but comparing it to a weaponized smallpox virus ...not even close.

He had given his final report and recommendations to Dr. Brilli, the department director earlier that morning. At this moment, Dr. Brilli was in Washington, D.C. giving a briefing to the Secretary of State and a few members of the foreign affairs committee. It was their job to reassure the Saudi's that the outbreak, although serious, was not an act of bioterrorism.

W.H.O. (the World Health Organization) had called an emergency committee meeting to decide whether MERS-CoV necessitated a public health alert based on the findings of his department and a few other agencies. Jonas was sure the Saudi's would ease up a bit once the evidence was presented. Still, with the tensions running so high in the region, every little thing that happens there seems to sprout accusations of covert operations by someone. Besides, with W.H.O. all over this situation, the pressure was now off his department and he could turn his attention to other pressing issues that had been set aside.

As Jonas sorted through the files piled on his desk, the phone rang. "Dr. Matthews here," said Jonas. It was Walter on the other end of the line.

Dr. Walter Fredrickson, or just "Walter" as he preferred to be called by his co-workers, was about as good a lab manager as you could get and one of the top DNA guys in the world. He was organized, methodical, and did his job better than anyone Jonas had ever known. Few would ever guess that outside the job, Walter was "home-grown". He drove a slightly rusted out Trailblazer, loved to go bass fishing, and always wore an old worn out Atlanta Braves baseball cap. He was a walking contradiction. Walter had just turned sixty back in March and they had celebrated it at Jonas' house with the rest of the crew. It was the first time that Walter had come to one of the get-togethers alone. Meredith, Walters' wife of thirty-nine years had died the year before of pancreatic cancer. There was an obvious sadness to him now, but he still showed up and ran the lab as he always had. Jonas had become closer to him since his wife's death, trying to get him out with friends. Jonas understood his depression and made surDr. Walter Fredrickson, or just "Walter" as he preferred to be called by his co-workers, was about as good a lab manager as you could get and one of the top DNA guys in the world. He was organized, methodical,

"Jonas, this is Walter. Can you come over to the lab sometime today?"

"Sure, what's up?" replied Jonas sensing some anxiety in Walter's voice.

"I need to go over these Toxoplasma samples that you had sent to us," answered Walter. "We completed the DNA sequencing and I need you to take a look at something."

"I'm on my way," replied Jonas.

Walter hung up the phone without saying anything else, which furthered the anxiety Jonas was already feeling. It was not like Walter to be so abrupt unless something was not right.

Jonas made his way down the connecting walkway to the lab complex which was in a separate building on the C.D.C. campus. Lab building 18 housed various offices and supportive rooms, but most impressive were its newly constructed containment labs. Inside were all four levels of labs and Jonas had no intention of going into any of them if he could avoid it. Recent investigations into the lax safety practices and construction errors had shaken everyone who dealt with the labs and fostered some degree of distrust. Walter, however, had come though the investigations unscathed. In fact, he was actually recognized for his outstanding compliance record. Walter ran his lab like a dictator. He did not tolerate anything but professionalism inside his lab as evidenced by the trail of ex-lab workers he left in his wake. Anyway, with all the new high tech gadgets in the conference rooms, one could discuss findings with researchers in the lab without ever entering the facility.

Jonas entered the lobby of the lab building where Walter was waiting for him seated on the couch in the reception area. Jonas approached him trying not to look too surprised as it was uncharacteristic for Walter to wander out of the lab area let alone come to the lobby.

"Who let you out of the cage?" joked Jonas cautiously as he started to sit down opposite Walter.

"I've got the keys," replied Walter with a token smirk on his face. "Not here," he said getting up and grabbing the files on the cushion next to him. "Follow me."

Jonas and Walter walked down the hallway leading to a small cluster of meeting rooms near the cafeteria. Nothing was said along the way. Jonas was getting uncomfortable. They passed through the cafeteria where Jonas bought a couple of bottles of water as Walter stood waiting impatiently.

"Sorry, but my mouth is getting dry from the exercise," Jonas quipped. Of course he was lying. The mysterious behavior of Walter had stressed him and his mouth simply dried up. "I got you one also," Jonas said offering him a bottle.

"Thanks," said Walter as he turned and began to walk again. "This way."

They walked out the opposite side of the cafeteria and turned down a smaller hallway that ended with an emergency exit. To the left, were supply rooms, obviously for the cafeteria vending machines. On the right were two doors marked "private". Walter pulled out his keys, fumbling through several keys, he found the one that fit the lock. Walter unlocked the door and opened it. "In here, Jonas," said Walter holding the door for him. The both entered the small room as the door closed behind them.

This room was small by comparison to the other meeting rooms that were in this building. Small, about fourteen by twenty feet with a single vertical window. It lacked the high tech gadgetry found in other such rooms. It possessed a conference table and a large dry erase board...fairly spartan for such a high tech facility. They sat down opposite each other at the far end of the table away from the door.

"Christ, Walter, what's up with the secret agent behavior? Why are we meeting in a broom closet?" asked Jonas opening the bottle of water.

"It's quiet at this end of the building. The food service uses these rooms for their meetings so they are fairly safe." replied Walter opening the file he brought.

"Safe? What do you mean by that?" asked Jonas. "You don't have someone running around contaminating the place do you?"

"Of course, we don't. You know better than that. I meant safe from listening ears. The newer rooms on the other side of the building are state of the art for meetings but they are also bugged," said Walter intently. "Think about it. We get all sorts of scientists and diplomats from other countries meeting in those rooms as well as our own staff. Everything that is said is recorded and checked to see if there is usable information that is unintentionally leaked. Hell, they even record my meetings. They have to. There's always the possibility that insiders could be planning a theft of materials or even a bombing. It's simply covering all the bases."

"Isn't this room bugged also?" asked Jonas in a lower voice and leaning forward.

"Maybe, but probably only when it's in use by the service managers. Most of the time it sits empty so they don't monitor it as close as the others. Now I've got to get back to the lab shortly so let's get on with this."

"Sure, what do have for me to look at?" said Jonas.

Walter pushed a copy of a DNA sequencing report in front of Jonas. "Take a look at the sequences I highlighted," said Walter. "This is the bug they isolated from those dolphins. It's definitely the parasite Toxoplasma gondii and judging from the saturation of tissue cysts in the samples we looked at, a fairly virulent form of the bug."

"So are we looking at Type I?" Jonas asked examining the page.

The protozoan parasite, Toxoplasma gondii had remained unchanged for hundreds of thousands of years. It was perhaps the most successful parasite to ever exist. There were three variations of the single species of organism. Type I was the most virulent and most common in mother-to-newborn transmission. Type II was the most common genotype found in cases of human toxoplasmosis especially in immunocompromised patients and Type III was considered non-virulent.

"That's why I wanted to meet with you about this. Naturally, Type I would be the obvious choice of the three genotypes, but that isn't the case here. Over 70% of the samples characterized were predominately an unidentified variant of Type II," said Walter tapping his finger on the DNA sequencing printed on the page Jonas was looking at. "There are always other variations such as non-Type II or non-Type III, but this is different."

"Different how?" asked Jonas now realizing the seriousness of the meeting.

"The sequencing of DNA between the three strains of T. gondii and the various sub-types are essentially identical with the exception of some alterations of the SAG2 gene, but in the samples with the Type II variant there are noticeable variations in the sequences, in particular, in the region where we believe reproductive characteristics are recorded."

"Do you know how that variation may express itself?" asked Jonas.

"Not entirely," answered Walter, "it could be any number of traits that may be altered."

"But we have dead dolphins infected with a parasite that should not have killed them," said Jonas.

"That's not completely true," replied Walter, now removing his glasses, leaning back and rubbing his eyes. "The examiners in French Guiana found significant numbers of T. gondii in all four dolphins so they assumed it was the cause of death. In fact, as near as I can tell from the reports, only one of the dolphins actually died of Toxoplasma pneumonitis. The other three were certainly infected but not enough to kill them. I am assuming they knew that but did not have an answer so they sent the mess to us."

"Now I'm confused here, Walter, if the three didn't die of the infection what did they die from?" Jonas was now getting impatient with Walter, who seemed to be beating around the bush. "Walter, I need some answers."

"I don't have any right now, Jonas, and if I did I would give them to you. Here's what I have right now. All four dolphins had injuries consistent with blunt force trauma, a finding our friends failed to mention. I noticed it on the photos of the animals and the autopsy reports showed bruised organs and fractured ribs in two of the dolphins. I sent the photos and reports to Susan Cross at the Dolphin Research Center for her opinion. Based on the information I gave her, she believes the dolphins were attacked by another dolphin or dolphins and because of the type of dolphin and the geographical location, it was most likely an animal within their pod. She mentioned that dolphin to dolphin attacks are not uncommon even within a pod as males head-butt for rank, but she has never heard of any fatal attacks within a pod and certainly nothing as severe as what was seen in the photos."

"Is she sure that it was a dolphin and not another animal like a shark or killer whale? Jonas asked.

"Without examining the bodies directly, there is no way to be sure," answered Walter, "but she did say that the diameter of the bruising on the animals was consistent with the average snout diameter of that species of dolphin. She said that the dead dolphins were pan tropical spotted dolphins and they are about the same size as the other species in the area, the bottle-nose dolphins so she could not rule out an attack by another species."

"So the long of it is that we don't know if the infection had anything to do with the other three dolphins death, right?" said Jonas in a frustrated tone. "Honestly, Walter, I'm beginning to get pissed off. What is the deal here? We have four dead dolphins that were sick with Toxoplasma, albeit a new variant, and they were attacked by another dolphin or dolphins," he said emphasizing the "s". "So, why the James Bond treatment? This isn't that unusual. Microbes mutate all the time and sick animals are often run off or killed by the other members of their group. I don't see the problem here."

Jonas stared at Walter waiting for a response. Walter was obviously uncomfortable and was searching for words. Jonas noticed beads of sweat forming on Walter's brow.

"Walter, seriously, what is going on?"

Walter looked up at Jonas as he pushed a picture of one of the samples toward him.

"This is a picture of Toxoplasma oocysts. These are usually formed inside the T. gondii's primary host, a cat. The oocyst is full of Toxoplasma organisms and is highly infective. It can also survive outside a host for up to two years. It only takes ingestion of one oocyst to become infected with Toxoplasma." explained Walter.

"Yes, I am familiar with the life cycle of the organism," replied Jonas.

"These oocysts," said Walter tapping his finger on the photo, "were isolated from a sputum sample from one of those dolphins. Three of the four dolphins were actively shedding Toxoplasma oocysts from their lungs." Walter leaned back into the chair and waited for the response from Jonas.

Jonas sat silent, searching inside himself for the information he needed to put together some kind of intelligent response but all he could muster was a weak "That's impossible. It's too radical a change for it to be random variation."

"Jonas, believe me I am hoping I am wrong but based on the samples they sent us, these dolphins were infected with a new variant of T. gondii that may have become host-independent. Of course, this is one case in a single species of mammal so we cannot be sure. That genetic variation I uncovered must have something to do with this modification." Walter said almost apologetically. "I'm not an expert in protozoan parasites, but this may be some kind of adaptive modification by the organism."

"What do you mean? asked Jonas.

"Well, think about it. You have a parasite inside an aquatic mammal. It probably got there when a dolphin ingested an oocyst that got flushed out to sea by run off or sewage flushing. It's a dead end for the parasite. There aren't any cats in the ocean so what is it suppose to do? These organisms are not stupid. They have been on the planet far longer than us and their survival strategies are on point. The parasite only has one other way of spreading and that is to undergo some kind of genetic modification that allows it to sexually reproduce in another type of host and since it's a dolphin, the lungs make the most sense as an exit from the animal.

"Why is that? Jonas asked. "Why not through the digestive tract like cats?"

"Again, if this strain has been around for a while it may have done that at first. Unfortunately for the parasite, being excreted in feces in the ocean from a moving animal might not lend itself to infecting other dolphins because of the dilution factor, so it goes through another adaptation and concentrates its oocysts in the lungs where they can be expelled through the blow hole. Swimming on the surface, the infected dolphin clears the hole with an exhalation shooting the oocysts into the air where other dolphins in close proximity can inhale them and start the cycle over again."

Jonas just sat there staring at Walter again, "That's brilliant!" he said, "But that is one hell of a leap of reproductive behavior to place on basic gene modification. Do these organisms think at that level?"

"Again, I am not an expert but I do know that many parasites have survival strategies that involve very specific actions on the host that seem almost planned. This protozoan, Toxoplasma can surgically remove a rodent's fear of the smell of cat urine and replace it with a mating pheromone response and it does it without affecting any other fears the rodent may have. I doubt if it was created with that ability. Bacteria can sense the presence of antibiotics in their environment and almost instantly begin manipulating their DNA to turn on resistance factors to the antibiotics that weren't in place before. If that isn't intelligence, I don't know what is." Walter explained. "It may seem almost impossible and highly unlikely, but don't underestimate a microbes ability to adapt to new challenges. Most of our major health issues today are on account of that very type of adaptive modification."

Jonas paced a bit more obviously troubled by what he was hearing.

"Okay Walter, let's assume that is what's happened. Why hasn't anyone noticed this before?"

"They might have except they dismissed it for the very reasons we thought it impossible. The oocysts could just as easily been inhaled into the lungs as opposed to forming there. You would have to have reason to believe that the organism is actually sexually reproducing in the animal to even check it out." replied Walter.

"So what made you think that is what's happening?" Jonas queried.

"First, the oocysts I examined are about twenty percent smaller than the typical Toxoplasma oocyst. That makes it even more susceptible to become airborne due to its lighter weight and second, an animal may inhale anywhere from one to a few oocysts depending upon the conditions. These dolphins were loaded with them. That is not possible out in the ocean. They would literally have to surface in the middle of a cloud of oocysts to account for the numbers I estimated. Our colleagues that sent the samples most likely dismissed the presence of oocysts in the lungs for the reasons we discussed."

"My God, Walter, if this strain isn't limited to these dolphins and the cysts can become airborne, this stuff could spread like wildfire. It's possible that a large number of mammals including humans could be actively spreading this disease. Hell, a third of the planet is infected with Toxoplasma already," ranted Jonas now out of his chair and pacing. "Walter, we don't even know how long this strain has been out there do we?

"No," said Walter, "it could be months or years. There's no way of knowing without doing some sampling. Of course, it would have to include other mammals, including humans. The question is where do we start?"

"Sam Watson was sent up to Oregon last week to investigate an outbreak of Toxoplasma in black bears," replied Jonas. "I can call him to see if he can send us samples ahead of his report. I'll make sure he collects sputum samples too." said Jonas who had now switched into his investigator mode. "Terry was suppose to track down other reports of events like this. I'll get with him and see what he found. If there are any other recent events perhaps they will still have samples."

"Jonas," said Walter, "this dolphin outbreak occurred in South America. We don't know how virulent this strain is in humans and if it now spreads in much the same manner as influenza...."

Walter didn't finish his sentence as Jonas instantly understood what he was going to say.

"...and if this strain has upped its virulence," said Jonas continuing Walter's line of thought. "There's nearly 30 million people infected with AIDS in Africa alone who were already fighting off the unmodified disease." Jonas tried not to sound panicked, but the mere thought of a new strain of Toxoplasma infecting that many people without immune systems was horrifying to say the least. "We can't take any chances with this. I'll put in some calls and start having samples set here. Can you get your lab ready to start doing the samples as soon as they come in?"

"Definitely. I can be ready in two or three days. I'll shuffle the schedule around and send some of our work to other units. I'll need something from you giving this priority," said Walter as he rose from the chair.

"I'll speak with Brilli when he gets back tomorrow, in the meantime, let's keep this under wraps for now. I need to make sure there's a problem before I take this upstairs. In the meantime, find out as much as you can about this bug from the samples we do have and be sure to check for drug sensitivities," said Jonas as he entered the hallway. "Walter, I sincerely hope you are wrong."

The two men walked through the cafeteria and into the lobby without a word being said. Both their minds racing through the things that needed to be done. Jonas stepped through the lobby doors and into the courtyard. He stopped and took a deep breath before continuing to his office.

6

Sam's Field Trip

"It is highly unlikely that an organism is causing the recent outbreaks of violence. This has all the signs of being a form of mass hysteria, perhaps a new form of social mania much like the St. Vitus' dance outbreaks of the middle ages."

Dr. Nathan Ingersoll
Smythe Center for Psychological Research

"Put me through to Sam Watson. Tell him it's Dr. Matthews from the CDC," said Jonas as he sat back into his chair.

Jonas knew that Sam was up in Washington state investigating an outbreak of Toxoplasma in bears but he wasn't sure why the CDC sent him. Typically, they don't investigate outbreaks in animal populations unless there was a human component to the outbreak. He wondered if Sam was unknowingly investigating the very organism he and Walter had discussed the day before. *Wouldn't that be an odd coincidence?* he thought. If he could have anyone on-site to make that determination it would be Sam.

Sam Watson was one of the CDC's top investigators. He had a real knack for field work. Where Jonas was considered outstanding in his ability to look through mountains of reports and zero in on the problem at hand, Sam was his equal in the field. His on site investigation during the Four Corners Hantavirus outbreak in 2012 firmly established him as a major asset to Jonas' department.

Sam was 2 years older than Jonas and probably could have been in charge of the department were it not for his lack of organization. He was a hunter and did not like sitting behind a desk. His reports were often too brief and lacked details, if he filed them at all. It was not at all out of character for Sam to go to the director's office, and say something like, "That outbreak in Six Lakes....it's Campylobacter. I think the source may be Swenson's chicken plant in Arkansas." That was his report and the written version would appear sometime after the second or third reminder that he had not filed a written report.

Despite all of Sam's flaws in the administrative aspect of his job, he was seldom wrong.

Jonas, still waiting for Sam to come to the phone, smiled at the thought of Sam trudging through the overgrown forest looking for bears. He could hear Sam cursing about the mosquitoes...

"Jonas? Jonas how are you doing? Damn, it's about time you called me. I was beginning to think no one missed me," Sam said laughing. "What's the occasion?"

"I'm lonely," replied Jonas with a grin. "Honestly Sam, you say you're going out for some beer and the next thing we hear is you're doing a Grizzly Adams in the Pacific Northwest."

"Not by choice, believe me. I've just about reached my breaking point with this mess," said Sam in a frustrated tone. "Jonas, this may have been the most unnerving week and a half in my life."

"What is going on out there? Why are we investigating Toxo in bears?" asked Jonas. His curiosity was showing. Jonas noticed a long pause on the other end of the line.

"I think we're looking at the beginning of something very bad," replied Sam in a lowered tone. "Jonas, we looked at about twenty bears, browns and a couple of grizzlies. Eighteen of them were positive for T. gondii."

Jonas sensed some degree of anxiety in Sam's voice but still bears testing positive for Toxo was fairly common. "What's so unusual about that? Jonas was uncomfortable with the knowledge that this was the second time in two weeks he had a conversation about Toxoplasma with one of his fellow workers and both conversations indicated something was up with this parasite.

"Jonas, all but one of the bears were asymptomatic. Dr. Yakashima, the director here, was able to isolate oocysts from each of the bears with a nasal swab. He told me that the oocysts he found in the nasal passages were smaller than typical T. gondii oocysts. Out of curiosity, he took the oocysts he had isolated and injected them in a number of mice. All of them died. So we're looking at a mouse-virulent strain of this damn thing."

Jonas felt himself weaken and pulled a nearby chair over to sit down.

"I know this organism, Jonas, and there are three problems with this scenario if you haven't already guessed," Sam continued, "One, what the hell are Toxoplasma oocysts doing in the sinus passages of wild bears? Two, why are they a different size? And three, since when did Toxoplasma become that damn virulent in mice?"

"I'll need to see your report and I want you to send whatever specimens you can spare to Walter. I'll have him go over everything." Jonas was now a bit unraveled. *Could it be the same strain that killed those dolphins? How in the world did the organism get from Guiana to the Pacific Northwest?*

Jonas became lost in thought.

"You didn't answer my questions," Sam said. "Jonas?"

Still sorting through the scenarios in his mind, Jonas was oblivious to Sam's questions. *How did a parasite go from marine mammals to land animals?* he thought.

"Jonas! You there?" Sam yelled into the phone.

Startled, Jonas replied, "Dammit! Sorry Sam I got lost in thought. I'm going to tell you something that only Walter and I know about right now so you have to keep this to yourself until I say otherwise."

"Absolutely, what's going on?" Sam sensed the seriousness in Jonas' tone.

"A few weeks ago four dead dolphins washed up on shore in French Guiana. They had smaller sized Toxoplasma oocysts in there sinuses and lungs. According to Walters initial findings, this may be a new strain of Toxoplasma that is not only host independent but is also airborne."

Jonas waited for a reply.

"Are you sure?"

"Fairly sure," replied Jonas. "I'll have Walter go over your samples and compare them but it sounds like the same organism."

Sam was puzzled. "How would bears get it? I mean, South America is a long way away."

"I know." answered Jonas. "Since there isn't any direct contact between bears and dolphins, there must be an intermediate....maybe the same food source."

There was a brief moment of silence.

"Salmon!" both Jonas and Sam said simultaneously.

"That's got to be it. You need to get some salmon from nearby rivers and get them to Walter asap," Jonas now a bit anxious. "Sam, if this parasite is that virulent we have to assume that anyone who comes in contact with it may be infected."

"I know," said Sam in a subdued voice. "I don't think we were exposed but there are so many ways an airborne infective could get through even the best barriers and we were out in the woods collecting specimens from live animals. Hell, those oocysts were most likely all around us."

"Exactly," Jonas said. "Let's play it safe. Everyone on the team gets swabbed, blood tested, and monitored for symptoms. That includes you."

"I'll get it going right away. Jonas. If any of us do have it...."

"It may not even cause a problem in healthy mammals so I'm not ready to push the alarm, Sam. If you test positive, it may not mean anything at all."

"Just the same," replied Sam, "these things can be a bugger to get rid of." He was now nervous.

"I'm way ahead of you. Walter is running a antibiotic sensitivity panel on the isolates from the dolphins right now. If you are positive, we'll get the right drugs into you immediately."

Sam felt more at east knowing that Jonas had the bases covered. Still, there was one more thing.

"Jonas, that other bear that did have symptoms..."

"Yeah, what happened to it?" asked Jonas.

"The rangers who went out with us had to put it down."

"Why? Was it sick?"

"Jonas, we were out tracking bears when the rangers got a call about a bear attack at a campground only a mile or so from where we were. We went with them to investigate the situation. A brown bear had trapped a young couple inside their rv and was tearing it apart trying to get to them. Jonas, we get there and what I saw happening scared the shit out of me. Here's this 400 pound bear throwing itself against the side of the camper. There was blood everywhere from it trying to claw through the metal skin. It was like this animal was possessed. To make a long story short, the rangers put a .50 caliber bullet into this bear and that only makes it worse.

Now the bear sees us and starts coming toward us making this horrible screeching noise. Anyway, the rangers end up killing the bear by shooting it a dozen times as it got near to us. I tell you, Jonas, it was like something out of a horror film."

"Did you test the animal for rabies?" asked Jonas.

"Preliminary tests showed it was negative. Of course it was positive for Toxoplasma. They're still testing for other bugs that could cause an encephalitis. I'm guessing that's what it was. It could be anything really," replied Sam.

"Just the same, make sure you include that animal in the samples you send. If they took any brain tissue I'd like Walter to have that analyzed as well." Jonas said being his usual thorough self. He was beginning to get a bit irked over the amount of time this Toxoplasma thing was beginning to take out of his already busy schedule. This summer was a busy one at the Center and there really wasn't much room to take on more, but it didn't work that way. If there was the possibility of a threat, he had to investigate it. It didn't deserve priority yet with other more pressing outbreaks already underway, but he instinctively knew he better keep a close eye on it.

"Sam, I can only say I'm glad I wasn't there. I don't need any more nightmares. Now, are you going to be finishing up there soon?

"It will take another two or three days and I will be out of here," replied Sam.

"Good, until then stay out of the woods," joked Jonas.

"Gladly," said Sam. "After seeing what that bear did, I don't think I will ever step foot in the woods again. Thanks for the call Jonas."

Jonas hung up the phone, took a deep breath and ran his hands through his hair. Sitting back in the chair, he closed his eyes and rocked slightly. He was feeling the stress a bit too much he thought. *A new strain of Toxo that appears on both sides of the globe*, he thought to himself. *Both reports have a violent behavior component. Is it possible that the behavior is a symptom as well?*

Jonas thought about it for quite a while, ignoring the work on his desk and the occasional call coming in. He was uneasy, and it was getting worse. Now he had two colleagues who were also alarmed about the situation. He respected both Sam and Walter. They did not get to where they were by crying wolf.

But Toxoplasmosis did not cause violent behavior, he thought to himself, at least the Toxo he knew. Sure there were some studies that supported the possibility that it caused schizophrenia in some victims, but nothing definitive had come out of those papers.

It was late in the day, about 4:30pm, and Jonas always dreaded the infamous commute around Atlanta. Even though he lived fairly close it still took a half an hour to get home if everything moved along right. The day sucked. His brain was in overdrive and he was tired of thinking.

"Screw it!" he said quietly to himself. "I leaving early today."

He pressed the com button on his phone that called his secretary, Amy.

"Yes, Dr. Matthews? answered Amy.

"Amy, I'm leaving for today. If anyone wants to get in touch with me, have them call my mobile."

"I will do that Doctor. You have a nice drive home," she replied.

"Like that will happen," Jonas joked to himself as he grabbed his briefcase and phone. He stepped out into the reception area and made his way down the hallway toward the walkway that led to the parking structure.

"Jonas! Hey, Jonas! Wait up!" came a voice from back down the hall.

Jonas turned and saw Terry half-walking, half-running toward him carrying a large packet of files.

"Terry, what on earth?" said Jonas, looking at his slightly out of breath friend.

"Jonas, I was hoping to get these to you earlier today but I kept getting called out to meetings." gasped Terry. "Damn! I better start working out again."

"No doubt, Terry. You're dripping sweat all over these files. What are they anyway?"

"This is the information you asked me to dig up on Toxo last week," Terry replied.

"All this? I meant within the last few years, not the last century," Jonas said looking at the large number of files.

"That is the last five years! In fact, it is only events I can verify. I thought the pile was too large so I culled it down a bit. I can always bring the rest," Terry replied.

"No, this will do for now," Jonas said pulling back. "I guess I'll have to go over them tonight. Thanks. I was wondering what to do with all that free time I had."

"Not a problem good buddy," Terry quipped slapping Jonas lightly on the back. "Have fun!"

"You know it's date night, so I'll have Ellie call you when she learns I have homework to do and can't take her out," Jonas said walking away.

"Hey, you needed an excuse...I delivered," joked Terry walking in the opposite direction. "Anything for my good friend."

Jonas stepped through the door into the walkway to the parking structure. Stopping for a moment he looked at the packet of files Terry had given him. *The hell with it!* he said to himself. Jonas began walking again but now with more resolve. He had his purpose. He and Ellie were going out tonight.

7

Cause For Alarm

"The closure of the New York Stock Exchange brought about by this global catastrophe has now entered its sixth month. Never in the history of the exchange has it closed its doors for this long. We do not know what the long term consequences will be on the global economy nor do we expect any recovery to happen quickly."

G. Thomas Anderson
Chairman, New York Stock Exchange

"Good morning, Dr. Matthews," said Jonas' secretary, Amy. "You're here bright and early."

Amy had been Jonas' secretary for six years now and she had gotten use to his routine appearance around nine-thirty each morning. Jonas explained his late appearance by stating that he had "rounds" to make, which meant he wandered around the building checking in on his friends and discussing what they were investigating or just to shoot the breeze a bit. Regardless, early appearances were rare.

"G'mornin', Amy," Jonas said as he walked by her desk carrying a cup of coffee and the files Terry had given him to go over. "Couldn't sleep much last night so I thought I get in early and try to get something done." Jonas entered his office and set down the files. Took a sip of coffee, grimaced, and then poked his head out of the doorway.

"Amy, can you get a hold of Dr. Brilli's office and see if he can meet with me this morning for about a half an hour?"

"Sure thing, doctor. I'll call his office right away and see if he has some time. What should I say this is about?"

"Just tell him I said it was important," Jonas replied. Brilli knew him enough to know that when he said it was important...it was important. Jonas hoped that Brilli would be able to help him make some sense of what was going on with this Toxoplasma issue. After all, it seemed to be important enough to send Sam out to investigate bears so he must be aware of some aspect of it.

Jonas sat back in his chair, took another sip of coffee, and began to sift through the days reports Amy had neatly arranged on his desk. It was the usual stuff. Mostly reports of food borne illnesses and a few updates from some health departments. *Well, let's get to it,* he thought as he opened the first file and began to read.

This was life at the C.D.C... A far sight from the glamour of field work or investigative research. Most of the tasks done by him and others at the department was paperwork. Jonas had gotten over his dread of doing paperwork early on in his career. He had developed an understanding of the need for it and how important it was to create the story behind any event such as a food-borne illness outbreak. In this way, you could develop a better understanding of the progress of diseases no matter how insignificant they may seem. Reports would often take on all the characteristics of a Sherlock Holmes type mystery.

The past several years, Jonas had noted (as had many others in the field) the rise in new types of infections as well as movement of existing ones into new areas. The prevailing thought was that global warming, human encroachment into pristine environments, and population stress was changing the nature of infectious disease. He had seen it happen a number of times. The rise of Ebola in Uganda and the Congo was certainly one of the newest problems, one that the world could certainly do without. AIDS was another example. Now, this Toxoplasma mystery had all the makings of another emerging problem, the extent of which Jonas was uncertain.

Jonas was startled from his thoughts by the sound of the phone intercom. It was Amy.

"Yes, Amy."

"Dr. Brilli's office called and said he could meet with you at ten o'clock. Oh, and Dr. Frederickson wanted you to call him when you get a chance."

"Okay, thank you, Amy"

Jonas looked at the clock. It was nine-fifteen now, plenty of time to check with Walter before the meeting. He dialed Walter's extension.

"Dr. Fredrikson's office." answered Walter's secretary.

"This is Dr. Matthews. Is Dr. Fredrikson available right now?"

"Yes, doctor. He's been expecting your call. I will put you through."

"Jonas, that didn't take long."

"You rescued me from a pile of paperwork," joked Jonas.

"Good. It's nice to know I am still useful,"

"What do you have for me Walter? I'm meeting with Brilli in about thirty minutes."

"I sent you most of the lab findings on our little Toxo friend. I think you'll find it interesting."

"Give me the short version, Walter. I won't have time to go through it all before my meeting."

"Okay.

"I've got some more lab results on that T. gondii variant we discussed a while back. I e-mailed you and Brilli copies of everything I have so far but I thought I should discuss a couple of items with you."

"What did you find?"

"Well, I've definitely determined that this is a new species of Toxoplasma. The variations in its DNA profile are significant enough to make this strain a stand-alone species. Second, the organism is highly virulent, at least in mice. I am not sure what its effects are in humans but I assume it is not much different than the T. gondii strain."

"What about drug sensitivity?" Jonas asked.

"It's fairly similar to common T. gondii strains. The usual drugs of choice: pyrimethamine, sulfadiazine, and clindamycin are minimally effective due to resistance. A couple of experimental drugs showed good results. Both Apicidin and the dinitroanilines both were effective in stopping growth in the mobile forms but not in the tissue cyst forms. The new class of triazines may be the most effective approach given this new species broad resistance but they aren't in large-scale production at this time."

"That doesn't sound promising," said Jonas.

"No it doesn't," replied Walter, "Remember, Jonas, this bug has been around a long time. Its survival mechanisms are impressive. It is very susceptible to treatment in the tachyzoite phase, that is when it's moving around in the body re-infecting tissues but once it encysts, it's damn near impossible to get to them. Also, the organism has an affinity to settle in the brain so trying to get an effective drug across the blood-brain barrier in sufficient strength is another major hurdle."

"What about some of the drugs used to treat schizophrenia? Don't they inhibit the growth of Toxoplasma?"

"I did test valproic acid and got the usual results. It does inhibit the progress of Toxoplasma induced schizophrenia but that is more than likely due to the inhibition of dopamine production by the organism. Also, it would be an impractical treatment agent in a large-scale event. The same goes for Haloperidol. Both will inhibit symptoms, but you'd be mass-medicating the population with mood altering drugs. Not very practical for the minimal effectiveness." replied Walter.

"Wonderful. So we have a new pathogenic species that is not very treatable without doping the entire population. This is what I'm going to tell Brilli?"

"Sorry, Jonas, but that's about the jist of it."

"Anything else I need to know?" Jonas asked in an exasperated tone.

"Yes, I got the samples back from Sam up in Washington. The bears, as well as some of the salmon samples, all tested positive for the new species of Toxo. Also, Sam and three other members of the team also tested positive."

"Sam has it? Did you tell him?"

"I've left messages on his cell to contact me and I sent an email. I also notified Brilli."

"That's good. I'll get a hold of Sam today to follow up. So this bug is already established itself," remarked Jonas.

"I would have to say yes to that. If this bug started out in the marine mammal population and it's showing up in land mammals, I would guess this thing has been out there for a few years slowly infecting coastal animals then working inland. It's probably already in the human population in large numbers by now."

"That's what I was afraid of when we first started to hear about this problem." replied Jonas.

"Jonas, there is also the possibility that a virus is involved in this somehow."

"How's that?" asked Jonas

"The additional serotyping I did on the newer samples showed additional DNA segments that did not come from the Toxoplasma parasites. I checked for contamination but came up negative. It's also not coming from the tissues themselves. I isolated the oocysts myself and double checked for outside sources...there weren't any. This extra DNA is coming from inside the oocyst or the parasite itself." explained Walter.

"What are you saying Walter?" asked Jonas, now becoming upset with the continued stream of bad news regarding this parasites appearance.

Jonas, had a bad feeling about this bug to begin with and now it was playing out like a few other major outbreaks had done in the past. He was keenly aware that anytime an outbreak began to feel like you were sinking in quicksand, the problem was going to get ugly in a hurry. He could feel the anxiety rising within him as he struggled to stay focused on what Walter was telling him.

"Jonas, my guess is that this parasite picked up a virus...a phage if you will. I don't know why or where it came from. Toxoplasma does not have any known viral phages. It's unique in that sense. Other parasites in the same family do like malaria with trypanosomavirus, but I have never heard of a phage that infects Toxoplasma."

"Could it explain the violent behaviors that seem to be associated with this new species? Like the bear that Sam saw and got samples from."

"Maybe, I don't know for sure. I took some pictures of the intact parasites from a number of samples and sent them and some of the data out to a friend, Dr. Alvarez, who is a virologist at Fort Detrick. I should hear back from him soon. He should be able to locate viral particles from the pictures if they are there. We should have Dr. Hoyle take a look at the data as well to get his take."

"I agree, but no time right now. I have a meeting with Brilli in a few minutes. I better get going." said Jonas as he gathered a few files from his desk. "I will call you later on to let you know what's going on." Jonas hung up the phone and proceeded to Dr. Brilli's office.

Dr. Antonio Brilli was the director of the D.P.E.I. (Division of Preparedness and Emerging Infections). He was a quiet man, very reserve, but he had no problem getting his points across. A world class epidemiologist, he had joined the C.D.C. after a long stint with the

National Institute of Health. Dr. Brilli was the consummate administrator and a master at surrounding himself with outstanding talent in the field. Jonas had joined his department at his request, eventually becoming chief investigator. Brilli had passed over other candidates with more impressive resume's and experience to get Jonas. He appreciated Jonas' intuition and relied on his advice on several matters.

Jonas entered Dr. Brilli's office.

"Good morning, Dr. Matthew's. Have a seat and I will let Dr. Brilli know you are here," said Brilli's secretary, Meredith.

"Thanks Meredith."

"Can I get you something to drink, Dr. Matthews?"

"Coffee would be great. One sugar. Thank you," replied Jonas.

Jonas sat back on the sofa and closed his eyes for a moment. *God I need a vacation,* he thought to himself. Meredith returned with two coffees in hand.

"Here you go, doctor. Careful it's hot." she cautioned.

Dr. Brilli entered the outer office from a hallway that led to his office.

"Jonas, come on back."

Jonas got up with a slight groan and followed Brilli down the hallway to a private conference room. Both placed their files and coffees down on the table and sat across from each other.

"Jonas, I hear you have things stirred up a bit around here. Walter sent me some information he had been gathering for you about this Toxoplasma issue. What is going on?"

"Tony (Jonas was on a first name basis with Brilli in private meetings) I wanted to make sure the findings supported my suspicions on this before I brought it to you. I am really getting a bad feeling about the appearance of a possible new strain of Toxoplasma that has appeared."

"Yes, I read Walters preliminary findings and it does raise some concern. Do you have any evidence that it threatens the human population?"

"Not anything direct. The mutation may have made it more infective and certainly easier to transmit. At this time, I see it as a major threat to immune-compromised patients and the AIDS population."

"I agree with that. We should look into whether that particular species has infiltrated those populations. I can request a number of clinics in the

U.S. to send blood and sputum samples for evaluation to determine how far it's spread. What else do you recommend?"

Jonas sat back a bit and looked away from Brilli.

"Tony, I am going out on a limb here with this but I think shit is going to hit the fan soon with this bug. I can't give you anything definite, but there seems to be an association between this bug and violent behavior. I only have a few situations to cite but if I am right, I think we are looking at a form of virulent encephalitis that causes psychotic episodes in its victims. Walter told me this morning that there may be a virus infecting this new species that may be part of the problem."

"I read that. That is somewhat surprising, but we can't be certain it has anything to do with behavioral changes. We can't even be sure that this new form of Toxoplasma has anything to do with the violent behavior as well."

"I understand that, but the possibility exists nevertheless. I know it's thin but we have a mutated form of a parasite that is known to cause schizophrenic episodes and modify host behavior, including humans. It is not unreasonable to assume that the few examples I have looked at that had violent behavior associated with them could have been part of the clinical presentation of the disease. So far, I have only seen it reported in animals, but there wouldn't be any reason to believe that it couldn't happen in human hosts as well."

Brilli sat up in the chair and looked at Jonas for several seconds.

"I don't want to cry wolf on this, Jonas, with everything else that is going on right now. We're spread so thin I have to decide what threats get attention and what resources we can spare. Jonas, you haven't given me anything to show this organism is a serious threat with the exception to the population it already infects in its other form. I am not sure I can recommend we launch a full investigation on this," said Brilli. "I just don't have the resources to check out a maybe."

"I understand, Tony. I hope I am wrong on this, but my gut instinct is telling me this is a bad one and we better get on top of it quick. Think about this. What if this organism has saturated the population as deep as T. gondii? What? About 1/3rd to 1/2 the global population is infected with it. Let's say, for the sake of argument that this phage causes the parasite to ramp up its deep brain effects causing a wide range of psychotic behavior especially violent behaviors. Look what has been going on since the early 2000's. Violent behavior has been steadily rising. Mob violence is not uncommon. Hell, we even have had face-eaters come out of the woodwork lately. What if there is a connection? This thing hasn't even gotten out of the box yet and if I am right, the number projections on this type of event could be staggering. I know I am reaching here but if we don't move now it may be too late, if it isn't already. Tony, you know I am fairly cautious with my recommendations. I wouldn't have come to"I understand, Tony. I hope I am wrong on this, but my gut instinct is telling me this is a bad one and we better get on top of it quick. Th

Brilli's eyes search Jonas' face. Again quiet for several seconds as he analyzed what Jonas had said.

"Jonas, you are scaring the hell out of me right now and I am not use to that. Okay, you have two weeks to come up with some definitive proof that this is a serious threat. Get a team together and get on it. I want something preliminary by next Thursday."

"You'll have it," said Jonas. "I will want to get Terry and Sam on this with me. I will also need a good parasitologist. I'd like to bring in Ben Hoyle, if I have your okay."

"Go ahead," said Brilli. "I will free them up from other cases to help you out. Two weeks, though."

"Right," replied Jonas. "Two weeks."

Brilli got up, gathered his files and his now cold coffee, and made for the door slowly.

"Jonas," he said, stopping for a moment. "I hope to hell you are wrong."

Brilli exited the room leaving Jonas alone in the conference room. Jonas could hear Brilli barking at Meredith.

"Meredith, what do I have to do to get a cup of hot coffee around here?"

Jonas shook his head. *Classic Brilli*, he though as he left the room, but the smile quickly disappeared from his face. He had a monumental task ahead of him and little time to accomplish it. He would spend the rest of the day organizing the team and coming up with a plan of attack. A sense of urgency had come over him as he sat down at his desk. *Where to start?* he thought.

8

Now You See Me...

"We are looking at the emergence of a new species of Toxoplasma. The alteration caused entirely due to the loss of host environment. The parasite modified its genetics to survive, but as we are now so horribly aware, it left the back door open."

Elizabeth Manning
Director, National Institute of Health

Traffic was lighter than usual that afternoon. Normally the drive home would take longer since it was mostly residential once you got out of the campus area and it as posted twenty-five miles per hour. It crawled at rush hour.

I'll have to leave earlier more often, Jonas thought. *All the traffic must be just getting onto the freeways.* He turned down East Rock Springs Road and made it to his driveway in just over twenty minutes. "A new world record," he said out loud. Ellie's car was not in the driveway but that wasn't unusual as her studio was closer to the downtown area near Ansley Park. It was about the same distance to drive in the opposite direction from their home but it involved driving out of the city at rush hour.

Jonas entered the house, tossing his packet of files on the kitchen table. He opened the refrigerator door and grabbed a cold bottle of water. Jonas checked the thermostat as it was very muggy outside and the house felt too warm. He was already sweating through his shirt as was typical of a hot August afternoon in Georgia. He finished the water and went upstairs.

Jonas turned on the CD player in the bedroom. *Something relaxing*, he thought. *Let's try one of Ellie's chill cd's.* Jonas picked a cd labeled "Midnight

Moves" and turned it on. The soft jazz began to fill the room as he closed his eyes and leaned his head back. "Perfect." he whispered to himself. Jonas took off his clothes, went into the bathroom off of the master bedroom, and ran a shower. As the water was running, he leaned onto the counter and looked into the mirror. He looked tired, he thought. He thought about taking a vacation, maybe a couple of weeks away from everything with Ellie would do him a world of good. He would talk to her about it when she got home. Even though he had come home a little early, Ellie was still out. She had a crazy schedule with her studio, anyway he had plenty of work to keep him busy until she got home. Thursdays were date nights. They had decided to go out on Thursday because Fridays were always too busy in the Atlanta metro area. Everyone blowing off steam at the same time. He and Ellie were more private. They enjoyed more sedate pleasures and tried to avoid the crowds. *Maybe a movie or a blues cafe' tonight*, he thought stepping into the shower.

Jonas faced the warm stream of water as it poured down upon his face and cascaded over his achy body. He slowly lathered up and washed himself finishing with his hair. As he leaned back into the water stream to rinse his hair, he felt a gentle cool breeze waft across his tepid skin. Sensing someone had entered the bathroom and having a good idea who, he turned into the water and closed his eyes. Moments later he felt Ellie's breasts press up against his back as her arms reached around him in a soft gentle caress. Her head laid upon his shoulder. Nothing was said, at least vocally, but as he turned and looked into her eyes he weakened. She still affected him that way after all these years. He was still a young college freshman and she was the beautiful sophomore photography student. She looked into him, her lips parted, and she pressed them against his. The water cascaded down upon both of them as they caressed, both lost in the moment, both needing each other.

Jonas woke up a while later. Ellie entered the room carrying some bath towels. "Some date you are," she joked as she sat down on the bed next to him. "I show you a little attention and you go to sleep on me."

"What time is it?" he asked.

"About 9:30," she replied. "I ordered a pizza a while ago. I saw the pile of work you put on the kitchen table. I assume you have homework."

"Geez, Ellie," Jonas said apologetically. "You should have woke me up. We can still go out to T. J.'s or someplace like that for a drink."

Ellie put her hand on his cheek then stroked away a tassel of hair from his forehead. "No, date night has been perfect so far," she said to him smiling. "We both needed that. We'll have some pizza. You can do your homework and I have a bit of photo shopping to do on some pictures."

Just about then, the doorbell rang. "Throw something on, pizza's here." said Ellie bouncing off the bed and out the door. "Hurry!"

Jonas threw on a pair of sweats and a t-shirt and made his way downstairs. Ellie had put the pizza on the kitchen table and left a cold beer next to it.

"Thank you!" yelled Jonas as he put a slice of pizza on the paper plate she had out.

"Welcome." she yelled back. "Let me know when you decide to go to bed."

"Okay." Jonas replied smiling.

Jonas sipped on the cold beer as he began to leaf through the files Terry had collected. They were chronologically arranged starting with the oldest report to the most current. He noted the subjects of the articles first to cull out the material he was most interested in.

-T. gondii in Hawaiian monk seals.
-Atypical T. gondii in bottlenose dolphins, American coastal waters.
-English river otters infected with atypical T. gondii.
-T. gondii found in Antarctic seals.
-Fatal toxoplasmosis in Antillean manatees.
-Systemic toxoplasmosis in stranded Beluga whales.
-Presence of atypical toxoplasmosis in black bears: Alaska, Pennsylvania, and Florida.
-Lethal toxoplasmosis in pigs, Gansu Province, China.
-Fatal toxoplasmosis in Australian birds.
-Atypical toxoplasmosis in Amazon parrots.
-Decline of baboon populations, Fongoli, Senegal due to fatal toxoplasmosis.

The list continued on, but Jonas had already seen enough to know what he was looking at. *What is this bug up to?* he thought to himself. For years the parasite had been infiltrating new environments. It was well-known that T. gondii was found easily in land mammals but now it had spread to marine mammals and perhaps entered the food chain there through fish and shellfish. Further, it was now found in the Arctic and Antarctic regions.

Jonas thought for a while wondering if it was the same atypical variant he and Walter had discussed. The only way to be sure was to evaluate specimens but those had been long discarded for most of these studies. He continued to leaf through the files. He stopped and looked at one that caught his attention. It read, *"A new atypical genotype mouse virulent strain of Toxoplasma gondii isolated from a wild panther in Guatemala."* He began to feel uneasy, as though he had witnessed a crime and new who committed it. If this was the same variant of T. gondii, it had already had time to implant itself on every continent and in the oceans. In Jonas' mind, this new bug was suddenly becoming the greatest threat to global health he was aware of. Typically, organisms like influenza or cholera start in one area and spread outward. You can follow the spread of the disease. In many cases, you can even track it back to the first case of the infection. This new strain of Toxoplasma was different. It seemingly was everywhere. Most likely a vast majority of animals, including humans, were already infected with it but the immune systems were holding it in check for now, much like the known strains of T. gondii. Jonas thought, *If something flips this bugs switch...*

The mere thought of the consequences made Jonas shake his head. He continued to leaf through the files. And then he saw a report that gave him chills. *"Outbreak of Fatal Human Toxoplasmosis from atypical genotype T. gondii in Surinam."*

This could not be a coincidence, he thought. The report claimed that a single atypical strain of Toxoplasma, not related to the three known strains, was responsible for the fatalities. It indicated that the organism is similar to the strain found in French Guiana that had caused a number of fatal human outbreaks there as well. It also reported that the victims were not immune compromised and the source of the organisms could not be detected, basically meaning this was a highly virulent form of Toxoplasma and it may be spread by pathways not common to the known serotypes.

Jonas laid the file down and sat back. *Why haven't we heard of this?* he thought. All indications were that the presence of this new variant had been going on for at least four or five years and was taking human casualties. Yet, he had seen nothing come across his desk about it. *Who else knew?*

He got up from the table, went to the refrigerator, and opened a beer. He wiped his forehead with the cold bottle then took a long swig. He looked at the clock on the wall...1:30. "Damn!" he said quietly. He did not realize how much time had passed. Ellie would be in bed by now. He turned off lights, went upstairs, and climbed into bed.

Jonas laid in bed staring at the ceiling for quite a while. *How did we not see this coming?* he thought. He turned over and closed his eyes. The morning would come soon and he had answers to find.

9

Sam

"We've been warning you for a long time. The government tried to get the guns...they put us in their healthcare programs to control us...they forced us to vaccinate our kids. It was about controlling the masses. They're the ones who unleashed this disease. They want to depopulate the country...the world. Resources are running out...water...food...energy ...too many people so they're culling the herd their way. Bet you're glad you have guns now, aren't you?"

Vance Masters
Publisher, *Survivalist Times*

"Hi, Jonas. What's up with you?" said the voice on the other end of the phone.

"Sam! Where have you been? I haven't heard from you since you got back from Seattle," said Jonas.

"I've been feeling crappy, Jonas, so I took a few days off to shake whatever this bug is. I've been working at home. Catching up on paperwork and stuff," replied Sam in a strained voice. "It's so damn wet out in the Northwest. I swear I get sick every time I go out there. I hate that area."

"Anything we should be worried about?" queried Jonas who, in the back of his mind, was aware that Sam had tested positive for the new species of Toxo.

"No, just a chest cold and a huge headache. Nothing I haven't had before. What is going on? I got your messages."

"I'm following up on the Toxo situation I spoke to you about earlier. Brilli gave me a couple of weeks to come up with evidence that it's a problem so I am putting a team together quickly to go over information. You, Ben, Terry, and myself. I will email you some of the things I need but for now you take it easy."

"Not a problem," Sam said coughing. "I just got to shake this damn headache. I will get on it when I get your info."

"Thanks Sam. Listen, you let me know if your condition gets worse. Walter mentioned you may have picked up that Toxo bug. We don't know if it does anything at this time but you can never tell about this stuff."

"Yeah, I figured that might be the case, but I don't think that's the problem here. Feels more like an upper respiratory thing. Walter had Dr. Branson call in a prescription for pyrimethamine just in case."

"Okay, just stay in touch. Let me know if your condition changes."

"I will, Jonas. Now quit your hen-pecking and go do something constructive,"

Jonas and Sam both laughed. Jonas was known for his, sometimes compulsive need to ride shotgun on his department staff. Sam was no exception, especially since he was out of commission and Jonas needed him now. He only had two weeks to come up with the proof he needed to convince Brilli that this Toxo issue needed priority.

"Call me if you need anything," said Jonas

"You got it!" Sam replied choking off a cough as he hung up the phone.

Jonas sat there for a while thinking about Sam. *What if he is infected? Walter said he tested positive.* Jonas picked up the phone and dialed Walter's extension.

"Dr. Frederickson's office," answered Walter's secretary, Maria.

"Maria, this is Dr. Matthew's. Is Dr. Frederickson available?"

"He's in the animal research facility at the moment. Can I give him a message?

"Yes, have him call me regarding Dr. Watson when he gets back. Let him know it's important."

"I will doctor."

"Thank you, Maria."

Jonas hung up the phone and began to shuffle through the papers on his desk. Terry had dropped off some more information earlier in the day for him to look over. *There it is.* Jonas opened the file and examined the contents. *Shit,* Jonas thought to himself, *"this damn thing is everywhere.*

The article reported the appearance of an unknown strain of T. gondii in Beluga whales in the arctic circle. *There was simply no way that it wasn't the same new Toxoplasma species, especially since it was so far removed from any major land masses,* thought Jonas. *Walter is right, this damn thing has gone airborne. Must be passed through respirations.*

Jonas spent a few hours reading reports from all over the United States... various reports of unidentified illnesses, unexplained deaths, anything that could be linked to this new organism. Nothing really jumped out at him. *It's showing up in all sorts of mammals...fish as well. It's got to be infecting humans but how? If Sam is infected then it might present as a upper respiratory infection, most likely not a very strong one. Is that it? If so, then great. We can deal with that, but still, there's the violent behavior pattern that seemed to be linked to some of the cases. Why haven't we seen any.....*

Jonas' train of thought was interrupted by a phone call. Jonas answered.

"Yes, Amy."

"Doctor Frederickson is on line 3."

"Thank you, Amy. I've got it."

Jonas pushed the flashing line 3 button on the phone.

"Walter, thanks for calling back."

"Well I'm surprised you're still here."

"Yeah, I got caught up in reading the reports that Terry had gathered for me and time got away. Anyway, I got a hold of Sam. He has some kind of upper respiratory cold going on. You mentioned he tested positive for this new Toxo bug. Anything we should be concerned about at this time?"

"Not sure yet. I've got a number of animals infected with the new organism. We're just waiting for the organism to saturate and start producing symptoms. I would suspect the respiratory thing is the first phase of infection as the organism proliferates in the lungs before moving into the body."

"Do you think Sam is in any danger?" asked Jonas.

"I don't have an answer for you, Jonas," replied Walter apologetically. "I certainly am not comfortable knowing Sam tested positive and now has symptoms of something."

"I know. Perhaps I should have him quarantined at Emory."

"Usually, that would be the prudent thing to do, but in this case it wouldn't accomplish anything but to isolate him for observation which isn't that bad of an idea. At least we could monitor him and record any symptoms and illness progress. As far as containment, forget it. If I have learned anything in the short time I have worked with this bug, it is that it spreads like fire in a lumber mill. I had to put down an entire room of test mice because one of our assistants took a cage of four infected mice into it by mistake. Two days later nearly every mouse in the room was dead. This is a seriously infective bug, Jonas, but I just don't know if it presents a major threat to humans yet."

"I understand. Still, I will call Sam tomorrow and have him check in at Emory. I'll make the arrangements to isolate him there for observation."

"I think that would be a good idea, but I don't think Sam will go without a fight. You know how he hates hospitals."

Jonas smirked at the comment. "Yes, I do remember what a pain in the ass he was when he had that gallstone attack. He did not make any friends during his stay. Hell, they may not admit him."

Both Walter and Jonas shared a subdued laugh over the incident, but both knew the possibility existed that Sam could be in trouble.

"Keep me up to date, Walter."

"I will Jonas. I should have some results for you shortly."

"Okay, thanks," said Jonas as he hung up the phone.

Jonas sat for a moment lost in thought. He picked up the phone and dialed Terry's extension.

"Dr. Andrews here."

"Terry, it's Jonas."

"Hey, Jonas. What's up?

"I've been going over these files you dropped off and I am wanted to ask you some questions about them. I also wanted to know if you had found anything else that may be related to this investigation."

"Anything in particular?" asked Terry.

"I am not sure. Maybe unexplained violent behavior, attacks, that sort of thing."

"I came across a story of a father and his daughter that were attacked by a beaver in a public park in Pennsylvania," Terry said half-laughing.

"What?" remarked Jonas.

"Yeah, it was on CNN last week. They were riding bikes on a bike path along a pond and a beaver ran out of some bushes and attacked them. Bit them up pretty good before the father hit it with his bike. Animal control took the animal in for observation. Tested negative for rabies."

"Did they give any explanation for its behavior?"

"No, but some people came forward and said that they had seen the animal acting strangely earlier that day."

"Strange like how?"

"One person who saw it said it was laying on the bank of the pond shaking and making weird noises, then it would get up and walk away or go back in the water."

Jonas thought for a minute, "Do you have anything involving humans?"

"Yeah, I came across some strange stuff but I doubt if it's related," replied Terry.

"You doing anything tonight?" asked Jonas.

"Not particularly. Why?"

"I'd like to go over what you found. You want to come over and watch the game while we look it over?"

"Sure, I can do that. I'll let Kim know. Will Ellie be home?"

"I doubt it. She has a showing tonight and will probably be home late."

"Okay, will seven o'clock work for you?"

"Seven would be great," replied Jonas.

"See you then," said Terry.

Jonas sat in his chair for a while and thought for a while. *Epidemics are loud*, he thought, *they're like a bull in a china shop*. You could usually track epidemics quite readily by back-tracking the trail of damage, or mortalities, but this bug was insidious. It appeared to be spreading silently, masking itself as nothing more than a mild respiratory infection. There was no trail of bodies to track. Worse, it had been infiltrating the population for a while without discovery. The only clue that seemed to be consistent was the fact that the new species of Toxo may be linked to some type of psychoses, at least in many of the animals that contracted it. *But what about humans?* he thought. *What is it doing to us?*

10

Terror At Sea

"We are in the process of establishing safe zones within the city. Residents are urged to keep off the streets. City police and local National Guard units are currently moving through the city to extract uninfected residents and move them to these zones."

Malcolm Weinberg
Mayor, New York City

"Radar reports target is 65 nautical miles ahead on our current heading, Captain." reported the conning officer.

"Maintain heading and speed, Mr. White. Launch Rescue One."

"Maintaining heading and speed, aye sir." barked ensign White.

"Captain, Rescue One is launching," confirmed Lt. Banks.

"Thank you, Mr. Banks. Let's make sure they have eyes on. I want to see what is going on aboard that ship." With that Captain Rodgers sat back in his chair looking forward toward the horizon. Rescue One, a SH-60 Seahawk helicopter with a crew of four, passed by the bridge on the starboard side and flew off toward a point straight ahead of the frigate, the U.S.S. Barry K. Atkins.

What the hell is going on aboard that ship? thought Capt. Rodgers. He had been on rescues before involving cruise ships but this was different. Last contact with the cruise ship, Kalypso, reported an outbreak of what was possibly meningococcal meningitis. According to the Northstar Cruise Line home office, the ship's doctor had reported an outbreak of a mild upper respiratory infection with debilitating headaches. He had requested more analgesics and the vaccine be flown to the next port, Cozumel. He reported several episodes of delusional behavior and a few attacks, all within the symptom profile of meningitis. A follow-up communication the next day by the ship's captain stated that the outbreak was out of control and there were rising episodes of violence occurring. He had decided to cut the trip short and was heading back to their home port in Galveston. That was over 20 hours ago. The Kalypso was not answering any hails and it's emergency beacon had been activated. Now, the Kalypso was a little over 200 miles from port.

Making it even more mysterious was the passenger that had been airlifted onto his ship. Mr. Alex Hollender, who presented Rodgers with a packet of orders including a letter from the 4th fleet Admiralty office instructing Rodgers to give this Mr. Hollender full cooperation. Rodgers had asked him for more information but Hollender stated that he could not discuss it at that time. Not until they were closer to the Kalypso.

Definitely CIA, probably some clandestine program director or something like that thought Rodgers. He hated mysteries, especially when it involved his ship and crew.

"Mr. Hollender, perhaps you would like to tell me what we are doing out here," quipped Capt. Rodgers as he turned to look at Hollender who was standing just behind and to the right of the captains chair.

"Can we speak somewhere privately?" replied Hollender without any facial expression.

"Mr. Hollender, on this ship nothing is private. You are on the bridge of a United States naval vessel. These are front row seats to whatever we engage and the officers and crew on the bridge are going to know what's going on in approximately twenty minutes. So, before I get extremely pissed off at you and turn this boat around despite your orders, I suggest you let us all in on the nature of our mission because I've got a strange feeling that this is not a routine rescue mission."

Captain Rodgers gave Hollender a look that had serious intent to it. Hollender looked around uneasily and then stepped in front of Rodgers leaning up against a console.

"You are right Captain, you should know what is happening. We have reason to believe that the outbreak onboard the Kalypso is not your run-of-the-mill infection. It is very possible that it was caused by a bio-weapon released by terrorists."

Rodgers looked at Hollender for a few seconds, staring right into his eyes. Then rubbing his forehead and sighing, "And you were going to tell me this when?"

"I was going to tell you when....."

"When what? After I had landed my rescue team on that ship?" barked Rodgers cutting of Hollender. "Mister, you are completely mistaken if you think I am going to put my men on that helicopter at risk because your bosses are curious.

"Captain, I'm not asking you to do that at this point. This is more of a reconnaissance mission at this point, but the mission could change depending on what we see when your crew gets on site. There may not be anyone alive on that ship. If there are then we have to determine if we can evacuate the ship safely at sea. Captain, if this is a biological weapon issue, we cannot allow that ship to get back to port. Do you understand what I am saying?"

Again, Rodgers studied Hollender's face intently and nodded.

"Mr. Banks," said Rodgers, without taking his eyes off of Hollender. "ETA of Rescue One."

"Under five minutes, sir," replied Banks. "They should have a visual."

Just as Banks said this the communications officer reported that there was an incoming message from Rescue One.

"Give me eyes and ears," replied Rodgers.

The overhead monitor in came on. Onscreen streamed live video from Rescue One's external camera along with audio. There, just ahead of Rescue One was the Kalypso, doing around 22 knots in calm seas.

"Rescue One, approximately one mile out. No answer to hails."

"Roger that, Rescue One. Notify us when you are along-side her," replied Lt. Banks, the Atkins officer-on-deck.

Moments passed as Rodgers and Hollender watched the monitor. The Seahawk was now pacing the ship along-side the bridge.

"Rescue One, we cannot see anyone on the bridge from this side. Still no answer to our hails. We are going to circle around aft," said the Seahawk pilot.

"Roger, Rescue One. Try using the loudspeaker."

"Will do," replied the pilot.

As the helicopter moved along the ship nearing the sundeck. The crew of the aircraft saw bodies laying scattered, lots of bodies. They also noticed movement. They aimed the camera toward the area of movement and zoomed in. What they saw shocked them.

"Mother of God! Are you guys seeing this?"

The entire bridge crew turned to look at the monitor. There, on the sundeck, were three survivors huddled over one of the bodies. As the helicopter neared, two of the survivors turned toward them and began to scream at them. They were covered with blood. They were eating the corpse. Suddenly, more survivors began to appear, attracted by the sound of the helicopter. They, also, were screaming and drenched in blood.

Rodgers was silent as was Hollender. Rodgers looked at Hollender.

"Mr. Hollender, can you explain that to me?" asked Rodgers in a subdued tone.

Hollender shook his head. "No. No, I can't. I was told there may be a possibility that the biologic could cause abnormal behavior, but nothing like this."

Rescue One continued to circle around to the portside of the ship. Images on the overheard monitor revealed the extent of carnage that had taken place. Two of the survival boats had attempted to have been launched only to hang loosely along the ship's hull. There were no signs of survivors, at least those that were not infected.

"Rescue One, we're waiting for further instructions."

"Rodger, Rescue One. Continue to hold position," replied Lt. Banks. "Rescue One waiting for orders, Captain."

"Keep them there for now, Mr. Banks."

Captain Rodgers looked at Hollender and spoke in a quieted voice, "Are we to assume everyone has this disease, if that's what you call it?"

"We can't be sure, but it's safe to assume that most of them are infected or have been killed based on what we see."

Rodgers looked out the bridge window, staring at the horizon, the Kalypso now coming into sight.

"How many people are on that ship?" he asked.

"We estimate twelve hundred with a crew of about two hundred, so about fourteen hundred."

Rodgers shut his eyes and sighed slightly. The sheer magnitude of the situation shocked even him.

Snapping out of his thoughts, Rodgers looked at Hollender.

"Well I sure as hell am not landing a search crew on that ship."

"Agreed," replied Hollender.

"Get Rescue One back on board," barked Rodgers, obviously upset over the entire situation.

"Aye sir," replied Lt. Banks.

As the Seahawk began to bank away from the ship, a flare shot up from one of the stored lifeboats.

"Rescue One, someone put up a flare. We are turning around to check it out."

"Rodger, Rescue One. We see it."

As the helicopter circled back along the portside of the ship where the flare had been fired, the hatch from one of the enclosed lifeboats flung opened and someone inside began to frantically wave a piece of clothing to get their attention.

"Rescue One, we have survivors in an un-launched lifeboat. Standby."

As the helicopter drew closer to the lifeboat the pilot could make out three survivors wearing life jackets. Two of them appeared to be crew members.

"Rescue One, we have three survivors in the lifeboat. They appear to be okay. They must have been hiding inside the boat."

Lt. Banks looked at Rodgers, "Orders, sir?"

Hollender spoke first.

"Captain, if they are okay, we need to get them off that ship. We need to know what happened. They may be the only survivors left."

"Aren't you forgetting that they may be infected, Mr. Hollender? If I bring them onto my ship I risk the lives of everyone on board, including you."

"Captain, I understand that, but the fact that they were isolated in the lifeboat and appear to be okay may indicate they are not infected. Besides we can quarantine them, right?"

"What about my rescue crew? Are we going to quarantine them as well?"

"Yes, we'd have to I guess," replied Hollender, "but I urge you to try and get them off that ship. We need answers, Captain."

Rodgers studied Hollender's face. He did not like the situation at all, in fact, he hated it. Now he was being put in a squeeze. He knew that Hollender had the authority to order him to save those survivors. It would be up to him to decide to risk his men or his career if he defied the order.

"Son of a bitch," Rodgers muttered to himself.

"Mr. Banks, get the medical officer on the com."

"Yes sir," replied Banks as he opened a line to the medical bay.

"Rescue One, we have a problem here."

"Go ahead, Rescue One. What is the problem?" replied Lt. Banks.

"We have large numbers of those things converging on the survivors position. They may be attracted by the sound of the helicopter."

At the same time, the Seahawk's crew chief, CPO Wurtz gave the order to stand by weapons. The Seahawk was equipped with a port window mounted machine gun. Wurtz spoke to the pilot on the intercom.

"Turn us around so we can get our gun on them."

The pilot acknowledged and the hovering helicopter rotated one hundred-eighty degrees putting the helicopter's port window gun on the lifeboat area.

Back on the lifeboat, the three crew members saw the oncoming crowd of infected and began to wave feverishly trying to get some kind of help.

"Rescue One. We don't have much time here. Can we lay down suppressing fire? What do you want us to do?"

Lt. Banks turned to Rodgers, "Captain?"

Rodgers stared ahead.

"Captain, we have to act now," said Hollender.

Rodgers turned to Lt. Banks.

"Get em' in the water, Mr. Banks. Lay down suppressing fire. Keep those things off of them."

"Aye sir," replied Banks, who immediately relayed the message to Rescue One.

The door gunner began to fire on the enraged crowd now very close to the lifeboat. Wurtz got on the loudspeaker.

"You are going to have to jump into the water. We will pick you up. Do it now!" he yelled as he watched the mob now at the lifeboat trying to break through the opposing hatch and windows. The gunner continued to fire on the crowd but he could not fire on those who had climbed onto the lifeboat without risking injuring the three survivors. The first into the water was a female crew member. By now, Wurtz had ordered the fourth crew member into the water and was lowering the harness into the water near them. The second survivor jumped into the water followed by several of the infected passengers. He was frantically swimming toward the rescue diver when he was overtaken by one of his pursuers. Wurtz and the gunner watched in horror as he was beaten to death in the water only fifty yards from the diver who was now being hoisted with the female survivor into the Seahawk. The pursuers seemed completely unhindered by being in the water. They tore the body apart in plain view of the rescue crew.

"Shoot them damn things!" yelled Wurtz.

The gunner began to open fire on the six infected passengers in the water who were now screaming at the helicopter.

Wurtz began to assist getting the female survivor and his diver onboard as the pilot banked the helicopter to pursue the cruise ship which had continued to travel several hundred yards ahead from the site of the rescue.

As the helicopter caught up to the ship and was moving along-side the lifeboat, it became obvious the third survivor did not make it into the water. Blood painted the side and top of the lifeboat. Highly agitated infected passengers crowded along the walkway, screaming a high-pitched scream at the helicopter. Several leapt into the air toward the helicopter as if to grasp onto it to get to the crew inside. From his seat, Wurtz could see several of those "things" fighting each other for what appeared to be the head of the third crew member that did not make it. Wurtz spoke into the headset and told the pilot the diver and woman survivor were on board.

The Seahawk slowed and turned away from the cruise ship, beginning its short trip back to the Barry Atkins. The woman, now covered in a blanket, was crying hysterically. Held by crewman Williams, the diver who had rescued her, she went into shock and passed out.

Back onboard the Barry Atkins, Rodgers had discussed the need to quarantine the survivor and the rescue crew. Chief medical officer, Dr. Vincent Allen immediately began to assemble equipment and gave orders to clear the passageway from the helipad to the medical bay to minimize the risk of exposure. His team of four had put on hazmat suits and were on their way to the helipad.

"Captain, Dr. Allen reports they are standing by," said Lt. Banks.

"Thank you, Mr. Banks. I want that helicopter secured the minute it's onboard. No one goes onboard that helicopter until the doctor gives the word it's safe."

"Aye, sir," replied Banks.

"Now keep us on a course parallel to that ship until we determine our next move," said Rodgers looking at Banks.

"Mr. Banks, take a breath. You look a little rattled."

"Yes sir, just a bit," replied Banks with a slight smile. "They did not cover this in naval training, sir."

"You are right about that lieutenant. They certainly did not so let's relax our sphincters and keep clear heads shall we?" said Rodgers looking around at the bridge crew.

Several officers and crewmen gave Rodgers nervous smiles and acknowledge the order.

"MAINCOMM reports an incoming message, sir. It's for Mr. Hollender," said Lt. Banks.

"Put it on my phone," replied Rodgers.

Rodgers handed Hollender the phone. "It's for you."

Hollender took the phone. Putting it to his ear, he turned away.

"Hollender here."

"Alex, this is Donaldson at Langley. We've been monitoring the events from the communications room. What's the status?"

"The ship is a loss, sir. Far too dangerous to attempt to find any more survivors. We recovered one, a female crew member. She is inbound and will be transferred to the medical bay upon arrival. We'll put her and the crew under medical quarantine. Sir, the sickness is far worse than anyone thought."

"I know. I saw the video feed here. It does not leave us too many options, does it?" questioned Donaldson.

"No sir, I don't believe it leaves us any."

"Agreed. I need to speak to Captain Rodgers."

Hollender turned back toward the captain and handed him the phone. "He needs to speak to you."

Rodgers took the phone.

"This is Captain Rodgers."

"Captain Rodgers, I am Clarence Donaldson, CIA special projects director. I believe you got that information from Mr. Hollender when he boarded."

"Yes sir, I did."

"Captain, I believe we all are taken back by what we have seen. I don't think there is any doubt about the seriousness of this situation and the extreme threat we face if this ship approaches a populated area."

"I agree, sir. What are you suggesting."

"As you are aware, the President and his staff are monitoring these events and has given us full authority to conduct this operation."

"Yes sir. I am aware of that. You are beating around the bush, sir. What are your orders?"

As Donaldson spoke to Rodgers, Hollender and Banks could see the disbelief in his face. Rodgers hung up the phone.

"Mr. Banks, move us away from the ship. Put us a thousand yards astern, match speed, and maintain that position."

"Yes sir," replied Banks.

Rodgers looked at Hollender. His eyes began to water slightly.

"Mr. Hollender," Rodgers said in a quieted voice. "I will have nightmares of this day for the rest of my life."

Hollender, having some idea of what Donaldson had said, looked at Rodgers and nodded.

"We all will, Captain."

11

The Order Is Given

"The disease decimated whole regions of the globe. Some countries, in particular, those on the African continent and extending into southeast Asia, saw vast areas where no humans could be found. Urban areas were hit the hardest owing to the dense population of potential hosts but they were also the first to recover as most of the resources were also located there. In the United States, the disease spread was slowed dramatically due to the aggressive quarantine and eradication programs put in place almost immediately."

Dr. Jean DuPont
Pasteur Institute

Donaldson hung up the phone. The staff in the communications room at Langley had become silent, shocked by what they had seen on the monitor. Behind Donaldson stood Tom Hutchinson, director of the Trojan Horse project, part of a top secret bioweaponry development program that existed outside the CIA. The joint project between Donaldson's department and USAMRIID (United States Army Medical Research Institute of Infectious Diseases) at Fort Detrick had been secretly developing new bio-weapons despite the ban put in place at the Biological Weapons Convention in 1975 in which the United States was a sponsor. Donaldson was the face of the program. In the unlikely event that the program was uncovered, it was Donaldson who would appear before any Senate committee and deny everything. Hutchinson was the "man behind the curtain".

Tom Hutchinson was a tall, thin man. In his mid-fifties, he was a native of Pennsylvania. He had multiple degrees in microbiology, parasitology and biochemistry. Hutchinson began his career as a researcher at USAMRIID and was approached by the CIA several years ago to run a clandestine bio-weapons program which would have him working between both departments.

Donaldson did not care for him at all. There was something unsettling about him. The nature of his work (based on what he had heard) was even more troubling.

"The effects are more terrifying than what I was led to believe," said Donaldson in a lowered voice as he turned to Hutchinson. "There's no way we can bury this. We are going to have to bring it out in the open."

"And do what, Alex? We don't know for sure if this was caused by the virus."

"Oh, bullshit, Tom!" replied Donaldson in a forced whisper. "There have been over sixty outbreaks like this in the past five months. I know for a fact that M'bera was us. This is only going to get worse and we have nothing to stop it.

If you won't do it, then I sure as hell will!"

All activity in the communication room had stopped as Donaldson's last exchange was not in a whisper but was heard by everyone. Hutchinson looked around the room and then back at Donaldson.

"You realize this will bring the house down on us."

"At the rate this disease is spreading, that may be the least of our worries," replied Donaldson.

"Okay....we'll start contacting people, but right now we have a ship sailing around the Caribbean Sea with several hundred infected passengers. Let's clean up that mess first."

Donaldson looked at him intensely.

"You give the order...you made this thing."

Hutchinson looked over to the communications chief.

"Get the president on a secure line," he asked.

Several tense moments passed as Hutchinson discussed the matter with President Grayson and his staff on a conference line. Finally, he hung up the phone. He turned to the communications chief.

"Contact the Vermont and have them proceed with their orders. Send through the proper verification codes. Also, contact Belle Chase and have them get the fighters in the air. Alex, you should let your man on the

Barry Atkins know we are going through with our orders. Also, notify your media relations department to be ready. I will send them the official cover story."

"I'm on it," replied Donaldson. "What about the female survivor? She's the only one outside the loop that knows what really happened."

"We can keep her on the ship for a while. Then we'll transfer her to a medical facility for observation. No outside communications and keep her under medical quarantine. That should buy us some time."

Time for what? thought Donaldson. *At the present rate, major outbreaks of this disease will begin to appear throughout the world within a few weeks.*

"Tom," he said as Hutchinson was walking toward the door. "Did you know this bug could do this to people?"

Hutchinson stopped and took a few steps back towards Donaldson. He thought for a moment.

"No...not really. It was suppose to cause a type of low-grade encephalitis in its victims. We tried for three years to get that virus to infect that parasite and it would not work. Finally, we gave up. I don't know what happened to make the virus finally work nor do I know how it got out of containment, but obviously it did. The results...well, let's just say I am more than impressed."

Donaldson stunned by his statement stood silent for a moment studying his face for some type of emotion.

"Your little bug has a body count of over nine thousand lives in five months and we're going to add another fourteen hundred in a few minutes and you're impressed? Are you insane? We may not be able to stop this thing, have you thought about that?"

Hutchinson moved quickly back toward Donaldson and got up into his face.

"Look you little shit. You're knee deep in this along with me. You knew what we were trying to do and you went along with it. It's our job. It's what we do to give our country...our way of life...an edge over those who would bring us down. And now that we've run into a problem you want to get all moral about it?

You better grow a set of balls, Alex and get back in the game. We have work to do. Now we just ordered the commander of a U. S. submarine to sink a cruise ship full of sick passengers, is there anything else you want to get off your chest?"

Donaldson, stunned by the attack, retreated.

"No...You're right."

"Great! Thank you. I will be going back to Fort Detrick. You can reach me on my mobile. Keep me informed."

With that, Hutchinson turned and walked out of the communications room. The communications chief who had heard the exchange looked at Donaldson.

"You okay, sir?"

"No...Not really...I'm anything but okay."

"We have contact with the Vermont. The authorization codes are being sent. Did you want to get a message to the captain?"

"Yes, I better. He deserves some kind of explanation."

The newly commissioned Virginia class sub, U.S.S. Vermont had been speeding along an intercept course with the cruise ship for several hours and was now within range. Captain Hollis, the commander of the Vermont, was looking over the orders that had just come in from Langley via USNAVSO (United States Naval Forces Southern Command) and the message from Donaldson.

"Mr. O'Connor, have the orders been authenticated?"

"Yes sir. Codes are a match. The message is authentic."

"Time to target?"

Lt. O'Connor, the ship's XO measured the distance to the target on the chart table. Checking with his figures with the navigation officer.

"Time to target is eight minutes. On course to intercept on this bearing, sir."

"Depth Mr. O'Connor?"

"We're at nine hundred-forty two feet."

"Steady as she goes, Mr. O'Connor."

"Aye, sir."

Minutes passed as the Vermont closed the distance between it and the Kalypso.

Lt. O'Connor approached Hollis, leaning toward him, he quietly asked, "Sir, may I ask why we are chasing a cruise ship?"

"Just about to do that Mr. O'Connor. Mr. Wells, put me on ship-wide intercom."

Hollis picked up the hand mike.

"This is the captain. Most of you already know we are on an intercept course with a cruise ship. I have been informed that terrorists may have unleashed a biological weapon onboard that cruise ship infecting the passengers and crew. It is assumed that all have been killed. The frigate Barry Atkins has been on site and confirms that there are no survivors. Our task is not to let that ship reach any populated area. That ship is considered a serious threat to our population and we have been ordered to sink her. I know that may be a shock to many of you and it's certainly not the type of action we wanted to be in our first tour out but those are our orders. That is all."

Hollis hung up the mike.

"Does that answer your question Mr. O'Connor?"

"Yes, sir."

"Weapons. Are we in range?"

"Coming into range now, Captain. Forty-five hundred yards and closing."

"Bring her up to periscope depth, Mr. O'Connor, and contact the Barry Atkins and have her back off. Weapons. Prepare to fire one and two. Open outer doors. Let me know when we are at four thousand yards."

Onboard the frigate, Capt. Rodgers was reading the message from Donaldson.

"Ahead slow, Mr. White."

"Ahead slow, aye sir," he replied.

"Well I guess we get to sit here and watch," said Captain Rodgers watching the Kalypso slowly pulling away from them. "The Vermont should launch her torpedoes within the next five minutes."

"Captain, inbound aircraft from Belle Chase. Twenty minutes out," reported the conning officer.

"Those must be our F-18's," said Hollender.

"As I understand it, that's the clean-up crew," said Rodgers. "For everything that doesn't sink with the ship. I have to hand it to you guys. You put a lot of thought into this for a spur of the moment situation."

"Captain, under the circumstances...."

"I know Mr. Hollender. We play the game too."

Back onboard the Vermont, Lt. O'Connor stood anxiously by the weapons console.

"Captain, we are in range. Thirty-five hundred and closing."

"Up scope," ordered Captain Hollis.

"Weapons. Do you have a firing solution?" asked the XO.

"Yes sir. Torpedoes ready."

Peering into the periscope, Hollis barked, "Flood tubes 1 and 2."

"Tubes 1 and 2 flooded. Green light Captain." said Lt. O'Connor.

"Range?"

"Passing three thousand yards, Captain."

"1 and 2, shoot!" ordered Hollis.

"1 and 2 away," replied Lt. O'Connor, as he pressed the launch buttons on the weapons control panel.

Instantly, two MK-48 torpedoes were ejected from the forward torpedo launch tubes. Their engines turned on immediately and they sped off toward the Kalypso.

"Target has been acquired, sir. Running true. Time to impact is 82 seconds."

"Thank you Mr. O'Connor," said Capt. Hollis as he sat down on the command chair. "Give me a countdown at twenty seconds."

Onboard the Barry Atkins, everyone on the bridge waited nervously.

"Sir, the Vermont has launched two torpedoes. Time to target is now under 70 seconds."

"Thank you, Mr. Banks," replied Rodgers. "Mr. O'Connor, get Mr. Hollender a pair of binoculars. I'm sure he'll want to see this."

O'Connor opened a cabinet and removed a set handing it to Hollender.

As the bridge crew looked forward, most having binoculars, the conning officer called out, "thirty seconds to impact."

Hollender watched through the binoculars intensely. The Kalypso magnified as if it were only a few hundred feet ahead.

The first torpedo went directly under the Kalypso's keel amidship. The second went under the keel further astern near the aft fuel tanks. Both exploded simultaneously.

A massive dome of water lifted the Kalypso almost out of the water. The huge steel structure bowed upward slightly from the explosion. Then, the ship came back down into a void created by the pressure wave, bowing it sharply downward. The sheer force of this snapped the keel of the cruise ship in two places. Fuel oil from the ruptured fuel tanks spilled into the surrounding water. Debris and bodies littered the water as seawater rushed into the now sinking ship. Those with binoculars could see the large numbers of the infected mob being thrown across the deck as it buckled and collapsed. The aft section was the first to submerge having the weight of the engines and the aft fuel tanks weighing it down. A series of large explosions ripped the section apart as fire spread into the fuel tanks. The mid-section now separated from the aft and bow sections was sliding into the water at a forty-five degree angle following the stern section and rolled over. The bow section was the last to go under. The largest of the three sections, it slid into the water nearly perpendicular. In all, it took a little over twenty minutes for the sea to swallow up the Kalypso. All that was left was a debris field of deck chairs and bodies floating in a fuel oil spill. Hollender stood in awe of the sheer power of the explosions.

"That was downright surgical," said Capt. Rodgers without any emotion, "I am glad the Vermont is on our side."

The bridge was abuzz with talk of the sinking, even a couple of high fives.

"People, may I remind you there were people on board that ship and though whatever disease they had that necessitated our sinking of that ship, show the proper respect. Lives were lost. Loved ones back home will suffer greatly."

The bridge quieted as they resume their tasks. Rodgers sat down in his chair, removed his cap, and rubbed his forehead.

"Captain, the Vermont is withdrawing from the area. She will continue to patrol the periphery until ordered out of the area."

"Send her our compliments on a job well done," said Rodgers.

"Mr. Banks, bring us to full stop."

"Full stop. Aye, sir."

Moments later a flight of four F-18's approach the site.

"Sir, the F-18 flight leader is requesting drop coordinates. They are inbound from the north, ETA of 3 minutes."

"Send them the coordinates and have them notify us when they start their runs."

Rodgers turned back to Hollender, "Here comes part two."

Once again the bridge crew peered forward out the bridge windows, some with binoculars. The F-18's began their runs each carrying two MK-77 incendiary bombs. Criss-crossing the debris field the bombs were detonated above the water raining a fiery napalm-like material down into the fuel oil. Immediately the fuel oil that was floating on the surface of the water, ignited. A thick black smoke lifted from the water's surface mixing with towering flames that burned everything floating within it. Hollender could see countless bodies aflame in the midst of the burning fuel. He lowered the binoculars suddenly realizing the impact of this event. M'bera had bothered him but he had just read reports and interviewed several survivors. Here, close to home, he had just witnessed the mass killing of over fourteen hundred people. His chest tightened. Capt. Rodgers, who sensed the emotional weakening of Hollender patted him on the back.

"It was necessary. They were already dead," he said looking directly at Hollender. "Mr. Banks, can you get a couple cups of coffee up here?"

"Yes sir, right away."

The F-18 flight passed over the frigate low and signaled they were done and returning to base. As they both watched the jets fly off to the north, Rodgers could not help but wonder about the events.

"Mr. Hollender. Someday you are going to have to tell me how you just happened to end up on my ship. It looked to me like you already knew what we'd find and had a plan in place to get rid of it."

Hollender looked at Capt. Rodgers, emotionally drained from the day's events.

"Captain, I doubt if I will ever be able to tell you that."

"Well, at least we stopped this mess here before it got to the mainland." Rodgers looked right at Hollender when he said that.

"We did stop it, right?"

Hollender felt his throat tighten, seemingly ready to explode as he held back the emotion running rampant within him. He knew the truth. He knew was lay ahead. He looked back at Rodgers, then out the window at the column of black smoke that continued to rise up from the burning fuel.

"I don't know. God help us if we didn't."

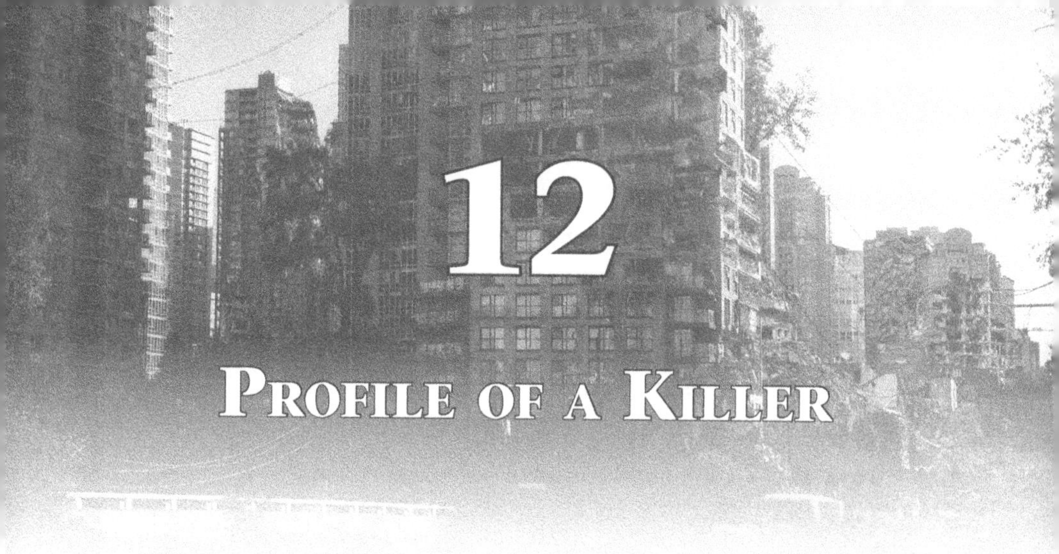

12

Profile of a Killer

"We cannot tell who is infected at this time. Our early attempts to evacuate seemingly healthy populations were met with disaster as outbreaks occurred within the confines of the refugee camps. Tens of thousands have been killed because they trusted us."

Emily Matheson
Ass't. Director, FEMA

Jonas had just finished eating a ham sandwich on the porch when his cell phone began to ring. It was Ellie.

"Hey El, everything okay?"

"Yeah, it's fine. Just thought I'd better call to let you know the showing is running late so I won't be home until ten. Evelyn is staying late with me so I won't be alone."

"Okay, but drive careful it just started to rain here. How is the art show going?"

"Well, the big problem right now is that this artist, Santos, is upset about the wine selection we chose for the showing. His agent is walking around here bitching about how we don't care for our guests and how we don't know what types of wine to choose for the art that is being exhibited."

"Seriously?"

"Hey it's news to me. I did not know that certain wines go with different types of art, but I do now."

Jonas stifled a chuckle.

"You know its bullshit, right? I mean it's just some guy with an over-inflated sense of self-worth making stupid demands to make you uncomfortable. Don't put up with it. If he gets out of hand, put him in his place."

"I will, don't worry about that. I would just rather be home with you right now than dealing with this."

"I know El, hang in there. It's only a few hours more."

"I'll wait up for you. We can have some wine," said Jonas laughing out loud. "What type would you like?"

Ellie began to laugh along with him.

"How about some hot tea instead?" she said to Jonas.

"Okay, it's a date."

Right about then Terry's car pulled into the driveway. Jonas waved to him.

"Hey El, Terry just pulled in so I have to go. Lots of work to do. Be careful driving home and I'll wait up for you. Love you."

"Love you too," replied Ellie as the call ended.

Jonas greeted Terry at the front door. The rain was just starting to fall hard. A warm, steamy kind of rain that was typical of Georgia in the late summer.

"It looks like it's just us two," said Terry taking off his jacket. "Ben had to go to his daughters play but he says to keep him in the loop. He does have some info to share with us and he'll get it to you tomorrow."

"Great," replied Jonas. "I know this is off the clock but I wanted to be able to brainstorm openly without worrying who may overhear us. I am not sure where all of this is going but I have a dark feeling about it and the sooner we have some kind of scenario the better we can move to avert it."

"I hear you, Jonas. I brought some info you may have interest in but it is not going to make you feel any better about this situation."

"Well, that's why we're here," said Jonas as Terry sat down at the dining table tossing a large overstuffed file onto the table before him.

"Can I get you something to drink?"

"I'll take a beer."

Jonas went to the refrigerator and brought back two beers. Sitting them down on the table in front of Terry. Jonas pulled up a chair and sat down, sipping on one of the beers.

"So what do you have?" inquired Jonas.

"Well, Jonas, remember that a lot of this may just be normal incidents and because we have no definitive thread to follow, they all may be unrelated."

"I understand that. Go ahead."

"Well, it seems that there has been a steady rise in violent behavior reports over the past three years. Not just here but world-wide. It also coincides with a rapid increase in the number of diagnosed cases of schizophrenia. It's pretty well documented in the industrialized nations but we have no numbers available for the third world countries, although some indications are that the numbers are far worse."

"Anyone offering up explanations?"

"A few. Some researchers claim it's a response to increasing social stresses, others cite depression, and there is even a study that claims electromagnetic field exposure in youth can be causing brain chemistry disturbances."

"You buy any of that?"

"No, it's the same blanket garbage we heard when we were dealing with that outbreak of echovirus two years ago. There we had encephalitis-induced behavioral disorders that painted a classical bi-polar picture. Everyone was convinced it was stress-induced at first. It wasn't until Larkin's over at John Hopkins isolated live virus from the brain of one of the victims that we realized the culprit was an echovirus."

"I remember that. Even now I know of some colleagues who claim it was coincidental."

Jonas took another sip of his beer, stretched his arms out, and then leaned forward.

"What do you think?"

"Honestly, Jonas, I am sure we are dealing with a biologic of some sort with many of these cases. Nearly all of the 40 to 50 cases of violent behavior I reviewed, including those involving more than one person, all fit the profile of schizophrenia. A more violent form of it of course. Common schizophrenia never makes it to the news. I'm talking about screaming, brutal attacks without provocation."

"And..."

"Well, I sent Ben my information as well and he went over it with me earlier this afternoon. He confirmed that our Toxoplasma bug is known to cause schizophrenic outbreaks including mass outbreaks in highly infected populations. It can also induce a very violent psychotic behavior pattern when it affects the deep brain region. That is not too common though. Ben's wife mentioned that it can cause a condition called "limbic seizure" which basically means the person suddenly is thrown into a psychotic state without warning and is capable of primal violence. She said she has even seen a few cases in her practice. Such an infection is not able to be seen on any brain scans and unless you specifically suspect Toxoplasma and test for antibodies, you will never know what cause it."

"Did Amanda say what could cause that condition to present itself?"

"Yes, localized immune-suppression, which I guess is uncommon. Concurrent viral or bacterial brain infections can cause it as well. There is growing evidence that schizophrenia is caused by deep brain infections"

"That would fit with what Walter was saying about the oocysts he isolated from the dolphins a few months ago. He found viral particles inside the oocysts. He wasn't sure at the time if it was something to worry about since the mutation of the parasite would cause the problems we were seeing at the time, but if there is more going on that what we are seeing, it may fit the profile."

Jonas sat back for a moment. Staring at Terry, trying to form his thoughts.

"If that's the cause then we're dealing with a dual infection, probably dual epidemics. Both causing such low-grade symptoms that they are under the radar but when they combine all hell breaks loose," said Jonas now in deep thought. "So we have already had the first phase of the epidemic and that is the spread of the new strain of Toxoplasma throughout the globe. Now we are in the midst of the second phase of the epidemic and that would possibly be the virus Walter took pictures of. It is not likely that that virus affects humans in any serious manner. Walter said the virus was inside the oocyst so I assume it is infecting the parasite."

"Jonas, that could possibly set up a third phase of the epidemic."

"What is that?"

"Well I would imagine that once sufficient numbers of people, animals, etc. are infected with both organisms, we should start to see the spread of infected oocysts as the primary vector for this disease. It may have its own unique symptom profile and effects."

Jonas rubbed his forehead, closed his eyes for a moment.

"Have you ever heard of anything like that?"

"No, never. I mean I have seen reports of a super malaria due to a viral phage that infects the malaria parasite, but it's not very common. That being said malaria and Toxoplasma are in the same family of protozoans. I would imagine it's possible."

"I agree with you," said Jonas. "But what doesn't make any sense is that if there was a Toxoplasma phage out there, we should have been seeing cases of it all along with T. gondii. I don't recall any evidence to suggest that a Toxoplasma phage exists."

"Yet, the evidence seems to be building up. There may be another possibility if we are to get somewhat dark about this. Viral phages are very specific as I recall. They don't infect organisms other than their specific host. So if that is the case, we may be left with one conclusion here. If Toxoplasma had no viral phage that infected it prior to our findings, then there was none. If that is the case, then there could not have been a T. gondii viral phage, yet here we are looking at one, maybe."

Jonas looked at Terry as if he realized what he was alluding too.

"Unless....someone made one?"

"That looks like what we are left with."

"But why, I don't see the benefit in creating a Toxo phage. Do you?"

"Not really," said Terry, "but an infected parasite could cause an amplification of symptoms. It just seems too slow to be considered weaponized."

"Is that what we are saying? That someone tried to make a weaponized form of Toxoplasma?"

"I know. It seems like a long way to go for that kind of result but we can't dismiss it right now. Either someone created a phage for this parasite for whatever reason or nature did it on her own."

Jonas pondered the information for a short time. He got up and returned with two more cold beers.

"Let's put this on the back burner for now. Do you have anything else?"

"I searched the database for unusually violent attacks over the past five years and up to about 18 months ago there wasn't anything out of the ordinary. But in the past 18 months there has been a notable increase in the number of bizarre and brutally violent assaults being reported globally.

I'm talking about the face-eaters, mutilations, suicides, cannibalism, etc. That type of behavior has always been out there but the incidence seems to be increasing. I can't quote any figures but I firmly believe I'm right about this."

"Anything as an example?" queried Jonas. "Something I may have heard about on the news."

"Certainly," replied Terry. "Do you remember that incident last year about the person who attacked that homeless man and began to eat his face?"

"Yes, I remember that. Didn't they determine that the attacker had been doing bath salts or some type of drug?"

"That's what the news reported, but I contacted some colleagues who were close to the case and they report that the attacker had no drugs in him at the time of the attack. He also was not being treated for any mental disorders. According to those who knew him, he was a nice guy who never showed any signs of mental disease. There were also several reports of brutal attacks by groups of people that seem to be far more violent that what is generally seen. There was an attack on inmates at the Kentucky State Penitentiary that left 34 inmates dead or critically injured and at least 8 guards dead. There was also some National Guard involvement to extract trapped personnel and they had serious casualties as well. That did not make it onto the six o'clock news. It was reported as an inmate riot that had only a few casualties."

"How did you find out about it?

"A mutual friend of ours, Dr. Henry Holmes, was involved in examination of the bodies of the inmates. They had transported most of the casualties to the Lexington VA hospital."

"Wait a minute," said Jonas, with a surprised look on his face. "Why the VA center? Why not to a local hospital?"

"I don't know. Perhaps because of the presence the military has in Lexington? You're guess is as good as mine."

Jonas leaned back into the chair and rubbed his face. He let out a long sigh.

"Why do I feel like there is more to this than just a weird parasite epidemic? It's getting late, Terry. Give me one more incident and we'll call it a night."

"Sure, Jonas," replied Terry as he shuffled through the stack of papers in the file he brought. "Okay, here's one that bothers me. About six months ago, the Guyanese government reported a similar type of mass violence incident about 50 miles up the Moroni River in a small village. They reported that at least 48 people were killed and several others severely injured. It was originally reported as an attack by opposition forces. The kicker is that the same type of thing happened at a militant camp about 15 miles from the village so it couldn't have been done by them. In both sites, bodies were found beaten and mutilated, some shown signs of being eaten."

"Animals?" queried Jonas.

"No, they found human teeth marks and footprints."

"Did the government request autopsies?"

"No. All the bodies were cremated right away despite an order by the ministry of health to autopsy and store the bodies pending an investigation."

"Were there any survivors that were questioned?

"I found nothing about survivors. No eye witness accounts...nothing."

Jonas sat silently for several moments staring at the pile of information on the dining table.

"Doesn't it seem odd that none of the events you have mentioned have autopsy reports or at least a statement from an official health agency regarding the cause of any of this? I mean, somewhere along the line, someone would have clearly done autopsies even if an illness wasn't suspected," Jonas said slowly looking up at Terry. "Certainly, the incident in Kentucky should have had some kind of report."

"There does seem to be a string of convenient oversights in many of these incidents," replied Terry equally concerned. "Jonas, one more thing that I thought you may find alarming."

"What is that?"

"On a whim, I contact a friend of ours, Dr. Jawad Patel, at W.H.O. and asked him if he had any information official or not on outbreaks of mass violence."

"And"

"He told me that there have numerous outbreaks throughout Africa and Asia involving mass killings by, what he could only describe as, brutally violent, rabid-like mobs. The one that we discussed the most was a reported outbreak at the M'bera refugee camp a couple of months ago. He had investigated the incident and interviewed one of the on-site physicians, Dr. Bashad. He claims that Bashad was an eye-witness to the incident. He described an outbreak of a mild respiratory illness months prior to the incident. The illness did not appear to be viral. There were complaints of moderate severe headaches and behavioral changes. Dr. Bashad reported that he witnessed several people develop minor facial tics that he described as a mild seizure and become suddenly violent to a degree he has never seen. Patel says that Bashad and several other had to fight their way out of the camp.

"Why haven't we heard of this?"

"Patel says there was pressure put on his team to play down the incident especially as the official report claims that a militant faction had attacked the site. He does not believe that was the case as he was on site shortly after the incident. He took video of the aftermath. He says there was no evidence of any terrorist attack, only bodies. The few survivors he could find say it was a madness that infected the people. People just started killing everyone they could."

"How many people were killed?" Jonas asked.

"Patel said that they estimated 2400 dead not including livestock."

"Jesus, Christ!" Jonas let slip out, shocked by the enormity of the incident.

"In a single event?" Jonas, again, slipped into silence as he tried to take in the thought of that many people brutally killed.

"Jonas, Dr. Bashad indicated that there was an alarming increase in Toxoplasmosis in refugee camp. He had reserved what little Septra he had for the AIDS-infected population who were dying at an alarming rate from the illness."

Terry paused and looked at Jonas. "Exactly, what we predicted the new strain of Toxoplasma would do."

Right about that time, the front door opened and Ellie walked in.

"Jonas, I'm home," she said loudly and walked into the dining room. "You guys still at it?

Jonas, shaking off the shock, smiled at Ellie, "You're home early."

"Not really. It's a quarter after ten and you don't look so good. What type of horror stories are you investigating now?" Ellie turned to Terry. "Hi, Terry. Why are you scaring my husband?"

Terry smiled and managed a slight chuckle. "Hey, it's usually him that scares me. Anyway, just the usual stuff. Trying to put out fires."

Ellie searched Terry's face then looked back at Jonas who was unusually silent. "How about that tea?" she asked.

"Yeah sure, that would be great," replied Jonas.

"None for me El, I better get home. Didn't realize it was that late. "Jonas, I'll talk with you more about this tomorrow. By the way, Patel said he had a copy of the video and he would send it in an email tomorrow."

Jonas nodded his head, "Great, I will definitely want to see it."

Terry hurriedly gathered up the files on the table and moved toward the front door. "See you tomorrow Jonas. Bye Ellie!"

"Goodnight Terry. Say hi to Kim for me."

"I'll want to meet with you tomorrow morning some time so don't get too busy," said Jonas as he opened the front door. "Keep this quiet for now. I think I'll approach Brilli with all of this if the video is convincing."

"I agree," replied Terry. As he stepped outside, he stopped and looked back at Jonas. "We're too late, aren't we?"

Jonas felt a lump in his throat as his emotions began to run amok. "Yes," he replied slightly nodding his head in agreement. "We've got work to do." With that, Jonas closed the door and turned around only to see Ellie standing behind him.

"Too late for what?" she asked searching Jonas' face. She sensed that he was troubled about what Terry and he had discussed. It was not like him to be this noticeably bothered by his work.

"Nothing. Just a problem that got in under the radar."

"Judging by the way you have been acting the past few weeks, I would guess there's more than just a problem. Jonas, is it bad?" Ellie sensed that whatever he and Terry were discussing was big. He rarely met with co-workers at home to discuss business and judging from what little discussion she had overheard, there was reason to be concerned.

"We're not sure yet, El. I can't really go into it with you now. Even if I could, I'm not sure that I know exactly what is going to happen. We're just grabbing at straws right now but..." Jonas hesitated. For a brief moment, he had a vision of violent mobs that shocked him. Staring blankly into Ellie's eyes, he felt himself losing composure.

"But what?" Ellie pressed, feeling that Jonas needed to let something out. "Jonas, don't you dare start keeping secrets from me. If it means that you're out there putting your life at risk then I..." Ellie stopped for a moment and put her arms around Jonas. "I couldn't handle anything happening to you."

"Ellie," Jonas felt her heartbeat against his chest. It was faster than normal. He looked at her and kissed her softly on the forehead. "I'm not in any danger right now so don't worry."

"Then what did Terry mean when he asked you if it was too late?"

Jonas hesitated. "Ellie, this is between you and me. It is important that you understand that."

"Jonas, you know I do."

Jonas nodded slightly, looking at Ellie. He knew she could be trusted. She had proven that repeatedly over the years. But still, the implications of this particular situation were mind-numbing. Despite that he decided to tell her.

"Ellie. We may be in the middle of a horrific global epidemic. It is unlike anything we have ever seen and I don't know what is going to happen, but I am sure it is not good."

"What type of epidemic, the flu? I haven't heard about anything on the news."

"It's not the flu. I wish it was. This is far worse. As far as we know, the symptoms are barely noticeable and once the person is infected, it causes severe behavior changes."

"What type of changes?" Ellie asked nervously. She could see the Jonas was not comfortable discussing this.

"Extremely brutal violence. The infected person is capable of killing others, perhaps without warning. At least that is what we think right now. Nevertheless, the possibility exists that a very large number of people already have the illness and are not aware of it."

"Can't you track down the infected people like you usually do? There's got to be a way to slow the spread down...right?"

Jonas looked away for a moment realizing that Ellie was asking the very questions the public would ask once this information got out. Now he realized it may not have been a good idea to tell her, at least until he was sure, but he had shown his hand.

"No, Ellie. It's too late. This illness may have already infected millions of people already, maybe more."

Ellie stood in shock at the statement. "I don't understand."

"I'm not sure I do either, at this time. That is why Terry, myself, and the others on my team are trying to gather information as fast as we can. We just don't know enough to make a call right now."

"Is there a chance you're wrong?"

"No...maybe...I don't know," Jonas replied.

It was the first time that Ellie could remember that Jonas was uncertain about anything and that alarmed her. She sensed she had pressed too far for now and Jonas was trying not to frighten her but she was. Jonas did not scare easy. He had confronted other serious outbreaks with confidence but here he was in front of her obviously rattled. She was sorry she had asked. She knew better to press further. She backed away a couple of steps and offered up a warm smile.

"I'll get us some hot tea."

13

Sam's Night Out

"Containment of this disease is no longer a consideration. There are few areas that have not been affected. Our focus here is a matter of survival of those that are uninfected or can be treated with a reasonable chance of success. We are now faced with very few options. Where the disease has caused the death of tens of millions in the U.S. alone. Millions more will die by our own hand in an attempt to preserve humanity."

Dr. Anthony Brilli
Director, DPEI
Center For Disease Control

Coming in and out of consciousness, Sam Watson struggled in his confusion to figure out what had happened. With each minute that passed his mind cleared a bit more. The last thing he remembered was driving to the local Winn-Dixie to get some ibuprofen and something to eat. He had kept himself at home for almost a week now fighting off the bronchitis he had come down with after his return from Washington. It had progressively gotten worse. Now he had a pounding headache that would not go away. He had made a call to his physician but it was after hours and he was not going to any emergency room for a damn headache.

Sam opened his eyes but his vision was blurry. Also, there was some kind of street light above him that hurt his eyes. After a few attempts his vision cleared well enough for him to see his surroundings. *Where the hell am I?* he wondered. It had to be late. He left for the store around eight o'clock. *Where is my car?* he thought. Sam became frightened. He had no memory of the past few hours and he did not know where he was. Looking around at the surrounding buildings he guessed he was somewhere closer to downtown. Quite a ways from Midtown where he lived. He struggled to get on his feet. Leaning against the brick building behind him, he was able to stand. His head hurt and he could hear his heart pounding. There were nothing but rundown storefronts around him. He noticed a few lights on in the upstairs apartments across the street. He tried to take a step in that direction but he was unsteady and fell back against the wall. "Goddamn it!" he mumbled to himself. He was just getting back upright when he heard voices coming toward him to his right. He turned and looked. Although still blurry, he could make out the shapes of four, maybe five people walking toward him. Sam became anxious. This could not be good.

"Hey, hey, look what we found," said one of the shapes.

As they approached him, he could make out more details. Five men, young, maybe 19-22. Sam's head began to pound even more as he became more anxious.

"I need help," muttered Sam, barely able to speak. *I must sound like a drunk*, he thought.

"You sure do man. You're in the wrong place. Whatcha' do get a little lost?"

Sam held up his hand in an attempt to show he was in no condition to deal with this but it just encouraged the group who now became aggressive.

"Give me your wallet...now," said one of the youths as they pulled out a knife.

The others began to encircle Sam. Pushing him and yelling at him to give up his money.

Across the street, curtains parted, as a few residents had heard the commotion outside.

Sam struggled to reach for his wallet but his coordination had not returned completely. Now the pain in his head was intense. A feeling began to come over him that could only be described as having a swarm of bees underneath your skin. Sam forgot about the gang surrounding him and now sensed there was something seriously wrong with him. He could feel rage welling up in him. His breathing deepened as he slowly sank back deep into his subconscious. Sam was gone and in his place something so horrible arose that his attackers stood stunned. The man with the knife was closest to Sam and he was the first to be attacked. Despite being stabbed in the upper chest, Sam had launched himself at him knocking him to the ground. Sam began to pummel and rip chunks of flesh off of his attackers face. Two other attackers jumped on Sam trying to pull him off their friend, only to have Sam turn on them. One had reached around Sam's head trying to pull him off allowing Sam to bite into his forearm and take out a large chuck of flesh, tearing an artery in the process. The second attacker was on Sam instantly. Sam's rage grew exponentially as he nearly ripped the attackers arm off at the socket and began to beat him to death.

Now the beast was in full charge. Looking at other two youths, Sam's face contorted, his lungs filled with air, and he let out a scream that could only be described as demonic. The two turned to run, but now Sam had quickly caught the slower of the two. Knocking him to the ground, Sam began to beat him relentlessly in the head until there was nothing but a flattened mass. By now, the other attacker was gone. Across the street, upstairs lights were on and people were looking down at the scene of the attack. Sam didn't notice. As quickly as the attack had began, now it ended and the beast withdrew back into Sam's exhausted body. Sinking into lethargy with only a slight facial twitch occasionally to animate the body that now sat motionless against the brick wall.

Minutes passed by in silence. A couple of people ventured out onto the street, curious as to what had happened only to rapidly retreat back inside once they saw the carnage that was scattered about across the street. Off in the distance, a siren broke through the silence, growing ever louder.

First to arrive, officers Tanner and Wilkins sat stunned in their vehicle, the headlights illuminating the street in front of them. Scattered about were four bodies mutilated beyond recognition. Blood was everywhere. They exited the car and walked toward the bodies. By now, a few residents began to emerge from their apartments, finding courage with the presence of the police.

Seeing the condition of the bodies, Mark Tanner fought the urge to vomit. He turned to Wilkins. "Call for back up and an EMT unit."

Wilkins hurried back to the car to call in the request. Two residents came up to him, pointing in the direction of Sam. "That's the guy that did it! He's just sitting there!"

Wilkins looked at them, "One guy did this?" he asked, incredulously.

"Yeah, it was like he was possessed. He was screaming and beating these kids. I saw the whole thing from up there," pointing to his apartment window.

Wilkins turned toward his partner Tanner, who had now noticed Sam propped up against the wall in a dark doorway a short distance from the bodies and was approaching him with his gun drawn.

"That's the suspect, Mark! Careful, it sounds like he is on something."

Tanner raised his left hand and waved slightly in acknowledgement. "Give me some light over here," he yelled back.

Wilkins got back in the car and turned the spotlight on, aiming it at the spot where Sam sat.

"Show me your hands!" yelled Tanner. "Show them now!"

Sam sat motionless, his eyes open and obviously looking at Tanner.

"God damn it, get your hands where I can see them!"

Sam did not respond. He sat there staring at Tanner. Tanner could see that Sam had been wounded. His clothes were soaked with blood. He still had a chunk of flesh in his hand.

Tanner became unnerved. This wasn't normal. He had seen his share of junkies before who had killed but this felt different. Meth...coke...bath salts...he had seen people do some serious horrible shit but this one was now at the top of his list. Despite his urge to slowly back away and give this guy some space until help arrived, Tanner approached Sam until he was standing in front of him. *He must be completely out,* he thought. Sam was motionless, his breathing barely noticeable. With his gun trained on Sam, Tanner lightly kicked him in the leg. "Hey, can you hear me?

Sam's muscles tensed as he let out a deep breath. With a single move, he lunged at Tanner, knocking him off his feet. Sam began to pummel Tanner, who had fired a couple of shots aimlessly before he dropped his gun. Sam was screaming as he bit into Tanner's face and neck tearing large chunks of flesh away from the bone.

The small crowd that had gathered near the patrol car screamed and ran to their doorways. Wilkins, seeing the attack, got back out of the car and fired several shots at Sam hitting him in the leg with one of them. Sam, turned his attention toward Wilkins and ran toward him. Wilkins panicked and dove back into the patrol car locking the doors. Sam began to smash his fists into the hood and windows breaking the glass. His assault was relentless. Wilkins grabbed the shotgun from the front seat bracket and began to shoot through the front window. The fourth round hit Sam dead center in the chest lifting him into the air and backwards. Wilkins got out of the car, his heart pounding in his chest, and moved around the front of the vehicle. Two more patrol cars had arrived, witnessing the attack, they too exited the cars with guns drawn. Wilkins approached cautiously. Sam lay face up on the pavement, his body still trembling from the infusion of adrenalin that moments ago fueled his rage. Sam was dead.

Within minutes, video clips of the attack were being posted on YouTube by bystanders who had filmed the incident with their cell phones. The face of the disease would be seen worldwide by the morning.

14

The Loss Of Our Friend

"We will fight back and we will be victorious over this great evil that has come upon our nation and our world. We will not rest until a cure is found. We will save who we can and we will mercifully eliminate those we cannot. There is no room for morality in our choices if we are to survive."

Sen. Charles Henderson, IL
Interim President, United States of America

Jonas exited the elevator at the floor where his office was located. He walked down the hallway reluctantly. He was tired. He had not slept well last night and now, he was late. Real late. He entered the waiting room of his department.

"Dr. Matthews. Thank God you're finally here. Dr. Brilli has been calling to talk to you. He says it's very important and to call him when you get in," said Jonas' secretary, Amy.

"I will. Thank you, Amy. Give me a minute," Jonas replied as he poured himself some coffee. *Great! The one day I'm late and my boss is trying to get a hold of me,* he thought to himself.

"Oh, I almost forgot. Dr. Andrews said he emailed you the video you wanted to look at."

"Okay. Thanks," he replied as he walked down the hall to his office.

Jonas sat down at his desk, sipped his coffee and looked out the window behind him. He turned back around slowly and began to go through the yellow post-its that Amy had placed on his computer monitor. Mostly, phone calls to return or make. He notice one from Walter asking him to call him. It was about Sam. He wanted to call Walter right away but he knew Brilli was waiting for him.

He picked up the phone and pressed the button for Brilli's office.

"Dr. Brilli's office," said the voice on the other end of the line.

"Good morning, Meredith. It's Dr. Matthews. Dr. Brilli wanted me to call when I got in."

"Right, Dr. Matthews. I put you right through."

Almost immediately Brilli was on the line.

"Jonas, I need you in my office right away."

Jonas sensed the urgency in Brilli's voice. He also detected fear. Something was seriously wrong. "I'm on my way." Jonas hung up the phone and walked out through the lobby. "I'll be in Dr. Brilli's office," he said to Amy as he exited into the hallway.

Moments later, Jonas entered Brilli's office.

"Go right in, doctor, he's expecting you."

Jonas managed a smile directed toward Meredith as he entered the director's office.

"Have a seat Jonas," said Brilli, giving Jonas a quick glance then returning to the report he held in this hands. "Jonas, I have some very bad news."

Jonas froze. His eyes studied Brilli's face. He was visibly troubled.

"Sam Watson was killed early this morning," said Brilli, struggling to fight back the emotion he was feeling.

Jonas felt the air rush from his lungs. He became sick and confused. His friend was dead.

"How...What happened?" Jonas could not hide the tears forming in his eyes.

"Jonas, what we are about to discuss doesn't leave this room...agreed,"

Jonas nodded his head, "Yes, of course." He knew when Brilli said that that something really bad was going to follow. It always did. He felt his throat closing. It was hard to breathe. Jonas sat back in the chair and readied himself.

"Sam was shot and killed by the police early this morning."

"What?" Jonas exclaimed, shocked by the statement. "But why? I mean what happened?"

"Jonas, Sam killed at least four people last night, and the police think there may be two more."

Jonas sat in silence looking into Brilli's face. Thoughts of Sam racing through his head. It was inconceivable that Sam could be responsible for such a thing. Sam had his moments but he was a very even-tempered and likeable guy.

"But that is impossible...are you sure?"

"Yes, it's been confirmed that Sam was the assailant. There were witnesses as well. I got the call early this morning from the county examiner. They found Sam's C.D.C. identification card and called. I had them send the body to Emory and quarantine the body. I sent Dr. Almont and Walter over to do the autopsy."

Jonas looked at Brilli, "Why Walter? Why the quarantine"

"Because of what you and Terry talked to me about a while ago. Sam was shot trying to smash his way into a police car to get to the officer. The killings were savage....beyond anything a sane individual could do. Jonas, I think Sam had the disease you're investigating. Walter seems to agree. That's why he went along. He is taking samples to confirm the presence of the organism."

Jonas remembered Sam describing the incident of the sick bear tearing away at the Airstream camper trying to get at the campers inside.

"We have another problem. Video of the attack made its way to YouTube. By the time we were made aware of the video and could get it removed, it already had over 400,000 views. By now, the news agencies have their investigation team on their way here to question us. I already contacted the director's office and will meet with her right after we are done here."

"Did we get a copy of the attack?" asked Jonas.

"Yes, we managed to make copies. I sent them to some key people already."

"Did you watch it?"

Brilli looked right at Jonas, "Yes...yes I did. It is horrifying."

"I need to see it," said Jonas now angry...angry at the organism for doing this to his friend.

Brilli turned the large monitor on his desk toward Jonas and struck a couple of keys on the keyboard. Immediately the YouTube channel came up with the video of last night's killings. Brilli enlarged the screen view and increased the volume.

Jonas watched in horror as Sam attacked and mauled the victims. Even more disturbing was the inhuman scream coming from Sam and his attack on the patrol car. The video ended. Jonas and Brilli sat in silence. Jonas went over the scene in his head repeatedly. The thing that attacked the victims was not Sam. He was sure of that....but what? What happened inside Sam to transform him into the creature that killed so viciously?

Brilli interrupted Jonas' thoughts. "You were going to report your team's findings about this organism. Please tell me this is an isolated incident."

Jonas looked at Brilli and shook his head. "No, it's not. We couldn't connect any of the incidents with the organism because of lack of autopsy records but the degree of violence is the same."

"How far into it are we?"

"Terry thought that this is the start of the third wave. The infected organism is spreading throughout the more heavily populated areas. He suggested the epidemic is already in its first year or two. Its spread has been slow and unusually stealthy"

"Son of a bitch!" Brilli said in a restrained voice. "So this is only going to get worse? Jonas, do you realize that...."

The phone rings.

"Meredith, I said no calls."

"I know doctor and I apologize, but it's a Mr. Donaldson from the C.I.A. He said it's extremely urgent."

"Put him on."

Brilli listened for several minutes. Jonas noticed the longer the conversation went the more solemn Brilli's face became. Finally, Brilli hung up.

"Well this simply isn't any good. That was Alex Donaldson, director of Special Projects at the C.I.A. He says he saw the video this morning and is coming here with a few members of his team tomorrow morning. He has already discussed the matter with our director and she is expecting us to meet with her in the afternoon. Make sure your team is at the meeting. Everything else is put on hold until further notice. Clear your calendars."

Jonas sat, lost in thoughts about Sam, oblivious to Brilli's words.

"Jonas!"

Jonas snapped out of it. "Sorry…I…"

"I understand. We all feel the loss."

"Tony, why is the C.I.A. coming here? Wouldn't it make more sense for the F.B.I. or Homeland Security? Why them?" asked Jonas

"I suppose you could answer that better than I could. What are you thinking?"

"Well, Terry and I came to the conclusion that the parasite was a mutation or a self-modification of the existing species. We made a second assumption that, based on Walters micrographs of viruses inside the oocysts we found, that a phage was infecting the organism and amplifying its deep brain effects. What we couldn't figure out was where the phage came from. We both came to the conclusion that it may have been engineered and now we have the C.I.A. special projects director giving us special attention?"

"I'm hesitant to agree without more facts but it sounds plausible. Anyway we will find out tomorrow morning. Keep working on this. Let's start looking for solutions as well. What drugs we have that may be effective. If we're lucky, the C.I.A. will have that already figured out…if it is them."

Jonas got up to leave. Turning around at the door he asked, 'What about Sam's funeral?"

"We aren't releasing his body. It's the only bit of evidence we have at this time about this disease. I'll notify his brother."

"I understand. I'll be in my office all day if you need me," and with that, Jonas walked out of Brilli's office.

It was almost noon when Terry walked into Jonas' office and sat down in the chair in front of his desk. Jonas knew he had heard about Sam just by looking at him. Terry sat silently looking out the window for a few moments.

"I feel the same way," said Jonas. "My insides are in a knot."

"Jesus, Christ, Jonas! You saw the video. Can you imagine a more horrible way to die? And what he did to those kids…" Terry began to break down. The shock of seeing a friend transform into a nightmare was more than most could bear.

"I know, Terry, but I'm sure that the person we knew as Sam was not even aware of what was happening. It's horrible but we don't have any time to mourn over Sam. He was in Washington, what, almost two months ago? That means that the illness is slow growing. Hell, by now, there's no reason to believe that it hasn't totally saturated most of the urban areas. We're past containment, Terry. What happened to Sam is most likely going to happen to a large number of people and I am having real difficulty grasping the severity of all of it."

Terry regained his composure. "I know. I think that is what affecting me the most. How are we going to stop this? I mean, we can't even tell who has it."

"I don't know, Terry, but we have to come up with some kind of plan and soon."

"Not wanting to add to the horror of all of this, but did you take a look at the video Dr. Patel sent me?"

"No, not yet. I haven't had the time this morning," replied Jonas as he began to move the mouse around looking for the email from Terry with the attached video. "Here it is." Jonas opened the file and began to watch the video.

"We are at the southwest sector of the M'bera refugee camp approximately 32 hours after the event," said a voice, obviously Dr. Patel's. "The area has been abandoned. There are only a few family members of the victims still here. We have Red Cross members as well as some of our military escort looking for survivors. As you can see there are a very large number of casualties," said Dr. Patel as he walked through the camp pausing to highlight the extreme brutal nature of the attacks. "The types of injuries we are seeing range from blunt trauma to stabbings to dismemberment. There are also a number of gunshot fatalities which is consistent with Dr. Bashad's report of panicked Peacekeepers opening fire on the crowd."

Jonas continued to watch the video. Terry sat in silence, already sensing the mounting anxiety in Jonas.

"We estimate 2400 dead. There were also a number of livestock killed in the same manner. We do not know nor do we have any way of determining which bodies are those of the attackers. If we had to guess, based on intact bodies that show no sign of mauling, approximately 25% of the bodies are attackers, the rest are victims."

Jonas suddenly closed the program. He had heard enough. It was far too much to take in. Seeing Sam's primal attack gave him a haunting image of what happened at M'bera. He had reached an overload.

"Terry, I need to be alone for a while. I will give you a call in an hour or so and we can talk more then. Besides I think Walter will be back from the hospital and may have some information for us."

"Okay, Jonas. Are you going to be alright?"

"Yeah, sure. I just need some time to sort things out and clear my head. I'll be okay."

With that, Terry got up and left, leaving Jonas alone in his office.

The day passed slowly. By now, news of Sam's attack was being aired on news stations around the world. The usual parade of armchair psychologists and drug experts had begun the dissection of Sam's character on the world stage. Suggestions by the "experts" implied that this had been a drug-induced incident, most likely something akin to bath salts or an overdose of PCP. The press release by Dr. Ellen Bern, director of the C.D.C. did little to quell these accusations. The official position was that no comment would be made pending the results of the investigation. The public had already made up their mind. Sam Watson was a drug addict and the attacks were caused by an overdose. Today, Sam was the most hated man in the country, but it wouldn't last long. A bigger story was about to break.

15

In The News

"For every one that is infected they kill four or five uninfected, even more sometimes. They're the most dangerous when they are in a group. The madness heightens the excitement and they become even more violent."

James Thompson
Survivor, Boston Rage Riots, 2018

It was almost three-thirty in the afternoon in Atlanta when television programming was interrupted for an emergency announcement by the Dept. of Homeland Security. Vincent Sanderson, director of the department, standing behind the podium, made the announcement.

"At approximately two-thirty this morning, central time, the U.S.S. Barry Atkins responded to reports of a possible terrorist takeover of the cruise ship Kalypso and subsequent sinking of the ship approximately 200 miles from her home port of Galveston. The last communication from the ship was from the suspected terrorists indicating they had seized control of the ship and had executed a large number of the crew. They gave no reason for the attack. It was originally reported that the Kalypso was returning to port due to a suspected outbreak of upper respiratory virus. We are unclear as to what may have caused the ship to explode and sink, however, it is likely that the terrorists had managed to place large explosive devices in key areas of the ship. There were no demands given by the terrorists and no group has claimed responsibility. Rescuers, on site, report no survivors have been found and rescue operations will continue for at least another 48 hours."

The news alert continued on, but by now, a nation was stunned at the loss of so many lives. By the time the six o'clock news came on, Sam's killing spree was no more than minor local interest story. Like so many other horrible events posted on the social media sites, Sam's night would be viewed repeatedly for the next several days and then the novelty would wear off. It would be forgotten.

The events that Jonas and his team feared may be happening were unfolding at an increasingly fast pace. At first the outbreaks involved smaller groups of people, often just one person, but it quickly became obvious to many that something was not right. Local law enforcement agencies began to suspect the appearance of a new drug on the streets but so far nothing new had turned up. In the months leading up to Sam's attacks, the disease had shown itself in numerous vicious attacks only to be dismissed as an "act of terrorism" or "drug-related". Terry had been right. This was the third wave of the epidemic. Now the new strain of Toxoplasma and its infecting virus were firmly established throughout the globe. Undetected, the disease took several months to produce the type of deep brain lesions that had caused Sam to brutally kill his victims. Many of the infected who were beginning to show neurological symptoms were diagnosed as having schizophrenia and placed on medications that suppressed the symptoms but did little to stop the progress of the infection. Prior to the attacks by Sam, many of the school shootings and other mass murders were done by those who had been diagnosed with schizophrenia and were either on medication or had stopped taking the medications. While the medical community was clueless as to the presence of the infective agent, the new disease was rapidly racking up a body count, both directly and indirectly. No other disease in the history of mankind behaved like this one did. Many of the infected simply got sick and eventually recovered or died, but far too many others went the way Sam did. The rage the disease caused within its victims caused them to commit horrifying acts of violence. Rape, murder, suicide to a scale never imagined were now possible, and no one was safe.

That evening, Jonas sat on the couch with Ellie watching television. Interrupted by news alerts about the ill-fated cruise ship, he held Ellie closer than usual. Both sat in silence, not knowing what to say. The day had seen the death of a close friend and now this historic tragedy. Jonas had turned his cell phone off. He needed time...time to regain his composure. Time to think things through. Tired of the repeated news reports and video of navy rescue ships in the area, both retired for the evening. As they lay in bed together, he looked at Ellie. *"Was she infected? Was he infected?"* He managed a weak smile and pulled her close. There in their bed, holding each other, they slept safe for now as the world began to come apart around them.

16

All On The Table

"New York City is under siege. Attempts by the military to expedite the evacuation of uninfected citizens from the island have stalled due to the inability of citizens to get to the safe zones. Estimated deaths now approach over 120,000 confirmed dead but on-site aide workers indicate that the actual number may be twice that. Similar scenes are being reported in nearly every city in the U.S. Attempts to enforce the quarantines have failed due to the lack of available personnel."

Karl Hedstrom
Reporter, New York Times

Jonas arrived at the Center early only to find the scene in utter chaos as a large contingent of news reporters had converged on the site.

What the hell? he thought as he passed through the congested parkway leading to one of the center's parking area. *Nobody could have linked Sam's attack with any disease this quick.* Jonas parked his car and walked toward the main building. As he made his way through the crowd of reporters and crew that had gathered at the main entrance he was stopped by one of the reporters.

"Sir! Sir! Could you give us just a minute of your time?" asked the reporter as he positioned himself between Jonas and the path to the front doors of the Center. "You're Dr. Jonas Matthews, aren't you? Chief investigator at the CDC?" he asked quietly as more reporters began to gather around pushing their recorders and microphones in front of him.

Jonas felt uncomfortable with the surge of bodies coming at him but knew enough to put on a professional stance. "Yes, I am Dr. Matthews. You've done your homework." Jonas said laughingly to reduce the tension.

"Yes I do, Doctor. Do you have any information about the situation in China? Any insights as to what illness they are dealing with?

More reporters began to shout their questions at Jonas.

"Is there any link between the killings by Sam Watson and the disease spreading through China?" yelled the reporter from a local station, WSB.

A CNN reporter asked, "Do you have any information as to how many people have contracted this disease?"

Jonas was confused. *What disease? What is going on in China?* He hadn't a clue as to what they were talking about...yet, they seemed to want to link it to Sam's attacks. Jonas stalled, "Please! Quiet please." Jonas raised his arms and signaled them to quiet down for a minute. "I am just arriving here as you can see, so I don't have any information to share with you. I am sure that the CDC will issue a press release regarding this situation as soon as they have some reliable information."

A collective moan was given by the crowd who began to yell questions at Jonas again. Ignoring further questions, Jonas turned and entered the Center's lobby.

There were several armed guards at the entrance of the building along with a few men in suits, obviously another departments agents. *The C.I.A. must be here already,* thought Jonas. *More fuel for the fire.*

Jonas hadn't been in his office for more than fifteen minutes before a call came in from Dr. Brilli's office directing Jonas to come down to the conference room on the first floor and bring all the materials he had on the Toxoplasma situation.

Jonas felt a lump develop in his throat. *This is it,* he thought. *Shit is going to hit the fan,* he mumbled to himself as he gathered up his files and exited his office.

As he entered the elevator he heard Terry yelling.

"Jonas! Wait up."

Jonas pushed the hold button as Terry and Ben both entered the elevator. The doors closed behind them.

"Well, this ain't going to be pretty," said Ben looking at the floor indicator.

"No, it won't," replied Jonas. "What do you guys know about some kind of outbreak in China?"

"You didn't hear yet?" said Terry. "It was on YouTube this morning. Someone leaked video footage of a rage outbreak, for lack of better terms, in a mall in some city over there. It just came out of nowhere. Dozens of attackers began to kill shoppers. When the police arrived, there was a big gunfight as the attackers rushed the police."

"It was gruesome," Ben chimed in. "Hardly anyone made it out of the mall. They estimate two hundred people were killed."

"Do you think it was our bug?" asked Jonas as the elevator doors opened.

"Jonas, the attack was just like Sam's attack. The scream, the brutality, even the incredible speed and strength...all the same. How could it not be?" replied Ben.

"And apparently, this isn't the first time this has happened over there," said Terry. "There have been at least six other incidents that we now know of. The Chinese government has been covering this up...calling them activist attacks."

"What about W.H.O.? Do they have anyone there investigating?" asked Jonas as they walked across the lobby toward the conference rooms.

"No. I checked. The Chinese government is refusing to let them into the areas." replied Terry.

Jonas stopped for a moment in the hallway and looked at Terry and Ben.

"I've got to tell you guys, I am scared shitless about this mess. I've been wracking my brains trying to see some way through this outbreak, but I can't. We've got no real evidence at this point that these events are being caused by this new infected strain. We have to get facts...evidence...about what we are facing otherwise we're screwed."

"Maybe we're about to get some," said Ben.

"Maybe," replied Jonas as they proceeded down the hall to a conference room that had guards posted outside it.

They entered the large room where Jonas could see Dr. Brilli and Walker talking to two men he did not recognize.

"Ah, good! They're here. This is Dr. Jonas Matthews, Dr. Ben Hoyle, and Dr. Terry Andrews. They are the team working on the Toxoplasma issue. Of course, you have already met Dr. Frederickson," said Dr. Brilli as he extended his arms toward the large table in the center of the room. "Please, let's all get seated and begin."

The group took their seats. Jonas and his team sat opposite the three strangers. Brilli sat at the head of the table. There were two other suited individuals in the room that Jonas had already pegged as security, especially since one of them had closed the door and was standing in front of it. The other had taken position just behind and to the left of Dr. Brilli at the far end of the table.

"Gentlemen, I am Alex Donaldson and I'm director of special projects for the Central Intelligence Agency. This is Dr. Carlos Alvarez, director of virology at ARAMID, and Dr. Marilyn Rice, Chief Medical Officer with Homeland Security. What we are about to discuss is a matter of national security and you are ordered to maintain the strictest confidentiality. Any violation of that confidentiality will be dealt with to the fullest extent of the law." Donaldson slowly looked at each of Jonas' team before his eyes came to rest on Jonas himself. "Do you understand?"

Jonas felt his face flush a bit. Not that he was intimidated, rather, he did not like being pushed. It angered him and Donaldson was already irritating him in all the wrong ways. Still, he understood that the need for secrecy in all things was a sacred cow at the CIA and other such agencies, so he suppressed the urge to respond in kind.

"We understand that without it being said," he replied. "I speak for my team, we have a grasp of the situation and its potential effect on our population. You have our complete cooperation."

Donaldson just held his gaze on Jonas for a few seconds and then opened up a file that was in front of him.

"We did not have time to make info packets for you so when we finish here, I will have my files copied and you will each receive a packet today. It is more important that you hear what we know so we can all get on the same page. I have already shared the information we have from you with the necessary contacts. Dr. Rice will speak of that shortly. First things first. We are very sorry about the loss of Dr. Watson. The video appearing on social media is what prompted us to contact your agency as well as Dr. Frederickson's photomicrographs of the infected parasite. Unfortunately, his highly visible death has brought a tremendous amount of attention to something we thought we may be able to contain. That, and other recent tragic events, has shown us that containment is not possible."

"What other tragic events?" asked Terry as he looked at Ben and then Jonas. "Are you talking about the outbreaks in China? Is that related to this Toxoplasma organism?"

"We cannot be sure at this time whether the attacks in China and other places..."

"What other places?" asked Jonas interrupting Donaldson. "What other events are you talking about?

"My team has been tracking outbreaks that may be related to this new variant of Toxoplasma for nearly a year. Since the first reported outbreak in Sierra Leone, there have been almost 300 similar outbreaks throughout the world that involved extremely violent attacks by one or more people. We have confirmed that a majority of them were infected with the new strain of Toxoplasma. There were others but we could not get access to the dead attackers to take samples for analysis. You are aware that China is dealing with these outbreaks as evidenced by the recent leaking of videos on YouTube. Of course, on the surface they deny anything is wrong, but the government of China has quietly approached the World Health Organization to help them contain the outbreaks. Apparently, they are unable to contain the disease and it has become a major crisis."

"Have they given any estimates as to how many may be infected or have died as a result of this disease?" asked Brilli.

"Nothing that is reliable. The agency did intercept a government transmission that indicated a major attack that occurred in the Jiangsu province, about fifty miles northwest of Shanghai. We know that troops were sent into the area but we have not heard anything else. It's important to note that that province is the most densely populated area in China. I cannot imagine the attacks were small."

"We know that a similar thing happened in M'bera. We saw a video of the aftermath. Do you know if that was caused by the new Toxoplasma species?" asked Terry.

"Yes, it was. We confirmed it through tissue samples and autopsies of some of the bodies."

"And what were the numbers there?" queried Jonas without looking up from his notes.

"Over five thousand died in the outbreak at the southern end of the camp," replied Donaldson.

Jonas looked up, stunned by the number. The other members of his team were similarly shocked.

"Over what period of time?" asked Jonas in a subdued tone.

"Less than a day from we can tell."

"That's impossible. It couldn't have been Toxoplasma that did this. It doesn't kill that fast. Hell, I can't even think of any disease that can do that," protested Ben. "I know this parasite and it can take months to kill its host even if the immune system is compromised. It had to be a chemical agent. Are you sure they were exposed to Ricin or some other agent?

"We're certain. There were no traces of any known chemical agents in the victims or in the environment. And as you know now, we are not dealing with the common Toxoplasma parasite. A majority of the victims were brutally killed. We could not tell how many of the infected actually did the killing. Our best guess is three out of ten, maybe more. By the time our team got to the site, it had been almost completely abandoned. Some of our team were attacked by a few of the infected that were too sick to move about much, but we had an armed escort that managed to keep them from being seriously hurt. We were able to do autopsies on several of the dead attackers so we know they had the disease."

"What were the findings?" asked Brilli.

"They were consistent with a type of Toxoplasma-induced encephalitis only a very unusual form. Based on the reports I have read, it would appear that the infected parasite infects the limbic region of the brain and can trigger a rage response to stressors that can last minutes to hours after which the host falls into a catatonic state until provoked again. We have no idea how long this can go on before the host dies but according to the autopsies, those lesions had been there a while.

"So someone like Dr. Watson could walk around infected and no one would really know until something triggered the rage response," said Terry.

"We'd assume so."

"But Sam was only exposed less than six weeks ago. The infection couldn't progress that quickly to cause brain lesions that severe. Ben?" Terry asked looking at his colleague.

"Generally, no. Toxoplasmosis is a slow progressing disease unless the host immune system is compromised," replied Ben.

"But Sam was reasonably healthy. His immune system was as good as any of us."

"That is not correct," said Walter, who had been quiet up to now. "Sam had been taking immune-suppressing medication to treat Lupus for several months before he was exposed. I had his doctor stop the treatment when we discovered that he was infected, but it takes months for the immune system to normalize."

"So his body couldn't stop the organism from rapidly infecting his brain and accelerating the process," added Walter.

"But that still doesn't add up. We see cases of Toxoplasmosis in AIDS victims and it still takes months to kill its hosts. We can assume this new parasite is much more aggressive but it still shouldn't kill its host that quick," said Ben.

"That's is where the virus comes in. It's the wild card in this mess," responded Donaldson. "Dr. Alvarez, can you explain the virus' role in this?"

"Certainly. You see the virus infects the parasite before it forms a cyst. That prevents the body's immune system from getting to it. Even though the viral particles are protected by the cyst, the immune system can still sense their presence and produces an exaggerated inflammatory response around the cysts causing more severe lesions in the deep brain. The protozoan alone might rarely produce the type of behavior response we are seeing, but add this viral phage in the mix and you get a type of super-toxoplasmosis whose main symptom is limbic rage."

Jonas had been quiet for a while. Listening. He had been studying the faces of the three strangers that sat before him and going over the information in his mind. He was becoming more and more irritated with the jabber that was being thrown at him. He knew. He knew what was going on. Their presence here confirmed it and yet, they had not confessed. He had heard enough.

"Why was the CIA in M'berra?" Jonas asked in a subdued tone, leaning forward in his chair, interrupting the conversation.

The conversation that had been going on suddenly stopped. Donaldson, who had been caught off-guard by the question, could only reply, "What do you mean?"

"I think the question is pretty simple. Why was the CIA in M'berra? I mean, that's a bit out of your neighborhood, isn't it? Also, you mentioned you thought you could "contain" it. I think I already know the answer, but for the past thirty minutes you have sat across from us and told us about things we already know about to some degree and you have not told us one single thing about why your agency seems to be connected to what is going on. So why don't you put aside the pretense and get to the fucking point."

"Jonas, that's not called for," barked Brilli, who was also surprised by Jonas' outburst. "I'm sure Mr. Donaldson was about to go into that. Weren't you?"

Brilli, who had also become somewhat impatient with the direction of the discussion looked at Donaldson and gave him a diplomatic smile and nod.

Donaldson regained his composure, looking at his colleagues, he turned toward Jonas and his team.

"The virus is ours, Dr. Matthews. We engineered this virus to infect T. gondii. Obviously, something went seriously wrong. We don't know where the hell this new strain of Toxoplasma came from, but like you, we assume it must be some type of natural mutation. Hell, we didn't know this strain even existed. We tried for a couple of years to make this virus infect the parasite with no success. Your garden variety Toxoplasma organism is immune to a viral phage. We abandoned the project over three years ago."

"How is it, then, that the virus is in the environment to begin with," asked Brilli.

Dr. Alvarez leaned forward. "We can't be sure. Since it wasn't technically a human pathogen most the work on the viral phage was done in a lower level lab. Later, when we began to do trials on the protozoan, we moved it into a more secure level containment. It's conceivable that the virus got out in the initial phases of testing. It may be that one or more of our staff was already infected with the new variant of Toxoplasma and it managed to get out of containment in infected cysts. Anyone who has worked with anthrax spores knows how difficult containment is, so early on if the virus found its way into one of the staff, if would be very easy to piggy-back out of the lab inside the protozoan cyst."

Jonas had been writing notes down. He put his pen down and looked at Alvarez.

"I don't understand why you wanted to develop a viral phage for Toxoplasma. Certainly, the organism is far too slow to use as a biological weapon. What am I missing?"

"Dr. Matthews," said Donaldson, "not all bio-weapons need to kill quickly. There are some organisms that can be used for other purposes. A more aggressive Toxoplasma infection could be considered an economy-buster. It can enter a population undetected, spread rapidly, and once the infected become symptomatic all hell would break loose. The affected region would assume it's a natural outbreak of some exotic disease and in the meantime, the sheer numbers of infected victims would collapse the economy and destabilize the governing body. Back in the early 1900's, the Yellow Fever outbreak brought the U.S. economy to an abrupt halt. It took several years to recover from it and millions of people lost their lives. Different disease but same results."

"Well you certainly seemed to achieve your goal with this bug," said Terry. "As far as we can tell, this....the organism...what the hell do we call this anyway? It's not just the protozoan, is it? It's both."

"Originally, it was named TGV-1 or Toxoplasma gondii virus - 1 but now, since the organism it infects is not T. gondii, and we really have not named the new species of Toxoplasma yet, we have been calling the infected organism Toxovirus," said Alvarez. "It's easier and it's assumed we are talking about the protozoan-viral phage complex."

"That's a hell of an ominous name. Toxovirus?" Terry said with a forced laugh.

"It just makes it easier to discuss when we know it refers to the virus-parasite complex," explained Dr. Alvarez.

"Let's get back to the real world here," said Jonas. "What information do you have about how far this thing has spread? It's obvious we have two organisms infecting the population. Does there seem to be any pattern?"

Dr. Rice, who had been silent up to this point, opened a folder in front of her.

"Globally, a majority of cases reported have been along the coastline and major river systems. It is more prominent in dense populated areas and is more often seen in warmer climates. There are random clusters of outbreaks but as of now we have not been able to trace any origin. In the U.S., there have been numerous reports of suspected outbreaks along the Gulf Coast and in major coastal cities. The further inland you go the fewer suspected cases are seen. Again, we do not have much data on this and we are going on outbreaks in individuals or groups that display the unique rage symptoms associated with this disease."

"When we first became aware that Toxovirus was a threat, we began to collect data throughout the country by having select hospitals submit blood samples of their patients to our research facilities. We tested for the presence of antibodies to either the virus, the new species of Toxoplasma, or both. We were alarmed at the findings," said Donaldson.

Jonas felt his stomach start to knot up. "What did you find?" he asked.

"In the past seven months we have tested over eighty-two hundred blood samples. Approximately fifty-eight percent of them tested positive for the combined antibodies."

"Are you telling us that over half of the population of the United States may be infected with this disease?" asked Brilli who had stood up and walked to the window.

"Based on what information we have now, I'd have to say yes," Donaldson replied.

"It may be even higher in densely populated areas. Since it is now airborne it will spread similar to influenza but it also can exist outside the body for prolonged periods of time so the area will continue to generate cases unlike the flu," said Dr. Frederickson. "The disease spread throughout my mid-level labs killing most of the test animals. It also found its way into some of the staff whom I have already begun a treatment regimen. I would hazard to guess this disease could be more infective than the Spanish flu."

"Except the Spanish flu didn't make you smash your neighbors head to a pulp," quipped Terry. "Seriously, we haven't even discussed the additional impact on the non-infected. If M'berra was any indication of what we can expect then more people will die from these rage attacks than from the disease itself."

"I agree with you," replied Donaldson. "From what we have seen, the collateral fatalities are far greater than the number of infected involved in the events."

"Dr. Rice, have you done any preliminary mortality estimations based on the information you have been given? asked Brilli who had taken his seat and was now obviously uncomfortable.

"Yes, we have run a few simulations," she replied. Her voice became unsteady as she sorted through some papers in front of her. "Based on the information at hand and taking into consideration the minimal effectiveness of existing treatments and variations in patient immune responses, we can expect fifty-four percent of the population to become infected. Approximately one-quarter of the infected will develop brain lesions severe enough to become violent. Again, these figures are based on the information at hand."

"So right now we are looking at over a hundred million cases, of which, twenty-five million will become extremely violent. And if we assume that each of these manage to kill two people then the total mortality on a conservative basis is over fifty million people? Is that what we are looking at? I cannot accept this?" shouted Jonas. This is the nightmare he had sensed was at hand. He looked around the table. "Somebody tell me I'm wrong."

There was prolonged silence at the table. Each person there was uncomfortable as the gravity of the situation was made apparent.

Dr. Rice was the first to break the silence. Clearing her throat she spoke in a reserved tone.

"I don't think the numbers will be that high. We cannot assume that everyone that gets this disease bad enough to form brain lesions will become dangerous. Also, there is the matter of natural immunity. We don't know if previous exposure to T. gondii gives the person immunity to the new species. There are so many other things to consider we can't let ourselves assume the very worse-case scenario."

Jonas stood up and leaned toward Rice. Dr. Brilli cut in before Jonas could deliver his salvo.

"I think we need a break. We've been at it for a while and there's a lot of information on the table that needs to settle in before we continue."

Jonas looked at Brilli who had given him a slight shake of his head indicating that he should let it go for now. Jonas looked back at Donaldson.

"Yes, I think that would be a good idea," he said as he moved toward the door. "Walter, will you get with Dr. Alvarez and go over possible treatments? Let's meet back here in an hour."

"Certainly Jonas."

Brilli gestured to the door, "Drs. will you follow me to our commissary. We have a side room set up with a lunch for you."

17

Secrets Revealed

"The crew came down with some kind of illness several weeks before on a previous cruise, nothing too bad. No one thought much about it. This last voyage was different. There was a lot of fighting. Lots of headaches. The passengers were upset because the crew was so ill. Then the crew went crazy. They attacked the passengers and killed most of them..they mutilated the bodies...and...some of them...they ate...Oh God!...it was a nightmare..I could hear the few remaining passengers screams. Then they started attacking each other."

Erika Winters
Lone survivor of the Kalypso

Jonas leaned over the sink splashing cold water on his face and looked into the mirror. He stood there staring, wondering how to process the information Donaldson and the others had just delivered. He had already developed an idea of the gravity of the situation before this meeting but hearing it from them in such a factual manner hit him hard. Right about then the bathroom door opened.

"There you are. We were wondering where you ran off to," said Terry.

"Yeah, you didn't look to well when you left the room so Brilli wanted us to track you down and check on you," said Ben.

Jonas managed a slight smile and chuckle.

"I thought about running away but I couldn't think about where I would go."

Jonas turned around and looked at Terry and Ben.

"You both know what is going to happen, right? This isn't influenza were dealing with here, it's far worse and it has a head start. We can't win this one," said Jonas in a quieted voice.

"Do you think Donaldson is holding out on us?" asked Ben.

"Sure he is, that's why they're here," said Terry. "If it wasn't out of control they wouldn't be here. Hell, he even has Homeland Security here so what does that say. They fucked up and they want us to clean up the mess."

"Doesn't matter at this point," replied Jonas. "The only thing that matters now is that we minimize the damage. They're here because they're out of options which means it is already out of control. Right now we need to know how much time we have before this situation blows up."

As Jonas and his team returned to the conference room, he noticed Dr. Brilli and Dr. Rice having a discussion further down the hallway. Brilli, seeing Jonas, motioned him to join them.

"Jonas, I have to join Donaldson and the others to go over some information they brought with them," Brilli said quietly. "Dr. Rice has something she wants to discuss with you before you rejoin the discussion."

Jonas nodded his head as Brilli moved toward the room.

"This has been a hell of a day, hasn't it," he said managing a nervous smile.

"That it has," she replied looking down the hall and then at Jonas. "Dr. Matthews..."

"Call me Jonas."

"Yes, okay, Jonas. I wanted to let you know that I was briefed on this problem by Donaldson only a few weeks ago. I am still greatly troubled by what is developing. I need to know that you and I can work together on this."

"I'm not sure what you mean. Why couldn't you?"

"Look Donaldson and his agency are not in the habit of giving out information without coloring it to some degree. I am sure I do not have all the pieces of the puzzle."

"Just enough to say they informed you," said Jonas.

"Right. The only reason I am at this meeting is because the President ordered Donaldson's superiors to involve my department. Otherwise, they would be trying to use your agency to bury this. Donaldson knows what is going on. He knows this is going to get ugly."

"What do you need from me?"

"I need honest answers. I cannot go back to Washington and brief the President without having some idea of what we can do to manage this outbreak."

Jonas laughed quietly. Her comment hitting him funny.

"Manage it? You gave us the numbers. How do we manage that? How do we tell the American people, let alone the rest of the nations on this planet, that our own government has just gave nature a big helping hand to get rid of humanity?"

"I understand, but I don't think it will play out as big as you think it will."

Jonas stood there for a moment looking at Rice, shaking his head, he looked away collecting himself.

"I'll be more than happy to be honest with you, doctor. It isn't about the disease itself. We could have dealt with that. It's the violence and chaos it's going to create. This may play out like some kind of zombie apocalypse crap you see in movies. More people will die because of the attacks than the disease itself. Donaldson was right, this will stop the economy dead in its tracks. Entire industries will shut down. Food, water, sanitation...all of these may not be available especially in urban areas and you know that. Make no mistake about this, Dr. Rice, if you have done anything, you have greatly underestimated the impact something like this will have. I'm scared shitless and you should be to. Tell that to the President."

Jonas turned and walked away. He felt the surge of adrenalin rushing through his body. He was now angry. He could already see the posturing that was taking place behind the scenes. Eventually, when the public found out about this mess, someone was going to have to take the blame. That would mean that every decision would be thought through and that meant delays. Time was not a luxury they had. *Months? Weeks? Years?* he thought. *When would the brunt of this disease take place?* He paused for a moment before entering the room to regain his composure. *Cannot risk alienating Donaldson, or anyone else, at this point,* he thought. *It wouldn't help the situation and they needed as much cooperation as possible.* He hoped he had not already lost Rice with his concerns.

Jonas returned to the conference room with Dr. Rice right behind him. There was some heated discussion going on between Donaldson and Walter. Brilli was doing his best to calm both parties down.

"It's inexcusable. What the hell were you thinking?" Walter yelled at Donaldson. Walter stepped back and turned to Jonas. "You're not going to believe this."

"Walter, sit down and relax," said Brilli who stood between Walter and Donaldson. "This won't get us anywhere."

"What now?" asked Jonas looking at Walter who was obviously irritated.

"We were discussing weaponizing viruses. Dr. Fredrickson stated that it was fortunate that we had a vaccine for the latest Ebola outbreak in central Africa," said Donaldson.

"And then he just happen to mention how fortunate it was that the outbreak was caused by one of their viruses," said Walter.

"You tested weaponized Ebola in Africa?" asked Jonas.

"Wait a minute, everyone. Let's let Mr. Donaldson explain," said Brilli.

"Thank you," Donaldson said. "Yes it was our virus. That's why we had an effective vaccine against it, but we didn't release it."

"Then who did?" asked Terry.

"Dr. Alverez, would you like to explain this?" asked Donaldson.

"Certainly. It was our weaponized Ebola that caused the outbreak but we believe it was a test release by a well-funded Arab terror group, Saifullah."

"How did they get it?" asked Jonas.

"Yes, you see back in the early 90's, we became aware that someone was taking vials of various organisms from the facility at Fort Detrick. Anthrax was the main concern at the time but several vials of weaponized Ebola also came up missing. We believed that they had been taken by a high level research scientist who had an Egyptian background but nothing was ever proven and the entire incident was swept under the rug. We hoped the problem would disappear."

"Sounds familiar doesn't it," quipped Walter obviously still upset.

"The recent Ebola outbreak is our organism. We released the vaccine we had developed for it once cases began to arrive in the U.S. The vaccine is fairly effective so in a sense it showed those who released it that we were prepared for it. I doubt if they would use it here. Once the organism was released, Mr. Donaldson's agency began tracking those who were responsible and eliminated the threat."

"Eliminated how?" asked Jonas.

"We made the problem disappear. That is all you need to know about it," replied Donaldson.

"Tell him about the Toxovirus vaccine," quipped Walter.

Donaldson looked at Walter, obviously irate over Walters's attitude.

"There is no vaccine for Toxovirus."

"What? Why not?" asked Brilli, now stunned by the response. "I thought it was protocol for any bio-weapon agency to develop treatments concurrent with any development of a biologic."

"Dr. Brilli, we realize we may have been short-sighted on this but at the time we were working with an organism that is assumed not pathogenic to humans, also, we could not get the phage to infect the parasite so there was no real priority to develop a vaccine for the organism."

"Dr. Alverez, I appreciate your honesty but this is a clear violation of protocols and I might add, criminal based on what is happening. Certainly, a vaccine could have been created,"

"Yes it could have at least been started. Again, I will remind you that this phage is engineered so we have no way of knowing how it would behave in the human body. We assumed it would be handled readily by the immune system since it most likely had no infective capabilities. It is very host specific. That being said, you know as well as I do, that it would take several years of testing including human trials to develop a vaccine for it. We would have to convince our superiors that it was of vital importance to justify the effort and resources to do so. We couldn't so we shelved it."

"I guess I'm not surprised," said Jonas. "This is becoming a tragic pile of screw-ups, isn't it? So we don't have a vaccine for the virus and Walter has told me that current medications are minimally effective against the parasite. Basically, we have no treatments for this. Am I right?'

Jonas looked around the room which had become silent.

"That's what I thought. Tony, this is your call. How do you want us to proceed?"

Brilli thought for a moment then leaned over the table.

"Mr. Donaldson, we will need everything you have on this organism and any events it was involved in as soon as you can get it here. Dr. Alverez, you will need to work with Dr. Fredrickson to bring him up to date as well. Dr. Rice, myself and Dr. Berr will be in contact with you to recommend further actions by Homeland Security and FEMA in regards to quarantines and treatment centers should we need them. Jonas and his team will begin to examine anyone infected with the organisms and determine if there are any treatments that can be brought to bear quickly."

Jonas raised his hand.

"Yes, Jonas. Do you want to add anything?

"Yes I do. You will need to inform your contacts within the military to have them begin plans for a potential civil uprising, at least that is the closest thing I can think of that will compare to what may happen."

"We've already done that," said Donaldson.

The members of the group all looked at Donaldson a bit surprised.

"The military has already been involved in a number of outbreaks. Our contacts know the problem at hand and are moving to set up safe zones if necessary and enforce quarantines."

"I will discuss that further with you in private Mr. Donaldson. Obviously, there is more to tell about these outbreaks," Brilli replied sternly. "We have a lot of work to do and no time to do it so let's get things going now. Thank you Mr. Donaldson, Dr. Alverez, Dr. Rice, for meeting with us today. We will be in contact."

With that the group left the conference room in small groups, the meeting was over.

Terry, Ben, and Walter gathered around Jonas in the hallway.

"What do you want us to do?" said Ben.

Jonas looked at each of them. "Wait. We have to wait for an attack to happen then get to the site as quick as possible. We need to know what actually happens, how this thing works. We need eye witnesses. We need to isolate the infected, especially those who attacked. Walter, we need to clear the quarantine section of Emory hospital and have it ready to receive cases. I suggest we have restraints and armed security as well just in case."

"I'm on it," said Walter.

"You guys start watching the reports coming in of odd illnesses or violent events. Be ready to go when it happens. That's all we can do. Oh yeah, hey Walter!" Jonas yelled as Walter walked away. "Make arrangements to have everyone tested for the organisms. We need to make sure none of us have it and if we do, we need to start treatment before it progresses."

Walter nodded his head, "I'll take care of it."

"Terry, you need to pick a couple of field staff to go with us when shit hits the fan. Field packs, especially specimen collection gear, cameras, you know what to bring. Fact-finding stuff only. Ben, likewise. Whatever you need to find this bug."

"Jonas, don't you think it would be a good idea to have some armed guards with us just in case," asked Ben. "You saw what this bug did to Sam. It's likely that we will come in contact with someone who is infected the same way."

"Yes, you're right. I will talk to Brilli and have him see if we can get a military helicopter and escort from Fort Gordon to support us. Now let's get going."

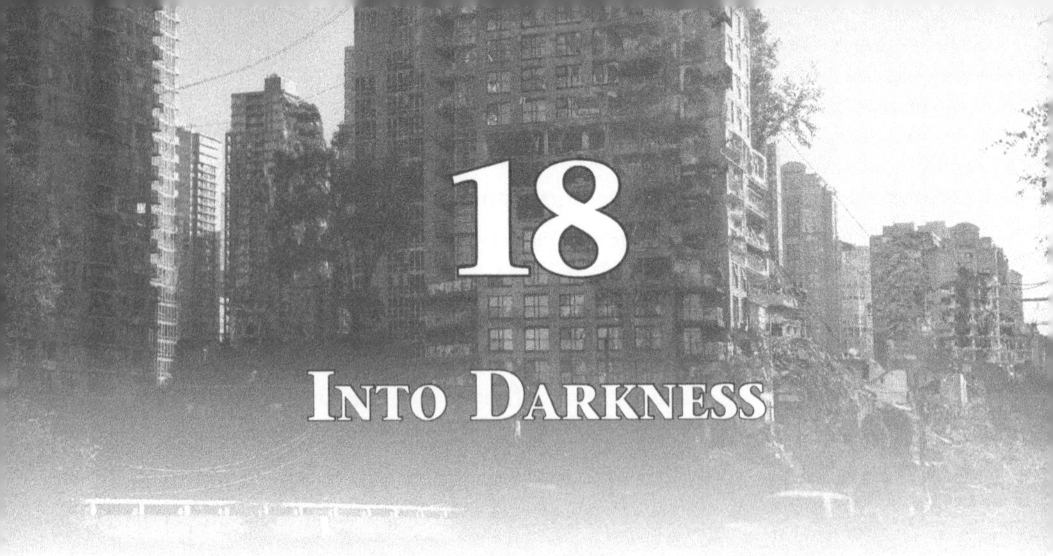

18

Into Darkness

"Every day we lost 2-3 of our staff to attacks by those who had been brought in with medical emergencies but were undiagnosed in regards to this plague. Something would trigger the victim to attack. I saw a man with a gunshot wound to the chest kill two EMT's before he was shot and killed."

Dr. Wallace Bern
Trauma surgeon, Henry Ford Hospital

Several months had passed since the meeting with Donaldson's group and it did not take long for the Toxovirus outbreak to take center stage on local and national news programs. More and more attacks were taking place and the scale of the attacks were getting larger. Jonas had been right. The disease had spread without warning throughout the population and only now were those who had been infected early were showing the final stages of it. Group attacks were becoming more commonplace as there seemed to be some kind of trigger that caused those with advanced brain lesions to suddenly morph into violent killers (called 'alphas' by the military) without warning. The results were nothing short of horrifying as evidenced by a recent attack outbreak at a rock concert in Austin, Texas. For unknown reasons, several dozen concert-goers converted into alphas during the concert and began to attack others. Of the more than eighteen thousand in attendance, over two thousand were killed or injured though the number of those directly killed was uncertain as many had been injured or killed by the crowds trying to escape the arena. It was estimated that the number of alphas grew during the violence to over one hundred, but no one is certain of the actual numbers. Many of the alphas were killed by police inside the arena but several who had followed the escaping crowd out into the parking lot and continued the attacks there managed to kill at least eight officers and a news reporter who had arrived on the scene with the police. Due to attacks such as this and others, FEMA declared a national emergency and enforced curfews and travel restrictions. Local authorities prohibited large gatherings of people and closed schools. They were treating the outbreak like a terrorist attack. The disease acted more like a terrorist cell, activating suddenly and attacking without warning. The results were similar.

Back at the CDC, Jonas sat across from Brilli reviewing several reports that had come in detailing the latest outbreaks and the fatalities. It had been less than a month since the Austin Texas incident and now the outbreak seemed to be going into full swing.

"Where are you at with the info that Donaldson sent over?" asked Brilli.

"I've gone over it and other than them sinking a cruise ship, I was not surprised by anything. Mostly, information we already had. Walter and Dr. Ames are going over the information on the virus they created. He has some samples in his lab and has been studying it with the parasite that Sam had sent to us. He also informed me that they're naming the new species, Toxoplasma aereus since it's airborne. It will help in labeling specimens to keep the species separate."

"That's fine. Let's get back to the cruise ship. What information did they get from the survivor? What was her name?"

"Erica Mendez. She was the assistant activities director. Not much we could use. The most of the crew was infected with what they thought was a URI, fairly benign. Weeks later, headaches started and some behavioral problems. This was the third cruise with the same crew. This was a smaller ship, mostly port to port travel for eighteen days."

"So we can assume none of the passengers were infected?"

"At least to the point the crew was."

"And all the passengers except her were killed by the crew?"

"According to her, the attacks began a couple of days before she was rescued. She wasn't sure if anyone else survived. Personally, I don't see how they could of under the circumstances," said Jonas shaking his head.

"Nothing about the crew, though."

"Nothing we can use."

"How is it she wasn't infected?"

"According to the test results, she has a natural immunity to the organism," replied Jonas. "Donaldson's group has already sent her blood specimens out to isolate any antibodies that may be present."

"How is she?"

"Not good. She requires sedation and is on suicide watch since her last attempt. She can't sleep. I can't blame her."

Both men sat there silently trying to imagine what she had gone through. Finally Brilli shook himself out of it and leaned forward putting his elbows on the desk in front of him.

"So what about your team. You have been on site after some of these attacks. What have you got so far?"

"Well, nothing major as of yet. By the time we get there, the...what are we calling them now? Alphas? The alphas are dead so we have nothing direct about their behavior or triggers. Eyewitnesses report a high pitched shrieking that seems to trigger other alphas so there may be a sound trigger to the behavior. Terry is working on a field test to see if we can isolate an alpha and trigger the response with certain sounds but it is dangerous. Also, some eyewitnesses noted that some, but not all of the alphas had a strong urine smell. I have to imagine that they probably don't have control of their bladder and may even defecate in their clothing but I am not sure why some of them do it and not others."

"Could it be that some are further along in the disease process?"

"Yes, it could, but that would mean the advanced stage is fairly stable and the infected host doesn't die very quickly. Some of the pathology reports we received on dead alphas mentioned that the lesions were fairly well developed and showed some scarring of tissue consistent with slow-growing tumors. If that is the case then we can assume the alpha stage may last months before the host dies."

"Damn it, Jonas. This is a damn nightmare," said Brilli rubbing his face with his hands. "We need to come up with something."

Jonas nodded his head in agreement but said nothing as he had nothing to suggest. Thus far, there was no way to quickly determine if someone was infected and if so, if they were in the alpha state without being attacked. Even if you could screen out the alphas, there wasn't any treatments that worked reliably nor was there enough medications to treat the entire population.

"Our friend, Mustafa Moefi, over at WHO spoke with me yesterday. Those poor bastards are up to their knees in this. He says they have already lost a number of their field staff and the military is refusing to send anyone into the outbreak areas. He offered whatever information he has but from what is sounds like they have less than we do. Dr. Berr has stayed in touch with our overseas contacts and the situation is far worse than it is here with the exception of northern Europe and Australia."

"I know that they are having similar problems in Central and South America. Dr. Rua, at the Brazilian Health Ministry is having difficulty with outbreaks occurring throughout the urban areas especially in Rochinha. They have already enforced a quarantine zone and limited passage into the cities."

Just as Jonas had finished, Brilli's intercom buzzed. Brilli answered, "Yes, Meredith. What is it?"

"Dr. Brilli, you have an urgent call from Dr. Larsen at the Broward County Health Department on line four."

"Thank you, Meredith. I've got it."

"Anthony Brilli, here. Dr. Larsen, how can I help you?"

"Dr. Brilli, I'm glad I could get a hold of you. I think you will be interested in what I have for you," replied Dr. Larsen.

Jonas was getting up to leave but Brilli motioned to him to sit down. He reached over and put the conversation on speakerphone.

"What do you have?" asked Brilli.

"We have two of those alphas down at the county jail under sedation."

"You what?" exclaimed Jonas. "They're alive, right?"

"Dr. Larsen, Dr. Matthews is with me here. He is our head investigator."

"Good to meet you, Dr. Matthews."

"Same here," replied Jonas. "You're saying these alphas are alive?"

"Hell yes. One damn near killed one of our deputies when they came across it. I got the message you sent to health departments about wanting to be informed should we have anything like this."

"Yes, yes, we want to examine them while we can," replied Jonas obviously excited about the prospect of examining alive alpha.

"Well you better get down here in a hurry. I was told by the sheriff he isn't sure how much longer he can keep them from killing someone or themselves. You have to see it to believe it."

"I will send Dr. Matthews and his team right away. Can you keep them sedated until he gets there?" asked Brilli.

"We can try. Dr. Isaacs is on site from Broward County hospital. I know he has taken blood samples for testing. I will let them know you are on your way."

"We'll be there in a couple of hours. I am leaving right now," said Jonas.

"Thank you, Dr. Larsen. I'll be in contact with you." said Brill.

"Not a problem. Just get down here as soon as you can."

Brilli hung up the phone as Jonas was getting up from the chair.

"Finally, a break," said Brilli.

"Hopefully. Won't know until we get there. Have Meredith send me the phone number of Dr. Larsen and the Broward County sheriff's department. I need to get Terry to the helipad."

"I'll take care of it Jonas. Good Luck."

Within minutes, Jonas and his team were boarding the awaiting helicopter at the helipad and were en route to the airport. Having transferred to an awaiting private jet, the team arrived at the Fort Lauderdale-Hollywood International airport where a Chevy Suburban had been waiting. Jonas looked at his watch. The trip had taken a little over two hours and had gone seamlessly. *Not bad,* he thought. He hoped the patients (for lack of a better term) were still alive.

The group arrived at the Broward County main jail facility and were greeted by Sheriff Bob Culhane and Captain Angela Baku, director of the facility. Terry and Jonas met with the two as their field staff got the equipment out of the vehicles.

"Sheriff. Captain. I'm Dr. Matthews and this is my team member Dr. Andrews," said Jonas as he shook their hands. Terry, likewise, followed the gesture. The group entered the facility, walking down a long corridor peppered with guarded doors.

"We're glad you're here," said Sheriff Culhane. "To be honest with you, this type of thing is scarring the shit out of me."

"It's scarring all of us, Sheriff. We've been desperately trying to examine some of the severely infected for a while without success. Hopefully, your two alphas will give up some valuable information."

"You can't possibly be thinking about talking to them?" asked Sheriff Culhane.

"No. Of course not. What I mean is we hope to find clues as to what triggers the violent response, the overall effects of the disease on its victim, and so on."

"What was the situation that they were captured in?" asked Terry.

"We had several people call in with complaints of alpha activity down near the Hollywood Hills Plaza, it's a local water and food distribution site. Callers were saying there were a number of people just sitting around not moving. They thought they were on drugs or something. We dispatched a couple of cars to the scene but in the meantime, two of the malls security guards attempted to move some of them and that's when they were attacked. Both the guards were severely injured by them as well as a few of the volunteers working at the distribution center there. Our deputies arrived just as the attack began. It started with only three of these things but soon three others joined in. The deputies shot and killed all but these two. We found these two huddled against the building in two different locations. They were just sitting there not moving. Our deputies tased both of them and put them in restraints. When they recovered from the shock they both went insane and we had to tase them again. We managed to get them here and Captain Baku's guards got both of them into restraint chairs and placed them in the detox unit until we could figure out what to do with them."

"We had our staff physician sedate the two and brought Dr. Isaacs over to supervise their care since this is a little beyond what we are trained to deal with," added Capt. Baku. "Dr. Isaacs has helped us in the past with violent offenders, usually drug related."

The group stopped at a double set of doors with a guard post between them. Passing through the stop point, they finally stopped at a wide hallway lined with four glass walled cells on each side. There were two armed deputies standing across from two of the cells where a makeshift table had been placed with two chairs. Seeing the group, Dr. Isaacs got up slowly and walked toward Jonas and his team.

"You must be Dr. Matthews and Dr. Andrews," he said softly. "Keep your voices down. These creatures are very sensitive to noise."

"Gentlemen, this is Dr. Isaacs," said Capt. Baku. "Let me know if you need anything. I must be getting back to my duties."

"Yes, of course," replied Jonas. "Thank you for your assistance."

"No problem, just let me know as soon as possible when you can get those things out of my jail."

"Dr. Isaacs, I thought the alphas were sedated?" asked Terry.

"Alphas? Alphas, oh yes! That's what you call them don't you. I guess that is as good as anything. From what I have observed, they aren't human anymore. At least when they turn violent. And yes, Dr. Andrews, they are sedated but they seem to react to noise anyway."

"How are they doing right now?" asked Jonas.

"They are both quiet. I had to give them a lot more of the sedative than usual to get them calm. Right now they are just sitting there motionless except for the minor twitches that come and go. Some kind of seizure I would suspect."

Jonas moved to the closed cell. Peering through the glass, he turned and asked, "Do we know who they are?"

"I can help you with that," replied Sheriff Culhane. "That one there is Antoine Diaz, age 42. The woman in the other room is still unknown. We haven't notified anyone yet. Not sure we should."

"I understand," replied Jonas. "Can we go in?"

"You can but I'm not sure how safe it is," replied the sheriff.

Jonas looked at Dr. Isaacs, "Doctor?"

"Yes. Yes, it should be fine. I have both of them heavily sedated for now."

Jonas turned back toward his team, "Get the video equipment set up on this one and get it rolling. Terry, can you do your sound evaluation with them sedated?"

"I think so. We should get some type of micro-seizure activity we can observe if they respond to sounds," Terry replied.

"Okay then," said Jonas as he entered the room followed by Terry and one of the field assistants. The last to enter was the sheriff carrying a taser.

The male victim sat motionless in the restrain chair in the middle of the room. The stench of urine was over-powering, obviously heavy with urea.

"Damn, that's awful," whispered Terry.

"You should smell our squad car," said the sheriff quietly. "The damn thing pissed itself when it was tased. We gave up trying to get the smell out."

"It may be an important clue though," said Jonas. "We have observed that alphas don't seem to attack each other, at least normally. It may be that pheromones or other compounds in the urine are signals. Kind of like animals marking territories or each other."

"Doesn't help the smell," replied Terry.

Jonas looked at Terry and managed a smirk. "Let's get this done quick."

Terry set up a small portable case with a set of headphones plugged into it. Carefully placing the headphones over the alphas ears, he moved back to the small machine.

"What is that?" asked the sheriff.

"It's a portable sound emitter," said Jonas. "It can create a range of sounds from audible to outside our ability to hear. We want to see if we can use sound as a way to screen for those who have advanced infections."

Terry turned on the audiometer, he began the test at 80 hertz and slowly moved up the scale, watching intently for any indications of deep brain activity.

"I'm at 300 hertz now," said Terry. "You see anything yet, Jonas?"

"No, keep going."

Terry continued to slowly increase the frequency. Now passing 400 hertz.

"Wait a minute. Go back a bit," whispered Jonas. "More. More. There. See the twitch near the left eye?"

Terry looked closer at the alphas face. "Son of a bitch. It worked. There's a definite facial twitch that fires when I pass by 397 hertz."

"What does that mean?" asked Sheriff Culhane.

Jonas turned back toward the sheriff, "It means that the sound frequency is being picked up by this man's brain...deep brain actually... and causes a physical response. A seizure, though it's a very small seizure. This indicates there is damage to the deeper portions of the brain. Most likely caused by the infection."

"It's set on a low intensity. I'm surprised we're getting any response at this setting," said Terry still looking at the twitching. "I'll increase it a bit."

Terry increased the intensity of the sound wave. The twitching became more noticeable. Rapid eye movement became obvious as the intensity increased.

"That's enough, Terry," said Jonas. "We got what we needed. Let's try the next step. What note does that translate to?"

Terry looked through a chart searching for corresponding musical notes for select frequencies.

"It would be an F#," said Terry. Looking back at the assistant, he motioned for the small case they had brought. Opening it up, he selected a tuning fork that corresponded to F#. He removed the headphones from the alpha. Striking the tuning fork with his hand, he brought it close to its ear.

"There! See it? The same twitching as before."

Terry tried a few other tuning forks but none triggered the response except the F#. As he turned to put the tuning forks back into the case, he knocked the case onto the floor resulting in a loud clang. Instantly, the alpha's eyes opened and turned toward the four standing within a few feet of it. Its face instantly filled with rage, it lunged at them but was held back by the chair restraints. It's face contorted and it let out a hair-raising shriek as it continued to try to reach Jonas and the others. Within seconds of the male emitting its horrific shriek the female in the adjacent room regained consciousness and she too, began to shriek and try to escape from the restraints. Terry and the other three got out of the room quickly as the male became more agitated and struggled violently to free its hands. Arching its back and straining with all its might against the restraints, its right forearm snapped and the broken bones ripped through its flesh spraying blood all about. It continued to struggle, impervious to the damage already done. The group stood in front of the glass wall and watched in horror as the two creatures shrieked and contorted violently in front of them.

"Jesus, Christ! This is insane," said Sheriff Culhane, as he hit the alarm.

"What are you doing?" yelled Jonas over the alarm.

"Getting some more armed guards down here. If these things get loose, I'm going to have them dropped instantly."

"Sheriff, can you tase them again?"

"I guess. It should work again," replied the sheriff, a bit unnerved over the scene playing out before him.

Two guards armed with shotguns appeared behind the group. Sheriff Culhane opened the cell door and cautiously entered just inside the cell aiming his taser gun at the convulsing alpha. He fired. Within seconds the alpha went silent. Dr. Isaacs followed close behind the sheriff with more sedative as well as one of the armed guards. Isaacs approached the male, who was now silent. He reached for the I.V. catheter taped on its left forearm that was still intact. As he began to inject more propofol, the creature turned suddenly, ripping away its forearm and lunged to its left taking Isaacs by surprise. It managed to bite into his left upper arm. Isaacs let out a scream. His lab coat was thick enough to keep the creature from biting through the flesh, but damage was being done as his flesh was being crushed by the creature's tremendously strong bite. Jonas quickly entered the room to help but within seconds of Isaacs being attacked the guard shot the creature square in the chest with Isaacs arm still in its mouth. The creature was dead instantly. In the adjacent cell the female, being further aggravated by all of the noise, was going berserk. She too had broken her arm trying to escape the restraints as well as being cut severely by the leather straps as it crushed and tore tissue under the intense strain.

Captain Baku, who had returned quickly to the area, moved toward the second cell summoning the other guard to follow her.

"Shoot this thing," she ordered the guard. "Before it breaks loose."

The guard hesitated, looking at her then turning his head toward Jonas and the group.

"Hold on Captain," said Jonas. "You can't just kill it."

"The hell I can't," she replied. "I won't take the chance of this thing attacking anyone else in my facility. Unless you can cure this woman right now and return her to her happy former life, the only thing left to do is to put it out of its misery."

Jonas starred at her. *She was right*, he thought. He couldn't keep her here indefinitely. Eventually, she would either hurt someone or would die from the disease. There was no cure, especially for someone so far along in the disease process. There were no alternatives. He turned to Sheriff Culane.

"Sheriff"

"I'm inclined to agree with the Captain, doctor. I don't know what I would do with her. There are so many of them out there, we can't just fill up a prison with them."

Jonas looked around, uneasy about the decision being discussed. Finally, he turned back to Captain Baku. "You're call, Captain. Come on, let's get out of their way."

With that, Captain Baku nodded to the guard as they entered the second cell. Pulling the 9mm out of his holster, he fired two rounds point blank into the female's skull. She slumped forward, killed instantly by the rounds.

Jonas and his team stood there quietly. The one field assistant, a young woman named Elise fought to hold back her tears. The reality of this horrific disease struck home to everyone in the hallway. At what point did the infected victims stop being human? Where was the point of no return?

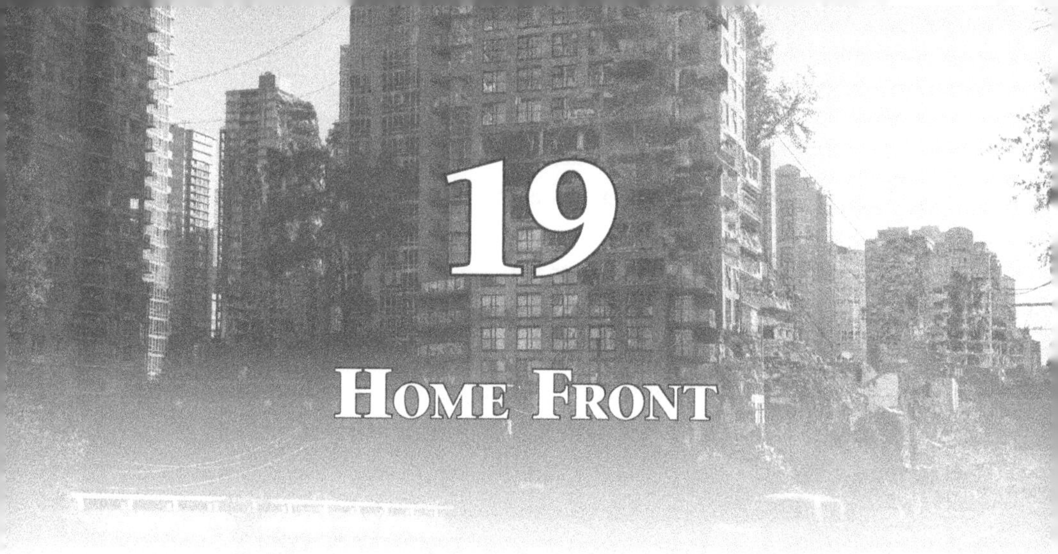

19

Home Front

"The Toxo-virus plague has brought the horrible reality of a global pandemic back to the modern world in a way never before imagined."

Dr. Malcolm Reese
Infectious Disease Research Institute

The flight back to Atlanta seemed longer this time. It had been fairly quiet as well. Terry had discussed the use of tuning forks for screening with Jonas but that was about it. Everyone on board was still reeling from the violent scenes they had witnessed at the jail earlier this afternoon. Soon they would be back at the Center and on their way home for the night. Jonas sat alone starring out the window as they came into Atlanta. He sensed that time had run out. That the silent killers that lurked within thousands, if not, millions of unsuspecting hosts were now coming out of the darkness in mass. *How would we stop this?* he wondered, already knowing the answer.

As the helicopter approached the Center, Jonas and the others could see that the area around the Center was lit with high intensity floodlights. There were numerous vehicles with flashers on throughout the compound.

"We're being asked to hold our position. There's a military helicopter in the airlift area ready to depart," said the pilot. "Looks like they're circling the wagons."

Terry looked at Jonas. "Brilli said that they may do this. Make the Center a safe zone if it got worse. It must be turning ugly quickly."

Jonas nodded and looked back out the window at the chaos below. All he could think about now was Ellie and if she was safe.

Moments later the helicopter was on the ground and the team was walking back toward the main building. All around the area, blockades and fencing was being placed at entry points to the Center's compound. Also, noted was the significant military presence. Jonas and his team were met by Brilli and two others just outside the main doors of CDC headquarters.

"Jonas. Good to see that you and your team made it back safe," said Brilli shaking both Jonas' and Terry's hands. "This is Dr. Lucille Walker from FEMA and Major Wallace Clark of the 878th engineer battalion of the Georgia National Guard. This is Dr. Andrews and Dr. Matthews. They are our lead team on this epidemic."

The group made their way to a conference room just inside the main building.

"We've recalled all essential personnel to the Center for safety concerns. Dr. Walker is overseeing the evacuation of uninfected citizens into designated safe zones with the help of the Guard," said Brilli.

"Tony," said Jonas. "I need to contact my wife before we go much further otherwise I won't be able to focus on a thing."

"Of course. Go ahead and make your call. Dr. Andrews, your wife called earlier and drove here. She is on site at your assigned quarters in the Emory Conference Center."

"Is it safe there?" Terry asked.

"As safe as we can make it," responded Dr. Walker. "All of the personnel have been screened for the disease. Of course, it's just a basic screening. Blood test take longer than we had to create these safe zones. We are anxious to learn what you discovered today. Dr. Brilli told us you got to evaluate two live victims."

Terry continued to talk to Brilli and the others as Jonas stepped out into the hallway to call Ellie. The phone rang several times. *Come on Ellie, answer the phone*, he thought to himself. Finally, the call was answered.

"Jonas?" she said quietly. "Oh, God. Jonas where are you?"

"Ellie, I'm at the Center. Where are you? Are you okay?"

"Jonas, I made it home, but the area has gone insane. There's screaming and gunshots everywhere," she said, her voice breaking several times. "I locked all the doors and windows and turned off the lights. I've barricaded myself in our bedroom upstairs. Jonas, they're right across the street. I can see them from our window. They're killing everyone. I don't know what to do."

"Ellie, stay calm and don't make a sound. Make sure your phone is on vibrate and the sound is off. I'm coming to get you. Go to the closet and get the shotgun out with the box of shells. It's loaded already. Use it if you have to."

"I've got it already."

"That's great. I'm going to hang up now but I will call you every few minutes until I get there, okay?"

Ellie began to break down crying.

"Ellie, you'll be okay. Just stay quiet and I will be there as fast as I can."

"Hurry Jonas. Please."

Jonas hung up and hurried back into the conference room.

"Tony, I need to go now. Ellie is trapped in our house. There are alphas on our street killing everyone. I have to go now."

"I'll get some men to escort you," said Major Clark, who then got on his handheld radio and issued orders.

By the time Jonas got to the front door of the building, three military Hummers were waiting for him. A soldier approached him.

"You're Dr. Matthews?"

"Yes," replied Jonas.

"I'm Lt. Avery. This way, sir. In the lead vehicle."

Jonas and his escort raced across town, the streets littered with abandoned vehicles. At one point, they saw an attack happening just off the freeway. There were flashers on site. *The police must have their hands full,* he thought. They couldn't stop to help. Ellie was priority, simply because she was Jonas' wife and he was the lead investigator of this pandemic. Jonas felt guilty about not stopping, but this once, with his wife in danger, he would take this benefit of his position. Just this once.

By the time, they got into the residential areas, it became clear that the suburbs had not been spared. Fires blazed throughout the neighborhoods, bodies littered the streets and lawns. Occasionally, the convoy would pass local police and fire trucks still trying to put out fires while fending off attackers, offering only several 50 caliber rounds from the mounted guns as they passed through taking down as many of the attackers as they could without stopping.

As the convoy turned down Jonas' street, they came to a halt. Several houses had small fires burning in them. About sixty yards from their position and very close to his house, there was a group of about ten to fifteen alphas running down fleeing residents, some of them children.

"Hurry, get down there," urged Jonas.

The convoy drove down the street opening fire on the attackers. The lead vehicle which Jonas was in, pulled up onto the lawn of his house near the front door. The other two took support positions on either side closer to the street. The 50 caliber and small arms gunfire shook the windows as more and more alphas appeared. Several residents who had been hiding began to run toward the convoy with their hands up, waving frantically for help. Many were brought down by the alphas, others were shot by accident as they crossed the lines of gunfire. Jonas had exited the vehicle and entered the house, yelling for Ellie. As he went up the staircase, he heard Ellie yelling for him as she appeared at the top of the stairs with the shotgun in her hand. They embraced.

"Come on. We have to get out of here," he yelled over the gunfire as he hurried down the staircase holding her hand.

By now the block was swarming with alphas who were now getting very close to the vehicles. Jonas and two soldiers helped Ellie and two other neighbors into the vehicles.

"Jonas! Jonas wait!"

Jonas turned around to see his neighbor, Jim and his family exiting their house. Jim had his handgun and stopped to fire on the attackers as Molina and the kids raced to the vehicles.

"Hurry! Come on, get in," yelled Lt. Avery.

Jonas turned to see where Jim was only to see an alpha come out from the back of the house and blindsided Jim as he was firing into the oncoming crowd.

"Jim!"

Jonas began to move toward his neighbor to help only to be grabbed by the lieutenant.

"It's too late."

Jim was on the ground with three alphas mercilessly beating him. Molina and the children screaming from the Hummer had to be restrained.

The gunner on the lead vehicle turned the 50 caliber toward Jim's attackers and began to open fire, but Jim was already dead.

"Come on," yelled Lt. Avery. "We have to get out of here."

The convoy turned around, still firing on the crowd, and quickly put distance between them and the enraged attackers, stopping only once to pick up three more survivors who had managed to escape the attacks.

Jonas held Ellie close as the convoy made its way back to the Center. The return trip was a stark reminder as to the seemingly hopeless situation that faced humanity. The night sky was lit by fires. The silence was pierced by gunfire and screams, and the horrible shrieking of alphas as they launched their relentless attacks.

Jonas turned to Lt. Avery.

"Thank you."

Avery looked back at Jonas and then looked down.

"I couldn't save my wife and son. They were visiting my parents in Savannah two weeks ago when the rage riots broke out there. I lost everyone," he said fighting to maintain composure. "I could, at least, save yours. Just find a way to end this nightmare."

Jonas nodded, unable to manage any words of comfort.

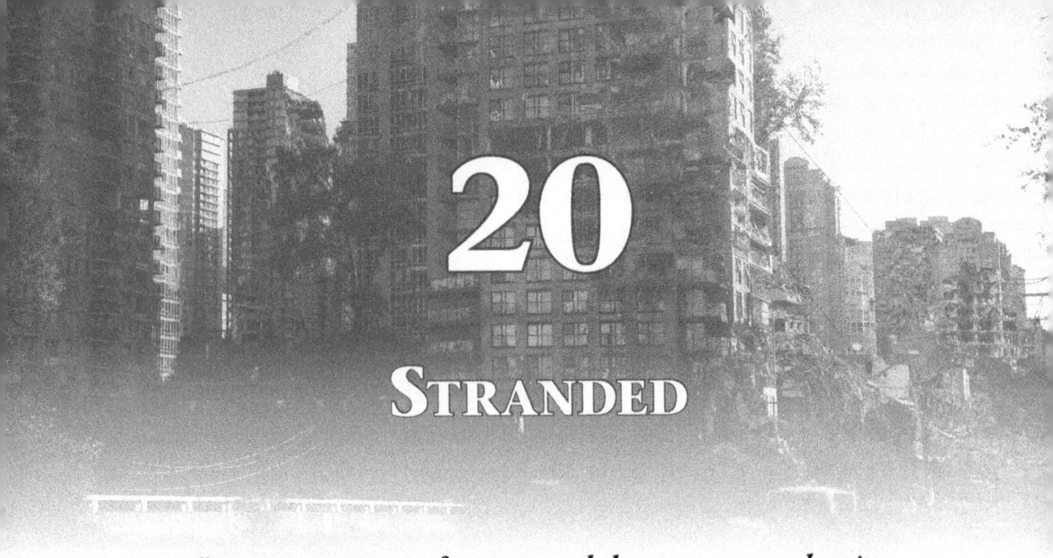

20

STRANDED

"Reports coming in from around the country are showing that the country's infrastructure is collapsing due to the increasing death toll and escalating violence. Public utilities such as electric, communications, water, and sanitation are at a virtual standstill in many areas of the country. The New York Stock Exchange remains closed for the third straight week as the economy continues to plummet into madness."

James Thompson
Associated Press

Angie had managed to get back into the elevator before the mob noticed her. Panicked, she pushed the 8th floor button on the panel and the elevator began to ascend. Moving between floors she could hear the occasional screaming of alphas. The lower three floors had a few alphas roaming through them, probably residents that turned. She stood with her back against the back wall of the elevator, clutching the 12 gauge shotgun in her hands, pointed toward the doors. Her foraging for food had been successful. There was a small diner on the ground floor of the building and no one had gotten to the cooler or supply room yet. She had grabbed a few pieces of fruit, some carrots, and some breakfast cereal. That's all she could get in her backpack. Outside the building a few survivors had tried to start an abandoned car, probably trying to get out of the downtown area to a safe zone, when they attracted the attention of a few alphas. Noise, any noise, brought them damn things running and screaming right to you. *They should have known better*, she thought. Once the alphas noticed them it didn't take long. They could outrun you and they had incredible strength. Against one, you stood a chance, but two or more, forget it. Just hope you had a gun to use on yourself before they got to you. She had managed to escape her attackers and fortunately, the infected were not very bright. They were animals so it was safe to assume they wouldn't remember how to use an elevator, she hoped.

The eighth floor light came on and the doors began to open. She pointed the shotgun forward, finger on the trigger.

"Don't shoot!" she yelled.

"It's Angie," said Marcus, who was positioned behind some furniture stacked in the hallway. "Stand down." He emerged from behind the furniture with Ryan.

"Girl, I thought you bought it," said Marcus throwing his arms around her. "We saw the commotion on the street below. Damn people ought to know better than to make that much noise. Oh man! You stink. Get rid of that thing!"

Angie untied a string that held onto a large piece of cut up men's slacks that had been taken off a dead alpha. It was saturated with old urine and it reeked of urea.

"Hey, don't be dissin' my invisible shield. This damn thing works and you know it."

"I know but you're beginning to smell like that all the time. Makes me sick," said Marcus.

They entered the large loft apartment which was the entire eighth floor of the small remodeled warehouse building. They had been lucky to find it last week. The building had been almost completely abandoned when the rage riots began downtown. Only a few tenants stayed behind. Some died, others not so lucky. Three others had joined them here on the eighth floor. Allan, a 37 year old graphic artist, Mrs. Jenkins, who lived with her husband in one of the third floor apartments before he was killed, and Ryan, who they had picked up along the way. Ryan may not have been on the right side of the law. When they had come across him, his car had died. They were driving when they noticed him waving them down. Keeping their distance and staying in the truck, they learned that he was on his way to a safe zone and he had guns. The guns sold them on him. He was in and Angie picked a Remington 870 tactical shotgun out of the abundant selection he had in his trunk. Angie had been in the Army and did one tour in Afghanistan back in 2010. She was familiar with guns and welcomed the newfound firepower instead of the metal baseball bat she carried around.

Marcus was Angie's younger brother and had worked as a handyman at a motel near their home. He and Angie had left their apartment on the north side of Atlanta when their neighborhood became overrun with the Toxovirus victims. They were heading toward the CDC safe zone. Angie had figured that they would have the largest military presence and maybe she could help, besides it was probably the safest zone to be in. That ended when they came across a large rage riot. Police were firing on the attackers but were losing ground. Marcus drove through the crowd without stopping until they reached the police line of defense, but by now, the vehicle was being pummeled by alphas trying to get to those inside. Ryan opened fire from inside the vehicle with an AK-47 automatic rifle and cleared the attackers off the Suburban. They opened the doors and made a run for the police. That was only two blocks from the building they took refuge in. They had been lucky enough to steal away as the alphas over-ran the police line moving down a narrow alley that kept them out of sight. Angie picked this building because it seemed defensible and being on the top floor with all the windows gave them an outstanding vantage point to the streets around them. In one of her earlier excursions out of the building she was able to locate the elevator and stairwell keys in the manager's office. That gave them control of the only access points to the loft. They'd be safe for a while. In the meantime, they had hung white sheets out the windows to hopefully alert any passing military convoy there were survivors inside. The alphas would not likely be attracted to them nor would any of them understand what it meant.

"We have to get serious about getting out of here," said Angie. "It's getting harder to find water. Everyone took it with them when they bugged out and I don't think the water department is going to restore water anytime soon."

"And go where? The CDC safe zone?" asked Allan. "It's still at least six miles from here and with hundreds of those zombie things running around out there it may as well be a hundred miles. We'll never get there. They swarm anything that moves and makes a sound."

"We have guns. Couldn't we shoot our way out," Mrs. Jenkins asked. "If we can get onto the freeway...."

"We'd be dead before we ever got near it. We only have so much ammunition and the gunfire will attract every crazy in the area. No. Its better we sit tight and hope that we can attract attention from a convoy or helicopter. They have patrols out there looking for survivors like us. We just have to be patient," said Ryan.

"Ryan is right Angie," said Marcus. "We still have electricity so we can keep the place lit at night, maybe get noticed. I can see if I can drain some water out of the lines in the basement. Should be enough in them to last a week or two."

Angie looked out the window facing east, toward the CDC. It was late in the day and smoke from burning buildings limited visibility to only a mile or two. Below in the street, she could see a small group of alphas eating a corpse.

"These things are starving. They're going to become more aggressive. I'm worried that they might figure out how to get in here."

"Angie, they're animals. They react, that's all they can do. They don't think anymore," said Marcus as he put his hand on her shoulder to comfort her. "I think we're okay for now. If it looks like they're becoming more of a threat, we'll get out of here."

"It it isn't too late," Angie replied looking down at the street scene below. "These things are attracted to noise right?"

"Yeah, of course," replied Ryan. "Why? What's on your mind?"

"We're gonna need a plan to get out of here. We can't just run out into the street and make a run for it. We have to have time to get a vehicle started, get it loaded, and make for the freeway, right?"

"Sure. What are you thinking, sis?" queried Marcus.

"We could use noise to draw them from us. Allow us enough time to get the vehicle and make for the freeway. I mean, once we get to the freeway...it's what three blocks from here...we should be able to make it to the safe zone, right? The military has to be using the freeways for their patrols. We could run across one on the way."

"Possibly," said Ryan. "But how are you going to draw them away?"

"There are more apartments about a block from here. One of those apartments has to have a stereo system, right? And we still have electricity so that isn't an issue."

"Hold on a minute, Sis. Someone has to move the speakers to the window and turn it on. Then what? There'll be dozens of those creatures in the streets the minute the music starts blasting. It's suicide. We'll come up with something else."

"That's not a bad idea," said Allan. "There's a parking garage just around the corner. If we could clear the zombies out of it, we could find a truck and get it started."

"Except we lose my sister in the attempt. No! It's not worth the risk."

"Look, I do this every day. I go out and scrounge around for food and supplies. So what's the difference? If I lay out my return route right, it shouldn't be a problem."

"No! I won't let you risk your life like that. What if they catch you? How are..." Marcus fought back.

Looking down at the creatures in the street, Angie looked back at him.

"We can't stay here. Every day we stay here there are more of them. When we first got here a couple of weeks ago we would see people driving by everyday but that has all but stopped. Now it's just those things and us. And what about us? How do we know if one of us is going to turn into one of those things? Then what? So far we've been lucky."

Angie looked back at Ryan and Mrs. Jenkins.

"We have to get to the Center. They'll have medicine...maybe even a vaccine. We won't survive here much longer."

Marcus put his forehead against Angie's and nodded.

"All right then, we start working on a plan to get out of here by the end of the week," said Ryan as he rubbed his hands together. "Mrs. Jenkins, what are we eating tonight?"

"Same as last night. Soup and cereal," she replied.

Angie looked off in the distance as the sky began to darken. Fires were burning in all directions. There was a heavy haze looming over the city making the air heavy and hard to breathe. She looked toward the northeast. She could see the glow of lights where the CDC safe zone should be. Occasionally, she could make out helicopter traffic in the area. Knowing that it was still there. That the lights were on and it was not very far away gave her hope. But between it and her group lie a sea of insanity, unforgiving and lethal. She bowed her head, *Please God, help us make it to safety,* she prayed silently to herself.

21

Numbers

"It's now a world without rules. Survival over morality. Us against them. The lines have never been more clear."

Gen. Ulrich Geissler
NATO Supreme Allied Commander, Europe

Winter had slowed the pandemic in much of the northern regions, however, the southern hemisphere was just entering the summer and the disease was progressing rapidly throughout the third world countries in South America and Africa. Despite the slowing of the Toxovirus plaque in the United States and Canada, the death toll was climbing as survivors were struggling to find food and water. Safe zone encampments were being decimated by the sub-zero temperatures from a harsh arctic air mass that hung over the Plains region. Further south, secondary diseases such as dysentery, food poisoning, and a host of viral illnesses claimed their victims as sanitary conditions at FEMA camps and militia camps declined. Just as Jonas had predicted the secondary fallout from this pandemic would be just as devastating as the actual disease itself.

The large conference room at the Center was buzzing with activity. Representatives from various government organizations had convened this meeting which was now in its second day. The fight against this Toxovirus pandemic was not going well and there was now, concern among the various government agencies that there may be no way to win the war.

Nobody really knew how far into the pandemic the world actually was. There was no set starting point. There didn't seem to be a "patient zero". The disease had a big head start and it did not draw any attention to itself like other diseases. Only now, when it had saturated the human population (as well as other animals), did it finally show itself. Jonas had been right. It was too late. There was no way to prevent it, to manage it, and no way to stop it. It was a stone cold killer in every sense.

"Are you sure those numbers are right?" asked Dr. Berr, director of the C.D.C.

"Yes, yes they are," replied Dr. Walker. "Of course, these are our best estimates and they may be higher but we aren't including more than we can verify, so yes, this is the blunt truth about our situation."

At this time there were six people in the room. Drs. Berr and Brilli from the C.D.C. and Walker from FEMA. Jonas' team was there as well except Terry who was doing interview exams with some of the people entering the safe zone.

Jonas sat in his chair, quiet, looking at the numbers being written on the board. Power point presentations had given way to chalkboards and dry erase markers in light of the rapidly changing situations arising throughout the country.

An estimated 22 million dead. Another 35 million injured, infected, or missing. The numbers were staggering and they did not appear to be leveling off. FEMA had projected another 8 million casualties by the end of the year and estimated that nearly 87.5 million would die either directly or indirectly from this pandemic by the end of the year. The global numbers were far worse rapidly approaching 500 million. The W.H.O. was predicting 78 million fatalities by the end of the year with no end in sight.

Jonas thought about it for minutes. Already they had reports of dysentery, typhoid fever, and other diseases that typically arise during pandemics. Most were the result of unsanitary conditions and then there were the countless bodies strewn about. The Toxovirus pandemic was one thing but the disruption of water, sewage treatment and garbage removal was creating another disaster. One that would surely double those numbers.

"Ben, do you have any numbers on the percentage of the population that is infected versus the possible conversion rate?" asked Jonas.

"Just rough estimates, Jonas," he replied. "Currently, we estimate approximately 107 million people are infected with the new Toxoplasma strain. We cannot be sure that all of them are also infected with the virus but it's safe to assume that they are since we have not found any cases were they weren't both present. Based on that, we're guessing a 42% conversion to alpha state rate. So approximately 45 million infected people will convert to alpha state, but that assumes the rate of new cases levels off which I haven't seen any indication it will."

"I understand. So we have a possible 45 million more alphas out there that will kill at least one other person, infected or not. If I assume half of the 45 million will represent the collateral deaths, then is it safe for us to assume that approximately another 20 million people will die along with the 45 million alphas as well as millions of infected that die from the disease itself."

"That's being conservative but yes, you could assume that," Ben replied.

"Christ, were approaching half the U.S. population. Is that what we are saying here? Dr. Berr said, obviously distressed at the figures being discussed. "Jonas, what do you have to say?"

"I think we'll hit that number easily," Jonas replied to the shock of everyone in the room. "We already have food shortages and failing water supplies. Add to that the unsanitary conditions being created by all the dead bodies, lack of waste treatment, runaway pollution, and now, we're in winter now with few areas in the north having the ability to heat homes. Hell, most of them are living in tents or shacks in the surrounding parks and woods. They're as good as dead."

Jonas got up and walked around the room stopping at the window he paused for a moment.

"We'll be lucky if we get through this with a third of our population intact. Also, I remind you that this is not going away. The Toxovirus disease is going to keep killing until we find a way to kill it. The oocysts are everywhere and highly infective. No, the deaths will slow down but they won't stop."

"Where are we at on treatments?" asked Brilli. "The information coming across my desk shows we are running low on the current meds.

"I can answer that," said Walter leaning forward. "The current protocol of pyrimethamine and sulfadiazine, as you are aware, is effective only if given early in the course of the disease. Most of you have already been on it. It is more difficult to treat brain lesions with it since it does not pass the blood-brain barrier as efficiently as we would like and I am not sure we should treat it. Our recent attempts to treat alphas were disastrous to say the least. Those we treated successfully either committed suicide or went entirely insane owing to the horrific memories of what they did while in the rage influence. Also, like you have mentioned, we are running out of it. FEMA has stepped in and begun rationing the meds according to critical need so we must pick and choose who gets the drugs until supplies can be restored."

"How soon will that be?" asked Dr. Berr.

"We have several pharmaceutical companies working to produce both of those drugs as well as a few others that we are running out of but it's not likely they can produce enough to treat the numbers we are talking about here," replied Dr. Walker.

"Also, the combination is only effective in about 65% of the cases. There was some cross-over resistance when T. gondii mutated. There are a few other possibilities we are looking at right now. The anti-malarial drug, JPC-2056 had just entered clinical trials for treatment of malaria at the onset of this pandemic. It showed remarkable effectiveness against Toxoplasmosis, reducing the number of organisms in just a few days. It has been named Apicocidin and I believe it has been rushed into production with the help of the FDA. Early clinical trials showed it to be well tolerated with less side effects than the current protocol," answered Walter.

"Still, without safety studies..." questioned Dr. Berr.

"What?" snapped Jonas. "What's the alternative? Let the parasite run rampant unchecked. Let millions of people turn into those creatures? Screw the safety studies. We don't have many things that can kill this organism and if this Apicocidin can be made available, I'll be the first to take it."

"I agree," added Dr. Walker. "The benefits outweigh the risks under the present circumstances. I have been informed that the first shipment of the drug, albeit a small amount, will be sent by the middle of next month."

"I must caution you. It's only one drug and it's untried against this new form of Toxoplasma. We don't know how it will perform. Also, it is not effective against the latent stage of the disease. Once the organism encysts, it is very difficult to treat it. So it will require multiple rounds of treatment to be effective," added Walter.

"Well we are in that boat now with the current drugs, right? At least this give us another option and we know there is not vaccine on the horizon. But to be honest with all of you, it may not even put a dent in this pandemic. It may be that we have to let the disease run its course before we can actually do anything."

"Jonas, do you really think that?" asked Brilli, who was surprised by the comment.

"I agree," said Walter. "This is like showing up for a four alarm fire with a gallon of water. Too little, too late. I agree with Jonas. This disease will have to burn itself out a bit before we can make any headway. We don't have millions of doses of anything to begin treatments. We are already having problems with our quarantine zones. Didn't the safe zone at Fort Benning recently collapse because of undetected alphas making it inside?

Dr. Berr, stunned at Jonas' pessimism, "surely we have some course of action, Dr. Matthews. I cannot....."

Dr. Walker's assistant entered the room quickly. Apologizing for the intrusion, she handed Dr. Walker a report that had just arrived. As Walker read the report, Jonas could see her losing composure. He walked over to her.

"Are you okay?" he asked, putting his hand on her shoulder.

Without looking up, she handed him the report. He read it and gave it back to her.

"It seems the Chinese government has already come to the conclusion we are coming to right now," he said as he took a deep breath. "They just detonated two low yield nuclear devices in the heavily infected cities of Xi'an and Wuhan. Apparently, they have decided to wipe the slate clean."

The room was quite for several moments.

"That's where we are at, people," said Jonas in a subdued voice. "Whether we choose to admit it or not, we're getting our asses kicked and if we don't come up a course of action quick, we'll be lighting up our cities next."

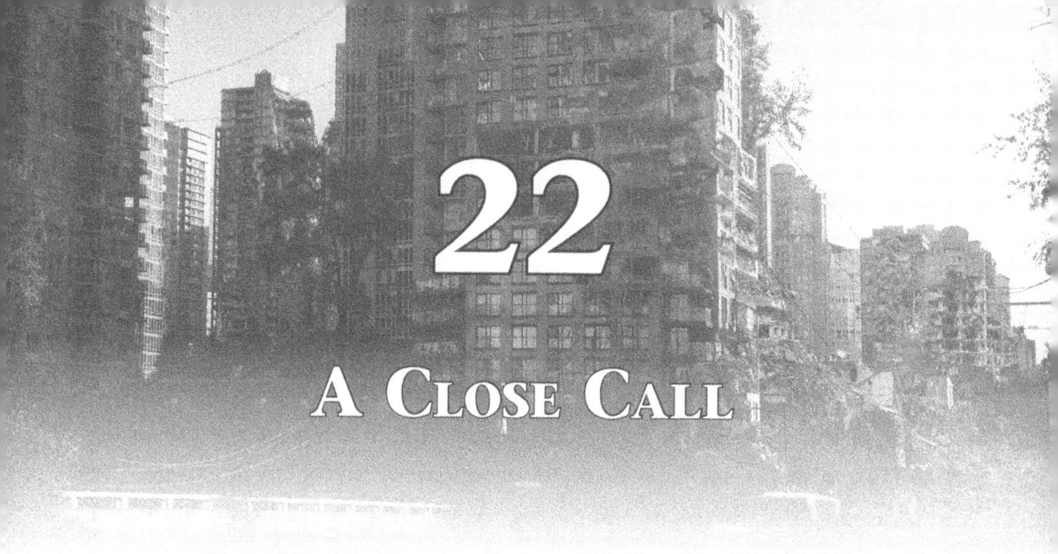

22

A Close Call

"In light of declining access to antibiotics to treat this disease, we have been forced to use anti-inflammatories and antidepressants to delay the onset of more serious symptoms. It is all we can recommend until such time when stocks are replenished and/or newer treatments are discovered."

Dr. Rene' St. Clair
Pasteur Institute, Paris, France

Jonas walked out the main doors and sat down on a bench along the mezzanine near the pond. Overhead, military helicopters flew by reminding him that the once quiet C.D.C. complex was now a military base of operations. He could hear the faint sound of gunfire in the distance. The sky was hazy due to the numerous fires still blazing uncontrolled throughout the Atlanta metropolitan area. He shook his head. This was all so surreal.

His cell phone rang snapping him out of the moment. FEMA had set up a dedicated cell phone communications system nearby which allowed all of the emergency teams to communicate with each other since the local communication systems were unreliable or not operating. He looked at the screen. It was a call from Terry at the safe zone encampment at Candler Field.

"Hey Terry, this is Jonas," he said.

"Jonas, it's me, Ellen."

"Ellen? How did you get Terry's phone? Where are you?"

"Terry's right here. We're at Candler Field. I talked him into letting me come along to do some photography. I thought I might photo-document what is going on here. Terry managed to get me a laptop from the FEMA supply tent and somehow managed to get a 35mm camera from someone."

"Well, I can't tell you I am okay with this. It's very dangerous out there and I'm surprised Terry let you go with him."

"He didn't have much of a choice and it's better than sitting around packing lunches or watching kids. Jonas, this is a chance for me to do something valuable. Who is documenting all of this? Here, I can get the stories and the photos in one outing. Also, there are soldiers everywhere here so I am fairly safe, so there is nothing to worry about. Terry already told me that if there is any problem we are out of here right away."

Jonas was quiet for a moment. "I am still not comfortable about it."

"Jonas, you're not going to talk me out of this so give it up. I need to do this, besides I'm already here."

"Alright. But I wish you'd give me a head's up when you decide to do something like this."

"I tried, but you were in a meeting."

"You be careful. Is Terry with you?"

"Yes, he's right here."

There was a moment of silence as Ellie summoned Terry to the phone. Jonas could hear some conversation in the background. He couldn't make out what was being said but judging from the tone it wasn't good.

"Hello. Jonas are you there?" said Terry.

"Terry. I'm holding you responsible for Ellie's safety," said Jonas a bit angered that his friend would put his wife in such a dangerous situation.

"Jonas, by the time she came to me and told me she was going with us, she had already got military and FEMA clearance. I was basically told I was taking her. They did assign us a guard so that makes us feel better. Besides, you know her, she wasn't taking no for an answer."

"What are you learning out there?"

"Basically more details about what we already know. There are varying degrees of alpha conversions. Some don't go all the way to the violent stage. They mostly become catatonic unless provoked. I haven't got any information showing that children under the age of 14-16 convert to alphas, so if they get infected they most likely die of the lesions or recover.

I am troubled by some information that seems to indicate that the alphas are becoming more violent and more organized in their attacks. Almost pack-like. I believe this is because of the lack of food. Hunger is driving the behavior changes and they are feeding on those they attack almost exclusively."

"That is disturbing. The last thing we need is for these things to organize. I didn't think the severity of the lesions would allow any type of rational behavior."

"I don't have the answer, Jonas. I can only assume that survival behaviors are kicking in under the stress and it's allowing some kind of social ordering within the alphas."

"We'll need to get that info to the others quickly."

"I agree," replied Terry. "By the way, Ellie was responsible for a new diagnostic for the disease."

"How so?"

"She was showing me some of the pictures that she had taken of the refugees here at the encampment. She complained that she was getting white eye-shine instead of red and couldn't explain it. I looked at the photos and it dawned on me that this may be leukocoria which could be caused by toxoplasmosis. I began to go through the camp looking at as many eyes as I could and I was shocked by the number of positives there were. Leukocoria would indicate a more advanced state of infection so it seems that we have another way of determining if a person is infected to the point of being a risk to convert."

"How did that correlate with the tuning fork test?"

"That's the alarming part. It seems that there were three times more people exhibiting leukocoria than tested positive with the tuning fork. That would explain why so many people still convert after entering the safe zones. We're simply missing a large number of severely infected people and allowing them into the encampments."

"Like foxes in a chicken coop."

"Exactly," replied Terry. "If Ellie hadn't been taking those pictures, we may have never noticed."

"Well now she'll be hard to live with," Jonas said with a small chuckle. "Terry, is everything okay over there? I heard a conversation in the background earlier. It sounded serious."

"Just a small problem with some unhappy refugees here in the camp. A few of them are stirring up trouble. They want to move into the Center area and are demanding they be moved now. Walker has had people over here warning them not to attempt to enter the CDC zone. Can't blame them really. It's overcrowded here and there's one or two alpha attacks daily. The military has it fairly well controlled but still, if they decide to over-run the compound in mass. Well the military has orders to shoot anyone crossing over the boundary markers."

"Sounds serious enough. What about the team and Ellie?"

"Just before Ellie called we were being told to pack up and get ready to return to the Center. It seems they don't want to take any chances."

"Good. It's just as well. I doubt if we will get much more info than we already have."

"Right. Okay, we're going to get out of here. I'll see you when we get back."

Jonas sat there on the bench for a while. He really did not want to go back to the meeting. It really wasn't going anywhere and he already had an idea of what the outcome of today's conference would be. Nothing. Agencies working against each other. No one willing to step up and take the lead. He had been here before. The field of global health was waist deep in politics. That is why so many previous situations got out of hand. No one wanted to get dirty especially on this one. Meanwhile, lives were lost and the infected population grew larger.

The sun began to set when Jonas heard a voice behind him.

"There you are," said Donaldson. "We've got people running around looking for you."

Donaldson spoke into his two way radio. "Found him. We're at the circle fountain south of the building. He's okay."

"Copy that. We're sending an escort to your location as a precaution," said the voice on the other end of the two-way.

"Understand. We'll wait here," replied Donaldson.

"Can't take chances like this. We've been lucky so far."

Jonas looked at Donaldson and smiled. "I suppose. I'm not use to having a chauffeur follow me around when I'm at work."

"You'll need to get used to it, especially if you aren't going to wear your sidearm you were issued. Hell, Jonas. You're just begging for it."

"No, you're right. I just keep thinking everything is okay. That it's not as bad as we think. I know better. I just forgot."

The military had issued a sidearm to everyone on the campus that had training as well as making it mandatory for those moving about in the open to have an escort. It was precautionary. Jonas thought about how excited, and serious, Ellie reacted when she received her M-9. Ellie was well-schooled on firearms, he father had seen to that. Growing up on their horse farm in South Carolina, her and her brothers would often go hunting together. She also carried a Ruger LCP in her bag for protection. Jonas had far less training but had learned to shoot at the gun range they both went to every so often. He had kept his pistol in the nightstand drawer next to the bed. Still, he was uncomfortable with the thought of having to wear a sidearm. It wasn't so much that guns made him uneasy, but rather the acknowledgement that they were needed.

"So what was on your mind that you needed to get away?" asked Donaldson.

"Just a bit overwhelmed at the moment. I wanted to get somewhere by myself and not think about anything for a while."

"I can understand that. This has been a lot to take in, of late."

Jonas looked at Donaldson.

"What?" said Donaldson puzzled by Jonas' expression.

"I just can't help but wonder how long your agency knew what was going on and why you didn't come to us before it got out of hand."

"Fair question," Donaldson replied. "I was under orders to keep quiet… or else. The orders came down from Tom Hutchinson to keep the problem under wraps. I suppose because we weren't sure we created the problem or if it was unleashed by another program. There were at least three countries that we know of that had similar experiments running. We weren't aware our lab had been breached and even when it became known, we were sure the virus couldn't effect the parasite so everything was put under wraps until we could get more intel. Unfortunately, we didn't know that nature was setting us up. By the time we figured it out it was too late."

"So why haven't we seen this Hutchinson person at our meetings? It seems he should be held somewhat responsible for this shit-storm."

"He's dead. Poetic justice if you ask me. He was killed in a rage riot outside of Bethesda back in August."

"So who's in charge now?"

"Me. I inherited this mess. Now, I'm just trying to do what I can to bring all of this to an end," Donaldson said looking over his shoulder. "Do you smell that? What is that?"

The hair on the back of Jonas' neck stood up as the familiar stench reached his nose.

"Shit," he whispered. "That's alpha stench. There must be one nearby… close."

Just as Jonas said that, they both saw a male figure moving around the back end of the pond about fifty yards away. It hadn't seen them yet. They were partially veiled by some small ornamental trees.

"Stay quiet," whispered Jonas. "It hasn't seen us yet."

Donaldson slowly reached under his jacket and pulled out his revolver. Jonas motioned for the two-way radio. Turning down the volume. Jonas pressed the speak button.

"This is Dr. Matthews. This is an emergency. There is an alpha at the south pond. Where's our escort?"

A few seconds passed and a whispered voice came on the two-way.

"We're behind you, Dr. along the west wall. We see you. Where is the alpha?

Jonas lifted his head to look over the back of the bench, as did Donaldson. The alpha had stopped along the walkway. Turning its head side to side and sniffing. It made a repeated grunting sound, almost ape-like. Within seconds, three more alphas appeared from the tree line near the Power House and joined the other alpha.

"They're on the west walkway, along the pond about 50 yards from us," Jonas whispered into the radio.

"Got em."

The pack of alphas hadn't moved. They were looking around. Occasionally, one would look in their direction. The alphas eyes glowed white with light reflected from the landscaping lights. Two more appeared near the pack.

"Son of a bitch," whispered Donaldson. "They're hunting. They must have heard us talking and were attracted to us."

Jonas didn't respond but he knew Donaldson was right. They were being hunted by creatures that weren't supposed to be able to hunt. The reports were right. The alphas, for whatever reason, were beginning to behave like a pack when looking for food. They obviously communicate with each other somehow. Other than them looking like humans, there was little else that was human-like. They walked spastically, stopping often and remaining motionless for minutes at a time. They were eerily quiet. As far as Jonas could tell the six alphas in front of them were four males and two females of different ages. It really didn't matter what age or sex as any one of them could easily kill an uninfected human.

"They're moving this way," said Donaldson. "We have to get out of here."

Jonas nodded and spoke into the radio. "We have to move. Any ideas?"

The area between them and the soldiers behind them was wide open. If they tried to make it to the soldiers it was possible they would be run down. If they stayed where they were, they would not stand a chance. They had to move.

"Give us a minute, Dr. We have backup arriving now," whispered the voice on the other end of the radio.

The alpha pack was now within thirty yards of their position.

"We don't have a minute. We have to move now," replied Jonas.

At that moment, one of the arriving soldiers had a call come in on their two-way which was at full volume. Jonas could hear it clearly. Both he and Donaldson turned their heads toward the pack who obviously heard it too. All of them began to screech wildly and began to run toward the sound.

"Go! Go! Go! Let's get out of here!" yelled Donaldson as he grabbed Jonas' arm and started to run toward the soldiers.

The soldiers moved quickly toward the two opening fire on the pack that was closing the distance quickly. Donaldson was struck from behind by the lead alpha and fell, dropping his revolver. Jonas stopped and went back to help him. Looking up he saw the other alpha already upon them. He grabbed Donaldson's revolver and fired at it hitting it in the head on the third shot. Turning back toward Donaldson, Jonas shot the alpha on Donaldson. Unfazed by the two rounds in it, the alpha continued the attack. Jonas jumped on top of the alpha and fought to pull it off of Donaldson. Plunging his fingers in to the alphas eye sockets, the alpha screamed and released his hold, allowing Jonas to throw it aside. Gunfire from a nearby soldier quickly finished it. By now, two other alphas had been killed but the other two had made it to the soldiers killing one of them. Finally, the final two alphas lay motionless next to a severely injured soldier.

Jonas, kneeling on the ground next to Donaldson, looked up at the soldier who had killed the alpha that attacked them.

"Thanks."

"Don't mention it, sir. Happy to help," replied the soldier with little emotion. He spoke in to his two-way radio. "Lt. Baylor reporting. Threat is neutralized. Six alphas. We have two injured and one dead here. Requesting medical team on site asap."

"Roger that. Medical is on its way." replied the voice on the radio.

Donaldson lay on the ground motionless but alive. The attack was short but brutal. He had a separated shoulder, multiple head wounds, and a large gash at the base of his neck where the alpha had bit into him. Despite all that, Jonas was sure he would survive. Off in the distance, the sound of gunfire and sirens broke through the background sounds of the night.

"That's coming from Chandler Park," said Jonas as he looked in the direction of the gunfire.

"Yes sir," replied Lt. Baylor. "They must have their hands full over there."

Jonas knew what he was talking about. A similar scenario was playing out at the safe zone camp that Ellie had been at only hours ago. He shuddered to think of the violence he had just experienced being thrust upon the families interned there.

The medical unit had arrived and Donaldson was being tended to when he began to regain consciousness.

"Doctor, the patient is asking for you," said the EMT from the back of the truck.

Jonas stepped up into the ambulance and knelt next to Donaldson who managed a smile when he saw Jonas.

"Thanks. You saved my ass," he said weakly.

"Don't mention it," replied Jonas. "Just keep quiet. They're getting you over to the hospital. You'll be okay."

Donaldson, nodded, his eyes closing. He was obviously in a lot of pain.

"You going with us, doctor?" asked the EMT.

"No, no I'm okay," he replied.

Stepping out of the ambulance, Jonas walked over to Lt. Baylor who was supervising the loading of the alpha bodies into the back of a truck.

"Lt. can you get me a ride to the housing center?"

"Right away, doctor," he replied.

Lt. Baylor spoke into his two-way and within minutes Jonas was on his way back to his room…back to Ellie and a hot shower. His body was now beginning to ache from the struggle with the alpha he had pulled off of Donaldson and fatigue was setting in. All he wanted to do now was to sleep but he knew that Ellie would want to know what had happened. Still, realizing how close he had come to being killed this night, it was a far better alternative.

Jonas and his escort were halfway to the living quarters when the distant gunfire coming from Chandler Park intensified. Suddenly, the night sky was illuminated by several flares that had been shot up. At the same time, sirens began to go off.

"There's been a perimeter breach at Chandler," said the soldier next to Jonas who replied back on this two-way radio. "We're re-routing now."

"Wait a minute," Jonas said, somewhat confused over the situation. "What's going on? Where are we going?"

"Sir, we've been ordered to bring all personnel to the main building for protection. Containment at Chandler Park is failing and there are multiple perimeter breaches by refugees and alphas."

"My wife is back at the residential quarters. I want you to take me there now," demanded Jonas.

"I can't do that, sir. I have to bring you in, now. If it helps you any, additional units have been deployed at the living quarters to protect the families, sir. They have priority. Your wife will be safe."

Jonas, realizing the futility of arguing, nodded his head and looked off toward the Arlen Specter building now lit up by flares and portable lights. The sirens became louder as they neared the center.

Those sirens have got to be making the situation worse, he thought. Sound, especially loud sounds drove alphas crazy and increased the conversion of those infected but at the edge of turning into an alpha.

"Who's in charge of those sirens?" Jonas asked the soldier.

"That would be Major Hopkins command. He's in charge of the defensive deployment."

"Where is he? Can you get ahold of him?"

The soldier nodded and spoke into his two-way.

"He's at the main ground post, sir. They've got their hands full. They're under attack."

"Tell them to turn off the sirens. They're attracting the alphas to the area."

"Yes, sir," replied the soldier as he began to speak on his two-way radio, attempting to reach the post.

"Sir, I can't make contact with the post. Communications just went down."

"Get me to the command center, quickly," ordered Jonas.

The vehicle sped across the mall toward the back lobby of the main building.

Jonas jumped out of the vehicle and ran inside. The command center had been set up on the top floor of the building. There, the various civil and military agencies had taken refuge behind the barricades that surrounded the CDC safe zone. Jonas entered the large command center room.

"Jonas, thank God your safe!"

Jonas looked toward the person who had said that. It was Dr. Rice of Homeland Security.

"We've got to turn off the sirens. Now!" said Jonas urgently.

Rice turned to the communications console, "Have them turn off the sirens right now."

Jonas moved toward the window that faced the front of the building. From this vantage point he could see the gunfire coming from several points along the barricades as well as Chandler Park. The sirens fell silent.

"How bad is it?" he asked, turning toward Dr. Rice.

"We're losing Chandler but we should be able to contain this shortly."

"Don't bet on it," Jonas said sarcastically. "Where is Major Hopkins?"

"He's dead. Alphas over-ran his post near the front gate. Major Ames of the Georgia National Guard has taken command of all troops until more troops arrive from Fort McPherson," replied Dr. Rice as she motioned for Major Ames to come over. "Major Ames, this is Dr. Matthews."

"Doctor," said Ames shaking Jonas' hand. "I heard you had an interesting evening."

Jonas went silent, still shaking the Majors hand. He was stunned by such a casual comment in light of the shit-storm unfolding outside the window they were standing next to. Dismissing the comment, he looked back at Dr. Rice.

"We may have a bigger problem," he said. "Do we have any way of seeing the area…say four or five miles around this complex?"

"We have a couple of reconnaissance drones in the air we can use," replied Major Ames.

"I need to see the area around the complex as quickly as possible," said Jonas.

Ames stepped away and spoke to a soldier at another console.

"We have a drone nearby that will circle the complex at a distance of five miles. Is that what you need?" said Ames.

"That should do," replied Jonas.

"The video feed will be on this monitor." said Major Ames assistant, pointing to a large flat screen monitor hung above the communications console.

A couple of minutes later the drone was in position and video was being displayed on the monitor using its night vision camera.

"Oh my God," exclaimed Dr. Rice as she looked at the screen.

The room fell silent. On the screen, images of thousands of enraged alphas were racing toward the complex, obviously attracted to the sirens just as Jonas had feared.

"They're all around us," said Ames in a subdued voice.

"It was the damn sirens. What a stupid thing to do. Didn't anybody think to ask us before setting them up? We've just called every alpha within ten miles to come and see what all the noise is about."

"But the sirens are off now. Won't they stop?" asked Ames.

"Normally, maybe, but they're close enough to hear all the gunfire so they'll just keep coming."

Ames, looking at the monitor. "There are thousands of them. We won't be able to stop them."

Jonas, looking at the monitor, suddenly had an idea. A crazy idea at that but maybe…just maybe.

"Where's the civil defense director?" he asked loudly.

"He is in the city command center across the hall.

"Get him, quick!" said Jonas.

Within seconds the civil defense director of Atlanta came into the room.

"I'm Bob Tullings what do you need?"

"Bob, can you activate the civil defense sirens from here?" asked Jonas.

"Yes. We have the controls in our center across the hall."

"Can you activate sirens in certain sections of the city?"

"Yes. The sirens are set up in groups so we can warn specific areas of the city if needed. Why?"

Jonas looked out the window and then turned back toward him. Looking at Ames and Rice. "We need to lead them away from here with a bigger distraction."

"You think that will work?" asked Major Ames.

"It's all we got," Jonas replied. "Bob, I need you to activate all of the downtown warning sirens including those in the metro area. If possible kill any sirens within two miles of our position. Do you understand what I am saying?"

"Absolutely. I'm on it." replied Bob as he made his way across the hall.

Jonas stood with Ames and Rice, looking out the window.

"We're still going to take a hit, major. Can your troops stop them?"

"If we can turn back most of the alphas on their way here, we should be able to stop any locals that make it here."

"I hope you're right, major. Otherwise we are going to lose everyone in Chandler and most of us as well."

Within minutes the wailing of the warning sirens downtown could be heard. More and more sirens went off, except those near the CDC safe zone. Those in the command center gathered around the monitor watching intently to see if the advancing alphas would take the bait. Seconds passed that seemed like an eternity. "There!" shouted Rice. "They're stopping!"

Everyone looked at the monitor. Dr. Rice was right. The alphas had stopped. Most moving about confused. Caught between the sounds of the sirens and the gunfire. The sirens won. The room erupted in cheers as the video feed showed the alphas were moving away from the CDC complex toward the sirens, but still the alphas closest to the complex, and the gunfire, were not deterred.

"Major, let's hope your troops can stop the rest," said Jonas, patting Ames on the shoulder as he looked around for a chair to sit in.

"They will," he replied as he began to call in orders to his field commanders which included arming the refugees at Chandler Park.

Within minutes of giving the commands, the wave of alphas attacked. Chandler Park erupted in a massive barrage of gunfire as it was outside the barricades. With only the two fenced barriers standing between the alpha horde and the camp defenders, they were the most vulnerable. Within the camp, those that could not fire a weapon were moved to the center of the camp for protection. Soldiers and civilians stood side by side firing upon the alphas as they breached the inner fence. The CDC complex itself, better fortified, was fighting off the alpha attack in every direction. Occasionally breaches would occur but any alpha that got through was quickly dispatched by the inner line of defense.

The attack began around nine-thirty in the evening and continued through the early morning hours. Just before sunrise, the gunfire had ceased for the most part. Those defending their posts, now battling fatigue, continued to watch for signs of another attack. It was quiet now. The silence broken only by the occasional sound of gunfire in the distance. The rising sun revealed the extent of the carnage. Hundreds of bodies both alphas and uninfected lie scattered around the compound, some still not dead. Already fatigued, medical teams began to wade through the bodies to attend to the wounded refugees and soldiers, while soldiers walked among the bodies euthanizing wounded alphas. Sometimes, it was impossible to tell the difference.

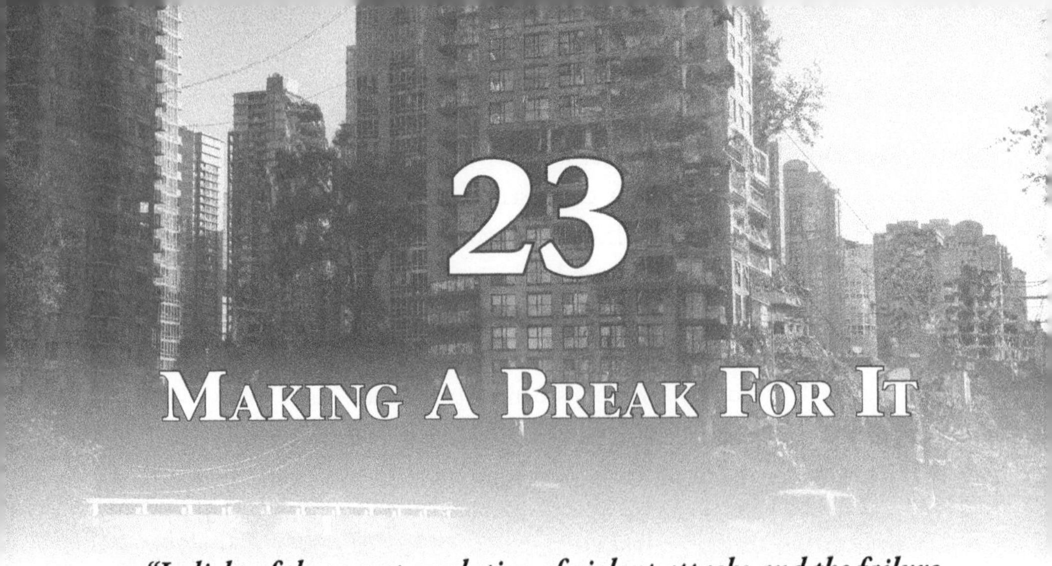

23

Making A Break For It

"In light of the recent escalation of violent attacks and the failure of medical teams to slow the progress of this horrific disease, we are ordering the extermination of all infected individuals that are in the alpha state. Other non-alpha infected individuals will be treated until such time that they are stabilized or determined to be too far gone to be rehabilitated, in which case, they too will be euthanized."

Dr. Marilyn Rice
Chief Medical Officer, Homeland Security

Angie slowly made her way down an alley moving north away from the building her and the others had been holed up in. She had passed by a few newly dead bodies of alphas. Some had been fed upon, but no live alphas so far. The others in her group were making their way to the parking garage where Ryan had located a vehicle he could start once they heard the music or time was up. They hadn't worked out all the details of the escape but last night's outbreak of gunfire, flares, and sirens coming from the direction of the C.D.C. safe-zone forced them to make the move now while most of the infected were out of the area. They had watched from their window as large numbers of alphas came out into the open and began to move quickly toward the sound of sirens coming from the safe-zone. All of them were stunned by the number of alphas in their area. *This was just the break we needed,* Angie thought to herself. *At least it would improve the odds of getting out of here alive.* They had heard the civil defense sirens go off throughout the downtown area shortly after the initial sirens fell silent and knew the defenders were trying to lure them away from the compound so they knew it wouldn't be long until the alphas began to move back into the area in search of food. The consensus of the group was to move first thing in the morning.

Angie reached the entrance to the building she had selected a few days prior. It was a smaller four story building with two storefronts at street level and apartments on the upper floors. It still had electrical service but the elevator was not working. She entered the building and quietly made her way up the stairway to the third floor. She stopped for a moment and listened, trying to detect any noise that may indicate the presence of an alpha. It was silent, but that didn't mean much. Alphas had a tendency to go into a type of catatonic state when not stimulated. This made them dangerous as one could walk right up to an alpha without realizing it and then it was too late. That is why Angie tied the alpha urine-soaked pants around her neck when she went out. Something in the urine, probably a hormone, prevented them from attacking each other. If she accidentally stumbled upon one, the odds were in her favor of being unnoticed.

She slowly opened the door to apartment 3C holding her breath as the door creaked. She had set up everything on her previous trip. She merely had to open the windows in front of the speakers, turn on the stereo, and get the hell out of there. The volume was set to the maximum and the CD was loaded. Angie had selected Guns and Roses, *Appetite For Destruction.* It was loud and she appreciated the irony of the title.

Angie made her way toward the stereo set up clutching the metal bat she had brought. It was a quiet weapon. Quieter than a shotgun for sure and it wouldn't attract alphas. She also had a Glock tucked behind her back. Ryan insisted she have a backup weapon but it was last resort. She set the bat down on the table and opened the windows, moving the speaker's right to the sill. She stopped. There was a noise. The hair on the back of her neck stood up. An alpha was in the apartment with her. She slowly reached for the bat but was violently hit from the side and thrown against the wall. An older male alpha was quickly upon her. Fending off the attack, she pulled the handgun out only to have it knocked out of her hands. She was defenseless. The enraged alpha began to pummel her viciously. Angie felt herself losing consciousness when suddenly, the alpha was pulled off of her. Her vision blurred, Angie made out the shape of a younger woman who now had her metal bat and was beating the alpha to death. It was another alpha. She passed out.

Angie was awakened moments later by someone shaking her. As she regained consciousness, her vision slowly cleared. The female alpha that had killed her assailant was squatting about four feet in front of her holding her bat now wet with the blood of the dead attacker. Angie snapped back to clarity and looked around for a weapon in a panic but there was none. Her gun was too far away. All she could do was sit against the wall and look at the alpha across from her.

Why isn't she attacking? Angie wondered. Obviously, the urine-soaked pants she had on didn't stop the attack this time so it couldn't be helping her now. Angie studied the female alpha across from her. She was young, mid to late twenties though it was hard to be sure because of the condition of her body due to the disease. She was filthy and her ragged clothes stained with dried blood. She was also very thin, *most likely starving*, Angie thought. Angie knew that although she was in better physical shape that the alpha across from her, she didn't stand a chance in a hand-to-hand fight against her. Even a dying alpha could inflict serious damage to its victim. Moments passed as the two stared at each other. Angie was now worried that the others were waiting out in the open for her to turn on the stereo to create the noise needed to draw the alphas away. Without it, they may not make it out of the area. Time was running out. *I have to do something*, she thought. *I have to turn on that stereo even if it means this thing attacks me.* Angie moved slowly to adjust her position which was immediately met with the alpha shuffling herself closer to Angie.

Shit! Angie thought to herself, becoming still again. The alpha reached out and touched Angie's face, studying her response. The alpha then backed away from her and pushed the gun toward her. Angie sat there confused by the gesture. *Was it offering her the gun*, she thought. Angie slowly reached out, took the gun, and quickly moved back into a defensive posture anticipating an attack. None came. Instead, the alpha, now on her knees, starred at her. The alpha began to move her mouth as though it was trying to talk. Angie was stunned. *Alphas don't speak*, she thought. *What the hell is going on?* The alphas face contorted as it tried to speak. First, a series of weak grunts but then words started to form.

"Heh...hep...meh...hep...me," it managed to say, fighting through the spasms

Angie stared at the alpha. "Help you?" she asked.

The woman slowly nodded.

"How?" asked Angie, shocked that she was talking to an alpha.

The woman slowly leaned forward, placing her head against the barrel of the gun that Angie had trained on her.

"Hep" she said pressing harder against the gun barrel.

Angie suddenly became aware of what the female wanted. She had killed a number of alphas over the past few months, but now she found it hard to pull the trigger. There was a person inside this alpha begging for mercy. *Perhaps...if we got it to the Center...maybe they could treat her*, she thought.

"We can get you to a doctor," Angie said. "They may be able to help you."

The alpha shook its head no and pressed again.

Angie struggled, finding it impossible to pull the trigger, she pulled the gun away.

The alpha backed away obviously agitated. Her breathing deepened and she looked up at Angie. Her eyes now revealing the rage taking over within. The woman was being pulled back as the animal re-emerged. Angie saw the change occur and pulled the trigger just as the alpha lunged toward her. The alpha dropped on top of her. Angie pushed her off and fired two more rounds into her. She jumped to her feet. Looking down at the woman, Angie couldn't hold back the emotions she was feeling. Tears began to form.

The sound of an alpha screaming nearby snapped her out of it. The gunfire had attracted the nearby alphas. *Shit!* She thought to herself. Angie went to the table next to the window and pressed the power switch on the stereo. Within seconds, loud music boomed out of the speakers. Angie didn't wait. She raced down the hallway to the stairwell and went up to the roof. She had laid out her escape plan days earlier. She could get to within a half a block of the meeting point without leaving the roof. It was the safest route.

"That's it," said Marcus, hearing the unmistakable sound of Guns-N-Roses, *Welcome to the Jungle* playing blocks away. "We have to hurry. I thought I heard gunshots."

"It's about damn time," replied Ryan. "She's running way late."

Ryan quickly spliced two wires together under the dash of the Suburban starting the engine without difficulty. With everyone in, the Suburban rushed out of the parking structure and onto the street outside. The pickup point was only three blocks away but the streets were a maze of abandoned vehicles and bodies. It would still take a few minutes.

Moments later the Suburban slowly stopped at the corner near the pickup point.

"There!" said Marcus. "That storefront with the sales signs."

"I see it," replied Ryan. "Anyone see anything?"

"We're clear to the right," said Allan.

Ryan slowly made a left turn onto the street.

"The alley is just up ahead on our left," said Marcus. "She should be there already."

"I don't see her," replied Ryan. "We can't wait too long."

"Bullshit!" said Marcus, irritated at Ryan even thinking about leaving Angie behind.

"I just meant…"

"I know what you meant. She put her ass on the line for us and we'll wait as long as it takes."

"There's movement between the cars on the opposite side of the street," said Ryan quietly. "Near that pile of cars."

Two alphas, both male, appeared from behind a box truck moving hurriedly, albeit spastically, toward the loud music Angie had turned on.

"I'm surprised they can hear it," said Ryan, his window rolled down halfway. "I can barely hear it."

At that moment, Angie darted out from the alley just ahead of them.

"There she is!" said Mrs. Jenkins, the only one in the car not watching the alphas.

Angie stopped suddenly and looked back into the alley. She drew her pistol and fired off three rounds. An alpha emerged from the alley behind her and fell to the ground. The two alphas across the street stopped and looked toward where the sound of gunfire came from. They saw Angie.

"Go! Go!" shouted Marcus.

Ryan floored the gas pedal and pulled the SUV up to where Angie was standing. Angie fired off two more rounds, hitting the lead alpha in the shoulder to no avail. Marcus had better luck with his shotgun, hitting both alphas with the first two shots. Allan had also struck one of the alphas with a 9mm round.

"Let's get out of here, there's more," said Angie as she got in the vehicle. The sound of agitated alphas nearby confirmed her fear.

Ryan once again hit the gas pedal and accelerated the SUV down the street and turned right at the corner toward the freeway. Looking back, they could see two or three alphas giving chase but the vehicle quickly put distance between them.

"What took you so long?" asked Marcus, who suddenly noticed that his sister had been injured. "What happened?"

"I was blindsided by an alpha in the apartment. I didn't see him until it was too late. It nearly killed me."

"How did you get away? Did you shoot it?" asked Mrs. Jenkins.

"No…nothing like that. Another alpha killed it. It saved me."

"No way. You sure you saw things right?" queried Ryan.

"No. I'm positive. It pulled the alpha off of me and killed it. Then it asked me to kill it."

"That's impossible. Alphas aren't human anymore and they sure as hell can't talk," replied Ryan.

"I'm serious. It pushed my gun to me. When I picked it up it put its head on the barrel and said 'help'. I froze. I couldn't pull the trigger. It got pissed off at me and lunged at me. I shot it twice at point blank range."

"Seriously? Son of a bitch. Talking alphas. There screaming is bad enough," joked Ryan quietly.

"It bothered me. I mean, for a moment there was a person there and then it was gone. What does that mean?" Angie looked out the window thinking about the incident and the woman who had saved her.

"Our turn is up ahead on the left," she said to Ryan.

"I see it."

Everyone in the vehicle turned their attention toward the parkway as they entered the entrance ramp. As expected, the highway was heavily littered with abandoned vehicles. Numerous decomposing bodies lay strewn about, more than they had expected.

"Christ! Did anyone make it out alive?" exclaimed Allan.

"I hope so, otherwise we're screwed," replied Marcus. "We've seen nothing but alphas and the non-alpha infected for the last few weeks. How many uninfected people have we seen?

"None," answered Ryan. "Except for those three that tried to start a car near our building last week and they're dead now."

"Are you saying that we may be all that's left in the area?" asked Mrs. Jenkins.

"Wouldn't surprise me any," replied Ryan. "Anyone healthy enough to get out early is gone. Only groups like us left now. Those that got trapped or chose to stay and ride it out."

"You're forgetting the C.D.C. safe zone and the other quarantine camps in the area" said Angie. "A lot of people made it to those areas when the attacks got out of control. There has to be a lot of people in those zones."

"Come on Angie," said Ryan. "Do the math. How many people lived in the Atlanta metro area? What? Roughly five million people, half of them infected. Even if three million people weren't infected a hell of a lot of them were killed by the attacks. I don't know how many camps or safe zones there are in the area but there is no way they could shelter and protect even a hundred thousand people let alone a million. We'll be lucky if there's anyone out there especially after last night's attack."

Angie, sensing the anxiety building in the others in the vehicle, fired back.

"Thanks for the optimism, Ryan, but I am sure that there are a lot of people that survived. Besides, before I left this morning, I saw helicopters off in the direction of the C.D.C. zone so there has to be people there."

"Maybe, but so what? What about other cities? What about the outer areas…farmlands…you know, rural areas. What happened there? Hell, it may be worse outside of Atlanta for all we know. None of us has heard a broadcast in weeks. How long has it been since the evacuation broadcasts? One, two months? I don't even remember. I'm just saying that we shouldn't expect things to be any better once we get to the safe zone."

"The parkway ends up ahead. Turn right at the intersection," said Mrs. Jenkins.

"How far is the C.D.C.," asked Marcus.

"Only a few miles," she replied. "We'll have to turn onto Briarcliff and it should only be another mile or so."

"Seems like the long way to go. Couldn't we go through the Emory Hospital area?" asked Marcus.

"No. It's too dangerous to go that way. I remember hearing broadcasts advising residents to evacuate the area because of really big alpha population to the south of the safe zone. Besides, I think they closed off all access from the south of the complex. I know the north approach is patrolled and it is still open."

"Nice to have a local in the group," joked Ryan. "I'm not familiar with the area at all."

"What? You never got out this way on....business?" quipped Marcus.

"Hell no! I did my business in the Cliff."

"You know, we've been holed up together going on six weeks now and I don't think you ever told us what it is you do," said Allan.

"That's because it was none of your business. Shit. The people I worked for are dead now. They got killed by their own clients. The plague went through that area like fire in a barn. All them sick druggies, stacked on meth and then they got the rage on top of it. Shit, I watched three of them rip apart a carload of Jack Boys like they were nothing. I got the hell out in a hurry. Took my guns with me too. Lucky us."

"Yeah. Lucky us for sure," replied Angie. "That must be when we saw you and picked you up."

"Kind of. I was actually on my way to the safe zone too with my girlfriend when we got attacked in Midtown. Ran into a bunch of alphas that came at us from the buildings. I tried to back out of there but they were on the car already. Had to shoot my way out."

"What happened to your girlfriend?" asked Mrs. Jenkins.

There was a long moment of silence as emotion began to appear in Ryan's face.

"She didn't make it. I didn't know she was infected. During the attack, she began to have a seizure of some sort. Shaking and all that stuff. Then she was gone.

I shot her as she came out of the car at me."

"She turned right in front of you?" exclaimed Allan. "I am so sorry for you, man. Having to kill your own girlfriend, I mean..."

"Allan. Enough," said Angie.

It became quiet again inside the vehicle as Ryan looked away out the side window. Pushing back the emotions, Ryan fought for control.

"It is what it is," he said. "Wasn't just her. Lots of people had the same thing happen to them. Might happen to one of us for all we know...right?"

"Hope not," replied Marcus.

The group got quiet again as the vehicle made its way toward the safe zone. Everyone now looking out the windows. Searching the surroundings for movement as they thought to themselves.

"Sir. We've got an inbound vehicle approaching the zone," said a young soldier who had been monitoring the video feeds from one of the drones patrolling the area around the C.D.C.

"Let's take a look," replied Lt. Harris as he looked up at the screen.

On the screen, appeared a dark-colored SUV approaching the intersection of Briarcliff and Clifton Rd., only a mile from the north check point of the safe zone. It was Angie's group.

"Stragglers," muttered Harris. "What's the area look like just ahead of them?"

"Not good, sir," replied the soldier. "They're still trying to clear out the alphas from yesterday's attack. The highest concentration of them is just north of the outer check point near the shopping center."

They're heading right toward them, thought Harris.

"Who's in the area right now?"

"Sir, Lt. Ramos' patrol is nearest to them."

"Contact Ramos. Have him intersect and escort that vehicle here."

"Yes, sir."

"There's a lot of movement in those storefronts to the right," said Marcus.

Angie leaned across Mrs. Jenkins to look out the passenger window.

"It's a shopping center," said Angie. "It's got to be alphas. There can't be any food left in there so it's not scavengers. The quicker we get out of here the better."

Ryan pressed the accelerator a bit more, trying go faster without attracting any attention. The going was slow, however. The road was littered with debris, abandoned vehicles, and bodies, lots of them.

As they passed the shopping center and neared the intersection where they had to turn, Allen looked back.

"We've been spotted!" he said loudly.

The group inside the vehicle turned to look back. Three alphas broke out of the tree line alongside the road, within thirty yards of the group.

"Go! Go! Go!" yelled Marcus.

Ryan pushed down on the accelerator, weaving the vehicle through the maze of debris. The road ahead worsened quickly as they approached the intersection.

"We're fucked!" Ryan yelled. "It's blocked ahead."

"Do something!" replied Marcus, in a panic. "There! On the right! The drive through."

"Got it!" said Ryan as he jerked the vehicle across the road toward the entrance drive of a fast food joint on the corner of the intersection. "Hope there's an exit!"

With the three alpha's still coming up from behind, Ryan came around the corner of the restaurant in an attempt to cut the corner and pull onto Clifton Road and hopefully, safety.

"Oh my God!" yelled Mrs. Jenkins as two alphas came out from the side of the building. Ryan steered into them to try and run them over. He managed to kill the closest one but the other charged the vehicle, jumping up into the windshield. The glass shattered from the force of the impact. The alpha, not fazed by the jolt, began to pound through the damaged windshield with no regards to the lacerations that were smearing its blood across the glass.

"I can't see!" yelled Ryan. "Kill that fucking thing!

Marcus shot three rounds from his 12 gauge shotgun and brought a halt to the alphas attack but unable to see ahead, the vehicle struck a light post in the parking area. The vehicle came to a halt.

The first of the other alphas to reach the group slammed against the back of the vehicle and immediately began to pound through the back window. Allen, who had been sitting in the back row seats, opened fire with his 9 mm Glock, but was so shaken by the attack that he missed the first three shots a point blank range. Angie turned in the seat in front of him and fired off several rounds from her handgun, striking the alpha twice in the head. It fell to the ground as the second alpha slammed into the shattered back window and forced itself halfway into the vehicle. Allen panicked and began to kick the alpha as he tried to get into the seats ahead of him where Angie and Mrs. Jenkins were. Angie attempted to get a shot off at the alpha but Allen grabbed her, trying to pull himself over the seatback. She couldn't get a shot. Ryan, shaking off the impact of the collision, was attempting to start the vehicle when another alpha slammed into his door and began to screech while hammering the door window with its fist. Marcus, who had been trying to train his shotgun on the alpha in the back turned quickly toward Ryan.

"Duck!" he screamed.

Ryan quickly leaned over toward the center console giving Marcus a clear shot. The first round hit it in the head. Marcus turned back to engage the alpha in the back but by now it had a firm hold of Allen and pulled him back through the rear window. Allen's screams pierced the air as the alpha began to tear him apart. Angie began to open her door to attempt to rescue him but it was too late.

"There's more!" yelled Mrs. Jenkins, who was now in tears.

Angie looked out the back window and saw a group of alphas rapidly closing ground between them.

"Get us out of here!" she yelled.

Ryan was still trying to get the car started through all of the chaos.

"It won't start!" he replied.

"Lock the doors!" Angie yelled. "We're gonna have to fight em' off."

Angie looked over to Mrs. Jenkins who was coming apart. She handed her a handgun with four clips and gave her a focused look.

"Don't let anything through that window," she said sternly. "Just shoot into the window when you see them. Reload and keep firing."

Mrs. Jenkins nodded nervously and turned toward her window. Angie positioned herself in the backseat where Allen had been. She had an AK-47 with several clips of ammo, a handgun, and a large knife. Marcus, armed with his 12 gauge shotgun and Ryan's AK-47, opened his door and got out of the vehicle. He jumped onto the hood and then atop the vehicle.

"Marcus! Get back in the car!" Angie screamed.

"No! I can do more damage from up here," he yelled back. "I'll be okay, just shoot these fucking things before they get to the car."

Angie knew he was right but he was her little brother and she was fighting the urge to get out of the car and join him. It was too late. There were several alphas coming at them from two directions. Too far yet to open fire. They had limited ammo and every shot had to count. She waited.

Ryan had stopped trying to start the vehicle. He turned to grab his handgun and a few clips out of the bag on the floor. When he turned back, an alpha was standing next to the window. It was the alpha that Marcus had shot a few moments before. Ryan yelled as he tried to bring his gun up to fire, but the alpha reached through the shattered window grabbing his head and pulled it through the window. Ryan struggled, his head completely outside the vehicle as the alpha began to chew on it. Marcus turned and looked down. The sight was horrific. The alpha had Ryan's neck twisted almost completely around as the remaining fragment of the shattered window sawed through the soft flesh of his neck. Stunned, Marcus hesitated, but it was too late. Ryan managed a muffled scream as the alpha pulled his head off. Marcus opened fire, unloading nearly a full clip before he came to his senses. The alpha was dead.

"Angie!" he yelled. "Save a few shots just in case. Do you understand?"

Angie looked back at Mrs. Jenkins, who nodded slowly.

"We hear you Marcus," she replied turning to look out the back window. She opened fire on the group coming in from behind.

Marcus, turned and saw three more alphas coming from the side of the building. He dropped two immediately but the third made it to the vehicle and attempted to climb on top of the hood. Marcus killed it only a few feet from him. The gunfire from the back of the vehicle was nearly continuous as Angie continued to fire into the oncoming group. Some had made it to within ten feet of the vehicle before they dropped. Angie knew she had shot some of the three or four times before they fell. *We're going to run out of ammo*, she thought to herself. She looked back out the rear window. Two alphas were moving toward them about twenty yards away. She raised the rifle, took aim, and squeezed of three rounds. Two of the rounds found their mark striking the thighs of both alphas. The alphas went down, their femurs shattered by the rounds. The alphas, still alive, could not get back up despite their incredible strength. *It's our only chance*, she thought.

"Marcus! Can you hear me?" she yelled.

"Yeah, I can hear you," he replied as he reloaded his rifle.

"Too hard to kill them. Try to take out their legs! Do you understand?"

"Yeah! I hear you! I'll try…heads up! More coming!

From his position on top of the vehicle, Marcus could see alphas coming from all directions. Most were individuals, but there were two groups of eight or more coming from the direction of the shopping center. He only had eighteen rounds of shotgun shells and one more clip for the AK. *We aren't going to make it*, he thought.

His heart sank with the realization that this is how he and his sister would die. Then anger came over him. He trained on the closest alpha and pulled the trigger. The round shattered its hip. *Close enough*, he thought as he took aim at another. Angie looked back at Mrs. Jenkins who had become uncomfortably quiet.

"You got both windows, right?" she asked.

Jenkins nodded, clutching her sidearm to her chest, still holding the two extra clips Angie had given her.

"Nothing gets through the windows," said Angie looking back out the rear window.

Jenkins nodded again. Not hearing a response, Angie turned and looked at her.

"Right?" she said forcefully.

"Yes. Nothing gets through," Mrs. Jenkins replied.

Just at that moment, an alpha raced toward the vehicle from the behind the building and slammed into the side of the SUV before Marcus could shoot it. It smashed the passenger side window next to Mrs. Jenkins. Startled, she pulled the trigger before aiming, firing a round through the roof, just missing Marcus who was standing just above her.

"The window," yelled Angie.

Mrs. Jenkins turned, pointed the gun at the alpha who was only feet from her and pulled the trigger. The bullet took the entire top of the alphas head off. She looked back at Angie who gave her a thumbs up. Nothing was said. Mrs. Jenkins moved her head from side to side, watching the windows. Her first kill had calmed her down a bit and focused her. She could defend herself, but for how long.

Angie took aim and dropped another alpha that was approaching the vehicle from the tree line near the road. It was then she noticed movement just behind the alpha she had just shot. From within the tree line that was between them and the shopping center parking lot, a large group of alphas appeared.

"Marcus! Alphas! Lots of them!" yelled Angie as she fought against the panic that was setting in.

"I see them!" he replied.

The three went silent as they watched the tsunami of violence break through the trees, spilling into the parking lot, rushing toward the SUV. Angie and Marcus opened up, pouring rounds into the large group of oncoming alphas. Angie's gun fell silent. She had used the last of her ammo for the AK. She pulled out her sidearm and began to fire at the closest alphas. Suddenly, she heard a gunshot from behind her. Mrs. Jenkins, unable to handle the situation, had put the gun barrel into her mouth and pulled the trigger. Not hesitating, Angie reached across the back seat and grabbed her gun and the two clips she still had in her hand. Giving her a quick final look, Angie turned back toward the rear window and continued to fire at the oncoming attackers.

The first few alphas of the group slammed into the vehicle with tremendous force. Angie kicked herself away from the alphas attempting to come through the back window, still firing her handgun. Suddenly, she was grabbed from behind by an alpha that was partially through the side window. She turned quickly and put two rounds into its head. She put the final clip into her handgun and grabbed her knife.

Outside, atop the vehicle, Marcus was still shooting into the group, focusing his efforts on the back of the vehicle where his sister was. The AK went silent. He had used his last clip of ammo. Casting the gun aside he grabbed the shotgun that was slung over his shoulder and resumed firing. He did not see the alpha that had climbed up onto the hood of the vehicle. It struck him from behind, knocking him down onto the roof of the SUV. Angie heard the thud.

"Marcus!" she screamed.

Marcus, now struggling to fend off the attack, could not respond. The alpha was on top of him. Marcus tried to push the alpha off but its strength was too much. The first blow struck him in the upper chest fracturing his clavicle. The second struck his skull. Marcus offered no more resistance as he began to pass out. Looking up he saw the alpha raise up, screeching. Suddenly, the alphas body exploded as several 50 caliber rounds hit center mass. As he lost consciousness, he could barely hear the deafening sound of two fifty caliber machine guns firing into the crowd. Inside the vehicle, Angie heard the gunfire and watched at the attackers began to fall in large numbers. She looked back out the side window. Two army armored vehicles and a Humvee had pulled up near the SUV and begun to fire into the crowd as soldiers exited from within the two armored carriers. Angie broke down and began to cry. Removing the clip from her sidearm, she saw that she had no bullets left. Two soldiers cautiously appeared at the back of the vehicle.

"In the car! Don't shoot," the one soldier yelled.

Angie fought to regain her composure. She threw the handgun and empty clip out the window.

"You're clear," she said.

"Come on, let's get you out of there," said the soldier pulling open the rear door.

Angie slowly exited the vehicle. *Marcus*, she thought.

"My brother. He was on top of the vehicle."

"Get the medic on top and check out the ladies brother," said the soldier with a smile. "I'm Lt. Ramos, ma'am. Sorry we didn't get here faster."

Angie nodded weakly, her eyes watering.

"Don't call me ma'am, Sir," she said weakly. "I'm Corporal Angela Moss, 1st battalion, 2nd marines, inactive."

Lt. Ramos smiled. Looking back at the bodies that lie strewn across the parking lot behind the vehicle, he shook his head.

"Yes, soldier. You sure as hell are but I wouldn't say you're inactive."

"Lieutenant! This guy is banged up a bit. He's got a head injury, but he's alive and should be okay," yelled the medic on top of the vehicle.

"Well let's get him packed up and out of here quick," replied Ramos. "We made enough noise to wake up every local within five klicks. Avery! Escort the corporal to the vehicle. Make sure they put her brother in with her."

"Yes, sir," replied Avery, as he put his arm around Angie and walked her toward the closest assault vehicle.

Gunfire erupted again as more alphas began to appear from the direction of the shopping center.

Looking back at the Humvee he rode up in, Lt. Ramos yelled.

"Sanderson! Get on the radio and give them the coordinates of that shopping center. We need it sterilized. There's a whole nest of alphas in there. Give us five minutes to get out of Dodge."

Sanderson flashed acknowledgement and began to call in to the command center. Meanwhile, the medic had Marcus on a stretcher and was securing him inside the assault vehicle with Angie.

"Fall back," yelled Ramos. "Let's get out of here!"

As the soldiers returned to the vehicles, the fifty caliber guns atop the assault vehicles began firing again, pouring rounds into the tree line or anywhere else alphas may be hiding. They continued firing as the three vehicles exited the parking lot and made their way toward the CDC safe zone.

Moments later, two A-10's began their runs dropping their loads of incendiary cluster bombs onto the shopping center area. Inside the armored vehicles, the report of exploding ordinance was felt.

"Wasn't that place we just left a barbeque joint?" said one of the soldiers.

The inside of the vehicle broke out in laughter.

"It is now," joked another soldier.

Angie managed to smirk despite her exhaustion.

The soldier next to her put his arm around her, rubbing her head and laughing.

"You're one bad-ass marine," he replied.

"Ooh-rah!" yelled the rest of the soldiers in the vehicle.

Angie looked around and smiled at them. She put her head on the shoulder of the marine next to her and closed her eyes. They were safe for now.

"Sir, Lt. Ramos is returning to base with two survivors," said the soldier at the radio set. "One needs medical attention."

"Get them to the holding area and alert the medical team," replied Lt. Harris. "and contact Dr. Allen's team and let them know we have two stragglers inbound. I'm sure they'll want to question them."

24

Throwing Curveballs

"We are faced with the impossible. We cannot cure them at the expense of not treating the uninfected. We cannot quarantine them because their numbers are in the millions. The only option left to us flies in the face of our humanity. The question now is how softly to pull the trigger."

Rev. Oliver G. Templeton
Director, Council of Christian Churches

To say the sudden escalation of violence took everyone by surprise would be an understatement. Like an out of control nuclear reactor, once critical mass had been reached, nothing could stop the explosion. In a matter of several months, entire cities fell to the massive outbreak of violence the infected unleashed upon the uninfected populations. No place was safe. Mass evacuations of the cities only served to spread the disease even further into the rural areas. Several cities were abandoned altogether as the infected far outnumbered the uninfected. Miami, Houston, Baton Rouge, among others all became restricted zones. The military, already dealing with their own problems of outbreaks, fell back to areas outside those cities and set up containment zones. Despite all efforts, the body counts skyrocketed with no end in sight. Humanity was becoming an endangered species.

At the C.D.C., another meeting was called to review a new set of directives coming from the White House.

"This can't be right," said Berr, who had been reading a letter handed to her by Dr. Walker. "When did they decide this?"

"I assure you, they mean it," replied Walker. "The President met with FEMA and other members of the government's emergency response team last week to decide a course of action. Most of the preliminary steps have already been initiated."

Others sitting at the table looked on anxiously as the focus was on the letter Dr. Walker had received from the White House outlining the new direction the government was taking in response to the escalating problems with the Toxovirus pandemic.

"What are they proposing?" asked Jonas. "The short version."

"Basically, they going to establish regional safe zones throughout the country, Atlanta is one of them. They want to focus their efforts in a few key areas rather than trying to cope with the pandemic on a town by town basis," replied Brilli.

"What exactly does that mean?" asked Ben. "It sounds like they are retreating."

"In a way, we are," Walker replied. "This pandemic has crippled the world economy. Many of the third world economies have already collapsed. We are not far behind. By most estimates the U.S. has less than a year to stabilize before the economic standstill becomes permanent."

"So what's the problem? We've been under martial law for almost a year now. The stock market closed around the same time. Our economy is already in the crapper. I don't see how that is our main concern."

"Ben makes a good point," Jonas added. "Shouldn't our focus be on getting the upper hand on this pandemic?"

"That's obviously not going to happen anytime soon, now is it?" said Donaldson, who had just entered to room, throwing a stack of papers down on the table in front of him as he sat down. "We have to face the facts here, people. Our best efforts have not been good enough. Quite honestly, this bug has kicked our ass and isn't going away."

"Considering the virus that has made this whole situation far worse that it should be came from one of your research facilities, you shouldn't be so goddamn cocky. Don't you think?"

"Walter! Enough!" yelled Brilli. "It's not helping!"

"Mr. Donaldson is right though," said Dr. Walker. "This bug has showed no signs of letting up. No one is to blame here. We got caught off guard by the wrong organism. All of us suspected something like this would eventually happen. Maybe not quite like this…with the violence and the attacks, but something on this scale has been in the back of all of our minds for years. FEMA has run projections on various scenarios over the years in order to make our response more effective. Nearly all of the models involving a runaway pandemic end poorly, not because of the disease, but because of the inevitable economic collapse that follows. We are running on fumes here."

"Unfortunately, I agree," said Berr. "It may be far easier to manage smaller zones than to try and clean up the entire country."

"I am not sure the people who are bunkered up outside those proposed zones would share that viewpoint," quipped Walter. "Basically, they're screwed in this plan."

"It can't be helped, Dr. Frederickson," replied Dr. Walker. "If we don't move fast to save these zones, there may be nothing left to save and then we're all screwed."

"How are they proposing we establish these safe zones? Jonas asked.

"They are calling for the eradication of all those infected with the disease, both alpha and beta states. They have recalled all remaining military personnel overseas to assist in the effort."

The room had become silent.

"How?" asked Jonas. "I mean how do they propose we do this?"

Donaldson having regained his composure after the confrontation with Walter, "by any means necessary I believe is what it says. Is that right Dr. Walker?"

"Yes. That's right. They are leaving it up to the safe zone managers to work with the military in the zone to decide how best to clean out the infected population. Of course, nuclear weapons are off the table."

"Why do we have to do anything?" asked Major Clark. "I mean they will eventually die from the disease right? Can't we just wait it out then go in and clean up whatever survives?'

"That's an odd position coming from the military director," said Donaldson.

"I'm not regular army, Mr. Donaldson, I'm in the Reserve and I have a family out there as do most of my command. I have lost nearly a third of the troops I started with over a year ago and I don't want to lose any more if I don't have to. If we can save lives by waiting it out, I'm all for it."

Terry, hearing the conversation as he entered the room, responded.

"Wish it were so, Major, but unfortunately the infection rate continues to create new alphas and while they are not as numerous as they were, I believe they are here to stay in sufficient numbers."

Terry sat down at the table next to Jonas and handed him a file. "Besides, there's been a new development."

Jonas read through the few pages in the file quickly, giving a sigh, he closed the file.

"Dr. Andrews is right. He has been interviewing patrol members and refugees coming into our safe zone for several months, gathering information. In some cases, he has gone out with the patrols to observe alpha behaviors. Terry, will you go over what you have uncovered."

"Sure Jonas. Our team began to notice some changes over the past few months in alpha behavior. When the disease first erupted, attacks by alphas were random, wrong place, wrong time kind of thing. Lately, there is more organization of the attacks. Roads are blocked for an ambush of military patrols. Even here, Jonas and Mr. Donaldson were hunted by a small group of alphas just outside this building near the pond. I have reports of alphas talking to people. One begged for the person to kill her. Another said we were all going to pay with our lives before it was killed by gunfire."

"Are you quite sure, they spoke?" asked Walker.

"Without a doubt. Something the alphas could not do earlier. I believe the disease is stabilizing. The infected are not going bat-shit crazy anymore, but rather they are entering a prolonged state of agitation that can easily be provoked into attacking. This means two things. They are living longer with the disease and they are more dangerous than ever since they can organize and think clearer. They're hybrids existing in a state of constant rage with moments of muddled awareness of who they are.

"How…how is this possible? Are you sure they aren't marauders that have gone rogue? I mean there have been reports of small groups of uninfected doing exactly what you described. How can you be sure?" Walker said, challenging the information.

"We're positive. We've even caught a few of them during an ambush. As far as what is happening to the alphas, I am not sure at this point."

"I can answer that for you, Terry," said Ben. "Higher order parasites such as Toxoplasma don't gain anything by killing their host. If it happens it is usually because of a mutation which catches the host immune system off guard. Given time the parasite will modify the effect it has on its host so that the host survives and thus, improves the parasites chance for survival as well. Viruses do not do this as well and generally kill their hosts so the highly lethal viruses become hard to find. In our case, either the virus is weakening itself to survive better or the protozoan is modifying its response on the surrounding environment or both. Whatever the cause, the disease is stabilizing itself and unfortunately, it still infects a part of the brain that causes it to be a major threat to us. Stabilized or not, we cannot have these things around."

"I agree," said Dr. Berr. "Besides we don't know what percent of the alphas out there are stabilized. It may be a few isolated cases."

"Don't bet on it," replied Jonas. "The way this whole Toxovirus thing has played out, it's unlikely we're going to catch a break anytime in the near future."

"One other thing," said Terry. "I can't prove this but these hybrids seem to have some kind of enhanced mental function. A hive consciousness for lack of a better term. They may be mentally linked in some way."

"There it is," said Jonas throwing his hands in the air. "Why not?"

"Is that even possible?" said Walker.

"Well, we know that it does happen with many animals. You've heard of the 100th monkey effect? It's like that. Plants are known to react in mass to the appearance of a violent person. So, with the right stimulation perhaps, maybe the infection can cause some kind of psychic ability," replied Terry.

"I'm not buying it. There's no way that crap is real," replied Major Clark.

"Hey, I'm just telling you what we are observing and hearing in the debriefings," said Terry. "We've observed groups of alphas operating in unison without any apparent means of communication. I can't explain it and I'm not saying anything definite. Just be warned that the possibility exists."

Dr. Berr tapped on the table to get the attention of all present.

"Let's not get too far off task here. We still have to come up with a plan. Major, what are your thoughts?"

"You're talking about a mass extermination on a very large scale. That's not something we practice. I guess the first thing we need to do is to determine what areas we want to clear. Atlanta is so spread out, it won't be easy. The downtown area is easier than the suburbs, so that may be a place to start. The next will be how to do it."

"It would be easier to transplant those people in the camps to the larger buildings nearby and downtown, so I think our objective should be to clear the downtown area out first," suggested Walker. "I can get supplies sites set up as soon as the areas are cleared."

"Major, can you do that?" asked Berr.

"We're going to need more troops to go door to door and we don't have any. We will have to send armed civilians out with the patrols. If we do that we should be okay."

"It doesn't mean anything unless we can get the numbers down to where that is even a possibility," said Donaldson. "I mean, we are kind of limited to how to go about this. We already know the door to door approach is costly and difficult to pull off. Besides, we're guessing as to the numbers of infected that are still out there, right?"

"No, you're right. I'd be guessing at best, but I believe the numbers to be smaller than we'd expect simply because most everyone, sick or healthy, got out of the downtown area early in the epidemic and most others left over time as supplies dwindled."

"Weren't we taken by surprise by the numbers of alphas that came out of the woodwork a couple of months back when they attacked Chandler Park?" said Terry. "We were looking at thousands of them before Jonas had them decoyed away from here."

"Maybe that's part of the answer," said Brilli. "The problem is that they are spread out. Hiding here and there in buildings. Hell, we haven't even looked down in the subway tunnels. There may be hundreds more down there."

"I think I know where you're going with this," said Jonas. "They're attracted to sound. We could use that to get them out in the open and concentrated. It would make it easier to eliminate them…however we do it."

"Yes, yes, that would certainly help out," said Major Clark. "If we could concentrate them in small areas. We could drop incendiaries on them…burn the whole area."

Everyone in the room turned toward Major Clark with disbelief. The thought of incinerating large groups of people, no matter how sick they were, struck the wrong cord.

"What? Hey, they're not going to leave on their own. What did you think we were going to do? Hell, the Chinese nuked their problem. You're going to get squeamish about some napalm?

"We can't use incendiaries downtown, Major. We have to preserve the buildings if we can. We have people to relocate there," Jonas said quickly to break the tension. "If we start multiple large fires, we don't have the fire crews to put them out. Atlanta will burn to the ground."

"Gas," said Donaldson, looking down at the table.

"What?" said Brilli. "What do you mean gas?"

"We use sound to get them in the open and in concentrated groups and explode warheads loaded with Sarin gas," replied Donaldson. "It's fairly quick. It breaks down rapidly so we could send troops in shortly afterwards without any danger and Sarin stays low to the ground so any uninfected people still in the area could be instructed to get to the upper floors in the buildings."

"You know, you're right. That could work," said Major Clark. "Unfortunately, we don't have any."

"How much do we need," replied Donaldson.

"Weren't our stores of nerve agents all disposed of a while back?" asked Terry?

"Yes, Mr. Donaldson. Weren't they? Or do you happen to know where we can get some," asked Major Clark.

"I do," said Donaldson, smiling slightly. "Now aren't you glad we don't follow the rules. Get me the numbers and I'll get it here."

"So we have a plan, sort of," Berr said getting up from her chair.

"I believe we do," replied Major Clark. "Mr. Donaldson I'll need to talk with you more about this before you leave."

Donaldson nodded and left the room with Major Clark and Walker to discuss the operation further.

Brilli walked over to Jonas who was now talking with Terry and Walter.

"Can this work?" asked Brilli, looking at Jonas.

"It makes sense, but..." replied Jonas quietly.

"But what?"

"I have some concerns about the long-term effectiveness of this action. Sure, it could clear the areas, especially if the military goes in afterwards, but how do we keep the areas clear? How do we prevent alphas from re-entering the zone? We're talking about trying to seal off a major metropolitan city with limited resources. How?

"Not to mention we haven't even addressed the suburbs!" added Terry. "Maybe the downtown area is doable but the outskirts is going to be a nightmare."

"I agree," said Jonas looking at Brilli.

"That's what I am thinking as well. Dr. Berr said the same thing to me moments ago. I am sure everyone else here is thinking that."

"Then why proceed with a plan that we think may not work?" Jonas asked.

"What good is it going to do us if we can't keep the ground we gain."

"None, I suspect, but it may give us some time to address other problems like food and water shortages, body disposal, road-clearing. Just the type of things you were warning them about when this mess first started."

Jonas nodded his head.

"History repeats itself," quipped Walter, shaking his head. "It's fucking ironic."

The other three looked at Walter, taken off guard by the odd statement.

"What do you mean?" said Brilli.

"Well, right now we are under siege, dealing with the same problems the ancient cities dealt with throughout history. You just mentioned them."

"I see what you mean, but I don't see the irony," replied Brilli.

"It's the nature of our problem that's the irony. Think back to the siege of Troy. How did the Greeks end up getting inside the walls?"

"The Trojan Horse. They built a large horse and…" Jonas paused for a moment. "I see it now. The project that created the Toxovirus was called "Trojan Horse".

"Precisely! What are the odds of that happening?" Walter said coyly.

"Not sure," said Jonas as he turned to walk down the hall. "Let's hope we fair better than the city of Troy did."

25

Awakening

"We should not deceive ourselves. We are in the midst of a global extinction event. Every bit as lethal as the meteorite that ended the dinosaurs reign 66 million years ago, so too this pandemic has the potential to erase humanity from the face of the earth."

Mark Johnson
American Red Cross

Robert stood at the window, looking out over the street below. It was uncomfortably hot outside and the humidity made it difficult to breathe. Still he and others across the street stood watch. Waiting for something, someone, to venture into their trap. He was starving, slowly, along with the others in his group. They had exhausted their food supplies weeks ago. Unable to find anything in their foraging through countless markets and homes, he (and the others) had resorted to feeding, once again, on flesh. Dogs, rats, anything...it did not matter, as long as it was reasonably fresh and healthy. Alphas had consumed most of the food sources, leaving only partially eaten bodies to rot in the streets. Early on, they had tried to eat alphas as there were large numbers of them in the area, only to find that a majority of the alphas were diseased. And there was the stench. The putrid smell of strong urine heavily ladened with urea. It burned his nostrils whenever he neared a body to eat. Finally, he gave up. Resorting to scavenging whatever he could. Like the others in his group, they found their sustenance by attacking stragglers still trying to make their way to the encampments. When that ran out, they began to attack the camps and military patrols. The attacks were costly. The heavily armed patrols could easily wipe out groups such as his and because of that, they had resorted to ambushes. Swift and sudden, with over-whelming numbers, they could overcome the patrols with minimal losses. A single patrol provided his group with four bodies, healthy bodies. With any luck, he and the other members of his group would eat tonight.

Something about that stirred emotions deep, very deep down inside him. He could feel them but his thoughts had become mere impulses broken occasionally by the voice of his own mind. Like someone calling out in a dense fog, trying to find their way home, his mind had been lost since the early days of the illness. He remembered nothing of his vicious attack on his own family that killed his wife and two children, his tattered blue dress shirt stained with their blood. Nor did he remember the countless other victims he had killed over the past several months. Up until the past few weeks, there was only rage and darkness. Now, something was happening inside him. He began to hear his thoughts more often. He could analyze the world around him. From the darkness of his primal mind, his former self was emerging. Not the Robert before the illness. The modestly successful research director at a local technology company. That Robert was gone forever. What was emerging was a primitive version of that person. Driven by base emotions, Robert understood what was happening around him, more than the others. He could think clearer. He understood the symbols painted on the walls around him. He could speak again, barely. Because of this, the others in his group let him lead. Most of them were still floundering in the darkness inside the minds but like, Robert, the darkness was receding. One by one his group was getting bigger. There were now twenty six in the group. He was the leader of sorts. Others followed him instinctively. Fights (usually over food) were common, sometimes ending in someone getting killed. The rage was still in them and although it had become more controllable, once loose there was no stopping it.

He continued to look out the window, glancing occasionally skyward to see if a drone was flying overhead. The plan was simple. He had become aware that the drones were what directed the patrols into an area. He was also aware that the drones would return to the area and circle as the patrol entered the area. Earlier that day, his group had caught the attention of a drone flying overhead by setting a car on fire. They stood out in the open, making sure they were seen. It had circled twice and then flew off. Robert new it would only a matter of time before the patrol vehicle arrived to exterminate them as they had to so many other groups of alphas. But they were not alphas, not anymore. Suddenly, he heard yelling down below. Some of his group had spotted the drone, pointing up. He looked and immediately saw the drone flying in from the south. He let out a barking sound and four members of his group moved out into the street, in plain sight of the drone's high resolution cameras. It began to circle. The patrol was coming.

Moments later, two military Humvees appeared down the street about a block and a half from where the alphas had been spotted. Slowly they approached the scene, a car up ahead still burning, as a few alphas stood in the middle of the street screaming at the oncoming convoy.

"Up ahead! Alphas!" yelled the soldier manning the 50 caliber gun atop the lead Humvee.

"See them!" yelled back Lt. Farzan, reaching for the two-way radio on the console. "Able 3 on sight. Targets confirmed. Proceeding."

"Roger Able 3. Good hunting."

"Let's go!" said Farzan signaling with his hand to the driver.

The Humvees sped up, closing in fast on the group of alphas they spotted directly ahead. When they were within about 70 yards, the alphas dispersed quickly, disappearing into some of the buildings along the street.

"What the fuck?" murmured the driver. The Humvee's came to a stop. "Lieutenant, I've never seen them do that before. Usually they rush us the minute they see us."

"I know," replied Farzan. "Keep your eyes open," he said reaching for the two-way. "Able 3 to Able 4, hit the horn. Be ready."

The gunner on the trailing Humvee gave a thumbs up signal. The loudspeaker on the back Humvee emitted a loud shrieking noise.

"Movement!" yelled the gunner on Farzan's Humvee. "Behind us to the left!"

Both gunners swung their 50 caliber machine guns around as two alphas broke from cover in an alley and rushed the vehicles. The guns opened fire, killing the two alphas quickly. Another alpha smashed a second story window to the right of the convoy, shrieking as it tried to find a way down toward the vehicles. It too was silenced.

"Somethings not right," said Farzan. "Those aren't the alphas we saw. They were ahead of us. Why aren't they rushing us?"

Lt. Farzan and his patrol had been on dozens of missions like this with predictable results. Get on site, sound the horn, and shoot the alphas as they rushed the vehicles. Alphas were violent and in the early days of the attacks, patrols such as his would have their hands full fending off large numbers of alphas. Now, the numbers were dwindling, at least here. But this group was different. They ran and hid. The horn had not brought them out.

"Able 4, deploy," said Farzan as he opened the door and stepped out onto the street along with three other soldiers. The gunners in both vehicles, each surveying their areas of coverage as the horn continued to blast.

Farzan gave the sign to cut the horn. It fell silent. He looked back at the soldiers from the other Humvee who had taken up positions on each side of the vehicle. He was glad they were with him. Normally, his group patrolled alone, but this time Able 4 was in the area as well and called in to give support since their area was quiet.

"It's too quiet," said Pvt. Bradley, one of Farzan's men. "Where are they?"

Suddenly, the silence was broken by screams as two people, a man and a woman, ran out of a doorway. They raced toward the vehicles screaming. The guns swung around and opened fire. At the same time, more alphas attacked from three other positions, racing quickly toward the vehicles. Others on the roof, began to throw large rocks and other objects down at the convoy. The attack came swiftly from all sides. Several alphas were killed, but a few made it through. Farzan watched in horror as the attackers swarmed onto the street. Desperately trying to get the convoy out of the trap, the driver of the Humvee behind him panicked and backed up quickly, the turret gunner still firing into the crowd of attackers. Suddenly, the gun fell silent, the gunner had been struck by a cinder block thrown from the rooftop. In a manner of seconds, the attackers had the driver out of the vehicle and began to pummel him until finally, he was motionless.

Farzan, now shooting into the oncoming attackers with his 12 gauge shotgun, saw an opening ahead. Turning to the turret gunner, who was still firing into the attackers, Farzan pointed to the front of the vehicle. The gunner swung the 50 caliber around and began fire at the alphas just ahead of the vehicle. The hole opened. Farzan jumped into the vehicle.

"Go! Go! Go!" he yelled, as two alphas made it to the vehicle door behind him. The Humvee jolted forward, plowing through the debris and the bodies, it quickly found its way out of the trap, the turret gunner still firing into the pursuing crowd. He paused, shocked at the sight of the crowd of alphas, carrying the bodies of his fallen comrades into the building they had been in front of, two of them still alive.

Farzan was shaking as he fumbled for the two-way radio, he turned to the driver, "Get us the fuck out of here."

The driver acknowledged with a nod and then the Humvee accelerated, moving as fast as it could through the debris-filled streets.

"Able 3 to base, come in," said Farzan into the two-way. "Come in, base."

"Base to Able 3, report," said the voice on the other end of the radio.

"They ambushed us! The fucking things ambushed us!" said Farzan, now unable to halt the flood of emotion welling up to the surface. "We drove right into a trap! They took down five. Able 4 is lost."

There was a pause…

"Understood, Able 3. Return to base. We have an escort on its way to you. We also have eyes above you."

Robert waked out onto the street, watching the Humvee speed away. His group having moved inside with their catch, he looked upward again to watch the drone follow the escaping vehicle. He slowly walked over to the other Humvee. Along the front passenger window, someone had chalked stick figures, a lot of them, just below the window. He knew what it meant. They were kills. The rage began to well up inside him. The small twitches appeared on his face. His brain was on fire. Robert looked away, desperately trying to fight back the animal, but it was too strong. His face contorted as he threw his head back and let out a loud, chilling shriek. Finally, after moments of convulsions and without an avenue to vent his rage, he went quiet. He sat down hard next to the Humvee and closed his eyes. The beast was receding.

After a few moments he stood back up, hearing the clamor of the group inside the building as they ate their catch reminded him that he had not eaten in days. He hurried inside, hoping they had left something for him.

26

The Gauntlet Is Thrown

"So this is how it will end. A disease-enslaved mind, driven by distorted base impulses of an invading microbe, creates the ultimate assassin of humanity...Man himself"

Vladislov Uradova
The Moscow Times

Several weeks had passed since the decision to clear Atlanta of alphas, the first phase of a lengthy and multi-phase plan worked up by Major Clark, Dr. Berr, Dr. Walker, Donaldson, and other members of various local and federal agencies operating in the area. What followed was a flurry of activity in and around both the C.D.C and the operating military bases nearby. Civil defense and the military began to broadcast warnings of the impending gas attack, urging whatever uninfected citizens that remained to get to the upper floors or rooftops of buildings at least 6 stories high when they heard the sirens going off. The date was given. The attack would be launched September 23rd, a Saturday, at 2 pm. (weather permitting). A secondary date was also given should the first not be able to be implemented. Leaflets with the same information were also dropped in case those who remained did not have radios. It was not likely that there were any remaining uninfected people still holed up in the downtown area but just in case, the broadcasts went out.

Donaldson had made good his promise as stockpiles of Weteye bombs armed with the Sarin ingredients were delivered to Dobbins Air Reserve Base because of its close proximity to Atlanta (only twenty miles northwest) and because it was the home of the 94th airlift wing which made transporting materials into the area far easier. Unfortunately, even with all the pluses, the logistics of the buildup were a nightmare owing to the fact that many of the airbases had become refugee camps creating crowded conditions and a strain on resources already. Further complicating the matter was that the military personnel based there had been decimated by the disease and was now relying on citizens within the camps to help them with their operations. This meant that things were going very slow. Scenes like this were being played out in every major metropolitan area through the U.S. as local military and civilian agencies prepared to launch whatever "sterilization" plan they had developed for their area. This created a fight for resources between the designated safe zones, but since Atlanta was the home of the C.D.C. and Donaldson had moved some of the C.I.A. special operations staff there, they were given priority. Slowly, Dobbins airfields began to fill with A-10's and F-18's. Planes were plentiful, it was finding enough pilots that was presenting problems. Because Dobbins was so close to Atlanta, it was determined that they could fly the number of sorties with fewer planes and thus, fewer pilots simply by having the planes rearmed when they returned from their runs and send them out again. It would be exhausting but it would work.

Jonas had questioned the practicality of using laser guided bombs filled with Sarin nerve gas. You obviously couldn't do this everywhere. There most likely wasn't enough Sarin in the stockpiles to cover the country. Also, the saturation level needed to cover a city like Atlanta and it suburbs would be difficult, if not impossible, to achieve even with the plan to lure alphas into specific zones. Still, the alternatives offered far less margins of error. There were still large numbers of uninfected citizens throughout the metropolitan area that were vulnerable to Sarin or any other "sterilizing" agent they might use. The Chinese had gotten around that by simply nuking several cities regardless of whether the uninfected made it out of the area. They had sent out warnings to citizens to evacuate the cities but to do so put them at risk of attacks by the alphas that, now, far outnumbered the uninfected. Their plan also meant that little would be left of the cities to come back too or rebuild. Fortunately, for the rest of China and the world, they ceased detonating nuclear warheads after the first four, under pressure from the global community as well as the threat of rebellion by the Chinese people themselves. Within weeks after the first detonations by the Chinese, other countries began to implement their own extermination plans. India and Pakistan, jointly detonated two low yield nuclear devices but stopped when they saw the global response to China's actions. Many European countries began military-type actions against the infected carrying out "search and destroy" missions with foot soldiers. Slow and tedious, this approach was not efficient and the casualties to the troops were very high due to the high numbers of alphas present, especially in urban areas where the alphas were most dangerous, hiding silently in dark alleys and buildings until provoked.

At least, this approach is more selective with less collateral damage, Jonas thought to himself as he moved toward the window. He stopped for a moment. *Odd*, he thought. *Genocide on a massive scale was about to take place in a few moments and we're worried about collateral damage.* This is what the disease had done to everyone. Morality gave way to practicality. Survival at all cost. Few in the room were talking and if they were, it was in quiet, sullen tones. They had front row seats to the spectacle about to unfold. Like spectators in the Coliseum, they awaited the Emperor's decision. In this case, that was a foregone conclusion. It would be thumbs down. Once the order was given the dozens of remote controlled sound trucks and civil defense sirens would be started up and begin emitting a range of oscillating sounds that would attract and enrage the alphas, luring them into small areas. After about fifteen minutes, laser guided bombs filled with Sarin would be dropped on the sites in a pattern to maximize the effective range. One by one, in a grid pattern across the city of Atlanta, this would be repeated. The drops and kills confirmed by drones flying over the city.

Now it was just a matter of waiting. Most of the staff had gathered on the upper floors of the Spector building to watch. Where Jonas was, the government agencies and the CDC had set up a small communications room to monitor the event. Ellie was there as well, taking photographs to chronicle the moment, but in reality, Jonas wanted her near him and safe. Jonas looked at his watch. *Four more minutes,* he thought to himself.

Jonas felt a hand on his shoulder.

"Any minute now," said Walter who had slipped away from a few of the FEMA observers. "Are you doing okay?"

"Not really. I can't help feeling like a vulture waiting for its prey to die."

"I can certainly see the similarity of circumstances."

Jonas looked at Walter and managed a smirk. Looking back out the window Jonas became sullen.

"I wonder how many uninfected people will be killed today."

"Try not to think about that, Jonas. We've done everything we could to get people out of the area or at least get them information to survive this. I think the numbers will be fairly low. The alternative was far worse. At least we gave them a chance."

"I hope so, Walter." said Jonas.

"At least the weather is cooperating with us. Typical late fall afternoon in Atlanta. The air is heavy with humidity and not even a hint of a breeze. I should contain the gas in the strike areas fairly well."

"It's starting," said one of the military staff who was on the headset. "The first sound trucks just started up."

The group moved closer to the windows. Outside, the shrill varying pitch of the sound being emitted from the remote trucks and warning towers could be heard off in the distance. One by one, they began to go off throughout the city.

Inside the room where Jonas was, the military has set up a few monitors linked to the drones that were circling over the city. Within minutes, live feed from the drones confirmed that thousands of alphas were converging on the trucks throughout the city.

Jonas drew close to one of the monitors where Dr. Brilli and Dr. Walker were standing. Both had surprised looks on their faces.

"There are more of them than I thought," said Dr. Walker, watching the alphas converge on the trucks.

"There were a lot of places to hide," replied Jonas. "Most of the confrontations occurred with alphas who were out in the open."

The group watched the monitors as more and more alphas gathered in an enraged, writhing mass. Some alphas even began to attack others. Something no one had seen before. Then, the report of a bomb being detonated lightly shook the windows. The group turned and watched as small flashes of light appeared throughout the downtown area. One by one, the Weteye warheads detonated on target releasing clouds of toxic gas.

"It's working!" claimed someone on the other side of the room.

Jonas and Walter moved toward the four monitors, one of which had zoomed in on the target site after detonation. The group watched as the horror of the effects of Sarin became apparent. Hundreds of alphas, now exposed to large amounts of the gas began to convulse. Some crawling on all fours in a futile attempt to escape the effects. Slowly, they succumbed to suffocation. For a few who did not die of asphyxiation, they lie comatose, one atop the other, muscles still twitching from involuntary spasms. Their death would be slower.

Many in the room hung their heads, others gave muffled cheers. Jonas stood there watching the monitor as if he was punishing himself. These weren't foreign invaders. They were neighbors, parents and children, whose only misfortune was that they were infected with a devastating disease. He felt shame.

"Jonas, there was no other way," said Ellie, putting her hand on his shoulder. She had been in the room quietly photographing the event. "You did everything you could to avoid this."

Jonas looked back at her and nodded, "I know."

Ellie looked into his eyes. They were filled with pain. She fought off the tears to look strong but Jonas knew. He gently squeezed her hand and managed a slight smile. Ellie pulled away sensing that she wasn't helping and he needed time, "I'll be down the hall with Ben and Amanda."

Jonas nodded approval as she left the room. He became lost in thought for a few moments.

"Hey, look there! There are people on top of some of the buildings!" said Donaldson who had been keeping remarkably quiet throughout the whole scene. "There are more stragglers than we thought."

The three other screens showed the rooftops of buildings around the target sites. There, atop a few of the buildings were small groups of people watching the attack from a safe height.

"They must have got the warnings we broadcasted," said Walter, patting Jonas' shoulder. "Thank God!"

"What building is that?" asked Jonas, squinting as he got close to the screen to see more detail. "How far from here?"

Brilli walked over toward Jonas looking at the monitor.

"It looks like a high-rise apartment building. I'd guess that's Piedmont Heights. Right?" he said looking around for affirmation.

"That's about three or four miles from here," said Jonas. "Can you zoom in on the people on top that roof?"

"Yes, sir. I can," said one of the soldiers working the drones.

"Major Clark, how far from the C.D.C. have your teams been doing searches for uninfected stragglers sheltering in place?"

"Only up to a couple of miles. That area we didn't bother with because we have a lot of military traffic along the freeway intersection so most everyone there was already evacuated."

"So there shouldn't be anyone on top of…" Walker stopped mid-sentence.

"There's your answer," said Jonas, as the high resolution camera zoomed in a group of about twenty people atop the high-rise. "They're alphas."

As the camera continued to focus in, the faces of the group became visible. Looking up, obviously aware of the drone circling overhead, they were screaming at it. Most of them hardly even resembled anything human anymore. Contorted faces, spastic movements, and tattered, blood stained clothing gave them away.

"They knew," said Walker. "But how? And why weren't they attracted to the noise?"

"They're hybrids. The one's Terry discussed weeks ago when we planned this," said Jonas. "Like the ones that attacked us." Jonas looked at Donaldson who nodded in return. "They understood the instructions and avoided the trap."

"So how do we get rid of them?" asked Walker's assistant.

Before Jonas could answer, Walker pointed to the monitor.

"What are they doing?" he asked

All eyes turned to the monitor. The drone's camera focused on the group of hybrids. Suddenly, more hybrids appeared on the roof escorting five people who had been bound. Four of them were wearing military khaki's.

"Major?" said Brilli.

"I don't know, we do have people unaccounted for but…" Just then, some of the hybrid alphas grabbed two of the hostages and threw them over the edge of the roof. The two plummeted eight stories down to the pavement below. Two more quickly followed, as the group in the room watched in shock. One hostage remained, a young woman in plain clothes. As the drone circled around to the front of the group, one figure seemingly gave an order. The alphas attacked the woman, tearing her body apart and showing their gruesome handiwork to the camera.

"They know we're watching," muttered Walker who was in tears. "How?"

"Some sort of enhanced awareness, I guess," said a subdued Walter. "Terry was right. Those goddamn things know what we're doing!"

"I can get a flight there in minutes to destroy that building," said Major Clark. "They can't leave there because of the Sarin. Not for an hour at least."

"Wait!" said Jonas. "Have the drones look at other roof tops around the city."

Major Clark gave the order to the soldiers at the drone station. Within seconds, the other three monitors focused in on roof tops throughout downtown Atlanta.

"Shit! There are more of them." exclaimed Donaldson.

The room went silent.

"You can't kill them all, can you Major?" said Jonas, sarcastically.

"No, not without leveling the entire city."

"Back to the Chinese solution. Maybe they were right," said Jonas.

"Sir, the group on screen four is moving inside," said the soldier at the station.

Jonas moved closer to the screen. The group was now moving back inside through the roof door. One remained. The one who had seemingly given the order to kill the hostages.

"Terry, that one," said Jonas, pointing at the monitor. "Is he familiar?

Terry looked closely at the monitor, the solitary figure was wearing a blue dress shirt, tattered and bloody, but a dress shirt nonetheless.

"That's the alpha that was at the ambush on the convoy a few weeks ago. We saw him on top of the rooftop then, too. Son of a bitch!

Robert stood there atop the roof looking up almost directly at the drone camera. He was holding the head of the young woman in its raised hand. Some in the room gasped and looked away. Jonas watched as the hybrid screamed at the camera and tossed the head over the edge of the roof. It too, disappeared through the roof door.

"My God! What was that about?" asked Walker, who was obviously shaken.

"It was delivering a message," replied Donaldson.

"But what? What message?

The room became quiet again except for the occasional report of the exploding ordinance as the bombings were still underway off in a distance.

Jonas looked around the room and then at Donaldson. Donaldson nodded.

"They just declared war on us."

Lightning Source UK Ltd.
Milton Keynes UK
UKHW011845250119
336225UK00001B/103/P

9 781532 055997